W9-AYN-216

Praise for the novels of William Goldman

The Princess Bride

"His swashbuckling fable is nutball funny. . . . A 'classic' medieval melodrama that sounds like all the Saturday serials you ever saw, feverishly reworked by the Marx Brothers."

—*Newsweek*

"One of the funniest, most original, and deeply moving novels I have read in a long time."

—*Los Angeles Times*

Boys & Girls Together

"[Goldman] succeeds where most novelists since Thomas Wolfe have failed. He carves a huge piece out of the heart of New York, and it has life, power, beauty, and truth."

—*San Francisco Chronicle*

"An extraordinary achievement . . . [that] will break your heart . . . will make you laugh . . . will make you weep. . . . It is impossible to praise this book too highly."

—*Cleveland Plain Dealer*

Marathon Man

"Superb . . . One hell of a read . . . There are two literary virtues that one wishes hadn't become cliches: 'It's a good read' and 'It exists on several levels.' One wishes these hadn't become cliches because they are two obvious virtues of William Goldman's *Marathon Man*."

—*The Washington Post*

"An exciting—often funny, often sad—chase . . . Goldman does a masterly job."

—*Associated Press*

FICTION

THE TEMPLE OF GOLD (1957)
YOUR TURN TO CURTSY, MY TURN
  TO BOW (1958)
SOLDIER IN THE RAIN (1960)
BOYS AND GIRLS TOGETHER (1964)
NO WAY TO TREAT A LADY (1964)
THE THING OF IT IS . . . (1967)
FATHER'S DAY (1971)
THE PRINCESS BRIDE (1973)
MARATHON MAN (1974)
MAGIC (1976)
TINSEL (1979)
CONTROL (1982)
THE SILENT GONDOLIERS (1983)
THE COLOR OF LIGHT (1984)
HEAT (1985)
BROTHERS (1986)

NONFICTION

THE SEASON: A CANDID LOOK AT
  BROADWAY (1969)
THE MAKING OF "A BRIDGE TOO
  FAR" (1977)
ADVENTURES IN THE SCREEN
  TRADE: A PERSONAL VIEW OF
  HOLLYWOOD AND
  SCREENWRITING (1983)
WAIT TILL NEXT YEAR (WITH MIKE
  LUPICA) (1988)
HYPE AND GLORY (1990)
FOUR SCREENPLAYS (1995)
FIVE SCREENPLAYS (1997)
WHICH LIE DID I TELL? MORE
  ADVENTURES IN THE SCREEN
  TRADE (2000)

SCREENPLAYS

MASQUERADE (WITH MICHAEL
  RELPH) (1965)
HARPER (1966)
BUTCH CASSIDY AND THE
  SUNDANCE KID (1969)
THE HOT ROCK (1972)
THE GREAT WALDO PEPPER (1975)
THE STEPFORD WIVES (1975)
ALL THE PRESIDENT'S MEN (1976)
MARATHON MAN (1976)
A BRIDGE TOO FAR (1977)
MAGIC (1978)
MR. HORN (1979)
HEAT (1987)
THE PRINCESS BRIDE (1987)
MISERY (1990)
THE YEAR OF THE COMET (1992)
MAVERICK (1994)
THE CHAMBER (1996)
THE GHOST AND THE DARKNESS
  (1996)
ABSOLUTE POWER (1997)
THE GENERAL'S DAUGHTER (1999)
HEARTS IN ATLANTIS (2001)

PLAYS

BLOOD, SWEAT AND STANLEY
  POOLE (WITH JAMES
  GOLDMAN) (1961)
A FAMILY AFFAIR (WITH JAMES
  GOLDMAN AND JOHN KANDER)
  (1961)

FOR CHILDREN

WIGGER (1974)

William Goldman's
The Temple of Gold

BALLANTINE BOOKS · NEW YORK

A Ballantine Book
Published by The Ballantine Publishing Group

Copyright © 1957 by William Goldman
Copyright renewed 1985 by William Goldman
Foreword and Afterword copyright © 2001 by William Goldman

www.ballantinebooks.com

Library of Congress Catalog Card Number: 2001118553

ISBN 0-345-43974-0

Cover design by Carl Galian
Cover photos: (bottle) © Jan Hakan
Dahlstrom/Photonica; (man's face) © Plaman Petkov/agefotostock;
(legs) © Brian Yarvin/agefotostock

Text design by Holly Johnson

Manufactured in the United States of America

First Ballantine Books Edition: October 2001

10 9 8 7 6 5 4 3 2 1

FOR

Marion

Contents

Foreword

The first time I ever had a catatonic fit was also the first time I ever sold a piece of writing. The two events are more than a little related and I think to try and understand my onetime catatonia, you have to know what corner of the room I was coming from.

I was born in Chicago, 1931, and brought up in a then small commuter's town, Highland Park. The 8:08 was the morning train of choice; the 5:40 p.m. brought the fathers home.

Mine was a businessman's family. There were two children, my four-years-older brother, James, and myself. He went on to win an Oscar for writing *The Lion in Winter*, but in his teens he wanted to be a music critic.

I had always wanted to be a writer, I don't know why. Probably because from my earliest memories, I have loved stories. I hid in books my first twenty years. I remember once picking up a play by O'Neill we had on our bookshelves, *Ah, Wilderness*—I hated it so much I could not believe he was this genius playwright, so I went to the library and over that weekend read everything he had ever written. Not such a big deal as I think back on it now. Except I was probably thirteen when I did it. So clearly, I read.

But my great love was comic books. I had many hundreds of them, all from what is now the golden age. My father was somehow on the mailing list for *Walt Disney's Comics and Stories*. He brought that home. And I would go to Larson's on Central with my allowance money for such wonders. The first Superman. Not just the first Batman but also the first Batman and Robin. Captain Marvel—and yes, I still know what SHAZAM stands for—the Sub-Mariner, on and on.

If you are wondering what my collection is worth I will tell you: zip. Because my mother, in an act of mother's evil bordering on Medea's, my mother, without asking or telling me, without so much as a word, *gave my entire collection away*. To the soldiers at Fort Sheridan.

I don't remember writing during these early years. Maybe I tried a one-page something or other when I was twelve or in my midteens.

Doubt it, though. I just had this vague notion that being a writer would be neat, whatever that meant.

Then Irwin Shaw came along to save me.

I was eighteen and an aunt gave me a copy of *Mixed Company*, a book of his collected stories. I'd never read a word by him, never probably heard his name. But I remember the lead story in the book was "The Girls in Their Summer Dresses." About a guy who looked at women. It was followed by "The Eighty-Yard Run."

Now you probably read this about me when all the millennium madness was going on—so and so was the greatest this, such and such was the greatest that—so you must have seen the headlines proclaiming me "Sports Nut of the Century." In truth, the balloting wasn't even close.

Point being? *The New Yorker*, by this time, had begun its endless publishing of bloodless stories about, say, an American couple, unhappily married, and they go to Europe maybe to change things and they end up at the Piazza San Marco where in the last paragraph a fly would walk across the table, and the story would always end like this: "And she understood." Well, "The Eighty-Yard Run" is about a *football player*. Shit, I remember thinking, can you do that? Can you write about stuff *I* care about?

I finished *Mixed Company* and probably didn't know the effect it would have on me. You see, Shaw wrote so easily. Never the wrong word. You just go happily along mostly unaware of the miracles happening around you.

Shaw is out of fashion today, which is too bad for you, because he is one of the great story writers in our history, and more than likely, you don't know that. He and F. Scott Fitzgerald are my two guys, and I have zero doubts on that score.

So I decided I would write like Irwin Shaw. (Easy money at the brick factory.) At eighteen, I began writing stories. Not a whole lot of instant acclaim. I took a creative writing course at Oberlin. Everyone else took it because it was a gut course. I wanted a career. Everyone else got As and Bs, I got the only C. It goes downhill from there.

I took a creative writing course at Northwestern one summer. Worst grade in the class. Oberlin had a literary magazine and I was the fiction editor. Two brilliant girls were involved with me. One was the poetry editor, one the overall chief. Everything was submitted anonymously. Every issue I would stick a story of mine in the pile. And wait for their comments.

"Well, we can't publish this shit," they would say when my story came up for discussion. Do you understand? *I couldn't get a story of mine in a magazine when I was the fiction editor.*

I go into the Army after graduation, am sent to the Pentagon by mistake. Every evening I would go back to Fort Myers for dinner, then return to the Pentagon to write my stories.

And of course, send them out.

I have, somewhere, hundreds of rejection slips. Never a comment from an editor. Never anything but the form note saying what I had written was not of interest at this time.

My confidence is not building through these years. I hope you get that.

Graduate school, Columbia. 1954–1956. My college grades are so bad I can't get accepted without pull, which luckily I had.

I kept sending out my stories. Kept getting the hated rejections. The suggestion is made I might return to Chicago after I got my master's and go into advertising. If I wanted to write, well, I could be a copywriter.

June '56, and the end is near. I am done with college, done with the Army, done with grad school. I thought for a moment of getting a doctorate, but then I realized I would have to pass a number of language tests and I have no facility for languages. The ad agency was smiling at me malevolently.

Where do you go when there's no place to go? Home. So I went back to Highland Park where Minnie was. Tomine Barstad came to work for my family five years before I was born, left when I was in my forties, and more than anyone is the reason I'm alive today. I would write and she would cook meals and sometimes I would take a break and we would have coffee in the kitchen. I had never written anything much longer than fifteen pages, but pretty soon I was on page 50 and that was scary because I'd never been there before. Then page 75 and finally, three weeks after I started, on July 14, page 187, and *The Temple of Gold* was finished.

I named it after the ending scene from *Gunga Din*, now and forever the greatest movie, where Sam Jaffe climbs up the temple of gold and saves the British troops and gets shot to death for it.

I held a novel in my hands. What a thing.

Query: what to do with it?

Cutting to the chase: a guy I knew in the Army knew an editor who hated dealing with agents so he became an agent so he could deal with writers. Joseph McCrindle. He read it, sent it to an editor he knew at Knopf. Who read it.

Now you are thinking the editor did one of two things—accepted it or turned it down.

Nope. He was kind of intrigued by what he'd read but he had no idea if I could write or not. So what he said was this: double it in length and submit it again.

That still seems among the nuttier directives ever given to a would-be first novelist. But after the standard days of panic, I did it. Submitted it again. And waited.

I was living in an apartment then with two others from the Midwest, my brother, who had now decided to become a playwright, and his oldest friend, John Kander from Kansas City, who wanted to be a Broadway composer someday but at that moment was stuck giving voice lessons. (Not forever, though. He went on to write *Cabaret, Chicago, New York, New York,* etc., etc.)

We had this sensational apartment. 344 West 72nd Street. Nine rooms, and the front three had what is still, for me, *the* view of Manhattan—straight up the Hudson to forever. People now who are told the three of us, all young and feisty, were together trying to crack Magic Town find the thought romantic. I never felt it was anything but three nerds trying to get through the day.

The rent was a total of 275 smackers. If you think that is amazing, know this: it had been on the market for six months at the gaudy number 300 and no one would take it. The rumor we were told was that the previous tenants were six Juilliard piano students who went mad one night and had a piano-playing contest, all six banging away at the same time for hours till the management got them out. (Van Cliburn was reputed to be one of the six, but I never checked that for fear that it might not turn out to be true. In my mind, he absolutely was.)

So one day, I am alone in the apartment, pacing, waiting to hear, hoping that somehow this time my novel might actually be accepted. But no one, truly, truly, had any faith. (A girl I was dating, when I picked her up later that night, gave me a present. When I asked what it was for she said it was something nice considering the publisher had rejected me.) But the phone rang—and it must have, but from now on I remember almost nothing—it was my agent saying that Knopf said yes.

I must have sounded pleased, but as I said, who knows? Jim was up in Boston and John was out somewhere, so I just wandered around the place.

When Kander came home he said, "Have you heard?" and I must have told him they took it and he said—probably—"Oh, Billy, that's wonderful." And I must have allowed that sure it was.

Then he asked, was everybody excited that I'd told? Hadn't told anybody, I answered.

By now he realized I was acting very weirdly indeed, so he saved me with these words: "Billy, would you like me to call people for you?"

How would we work that? I must have wondered.

"Well," Kander said, carefully, "what we could do is sit next to the phone and you could tell me who you wanted me to call and then I could call them and tell them the news and also that you were acting a little strange and didn't want to talk about it now."

I liked the sound of that so we did it. I remember sitting down next to him and he would say, "I think Sarah would be so happy for you, shall we call Sarah?" and I would nod and I can still hear him saying, "Sarah, Billy's book was taken by Knopf but he's not quite up to talking about it, would you like to say congratulations?" and then he would put the phone near me and Sarah would say, "It's just wonderful," and I would say "Thank you, it is," and then John would tell her that I would call tomorrow and we went on down the line of all the people I knew.

I didn't know at the time that I was in a catatonic state, maybe a medico would say it was something else. But looking back on it, I'm satisfied that's what it was.

By the next day I was able to deal with the phone myself and life went on. But of course, it had changed. Everything had changed. I was a writer now.

Later that week I went to a party and met a girl and she asked what I was doing in New York. I said I was a writer and she got this terrible look and said to me, "Oh, another one." But I was able to say I was, I really was, and Knopf was publishing my novel in the fall.

As I look back now, I guess the single most remarkable act of my decades of storytelling is that I somehow, in what desperation, what despair, what overall sense of failure and survival I know not, but somehow I wrote this book that you now hold in your hands.

But I do know: if Knopf said no, if all the publishers said that awful word, no, sorry, not for us, nothing we can use at this time, no, thanks but no—I never would have written again.

Which would not have greatly altered the course of Western culture and a number of people I know don't believe that I wouldn't have tried again.

But I do.

What I'm not totally sure of is why I went weird that day. I think the shock of suddenly being told I had talent after those early formative years of being told I had none, that had to be in there somewhere. So was the family fact that I wasn't supposed to succeed, my brother was.

Or maybe it's tied to an early and great Kander and Ebb song. A girl with no money and a lot of desperation has just gotten, amazingly, a job. This is what she sings:

When it all comes true
Just the way you planned
It's funny, but the bells don't ring,
It's a quiet thing

Could be that. That movies have prepared us for The Big Deal, whistles tooting, but life doesn't work that way.

All I know is, it sure got awfully silent on West 72nd Street that wondrous afternoon.

The Temple
of Gold

I . . . . The Family

My father was a stuffy man.

That is not meant as criticism but rather to be the truth. It is the word that best fit him. Stuffy. He always wore dark suits and ugly ties, and was forever pursing his lips and wrinkling up his forehead before he said anything. "Is that you?" my mother would call when he came home. Then he'd purse his lips and there would go his forehead and after a while he'd say: "Yes, my dear." He always called her that—"my dear"; never her real name, which was Katherine. And I was always Raymond.

It's easiest to begin with my father rather than my mother or Grandmother Rae for the simple reason that I knew less about him than the others. We lived side by side in the same house for many years, but I never really got to know him. That again isn't meant to be criticism; it was just the way things worked out.

Because, in the first place, he was a lot older than I was, being forty when I was born. And he was not the kind who enjoyed walking along the beach or playing catch out in the back yard by the ravine. He was a scholar, and I guess a good one, for he was far and away the most famous person at Athens College in Athens, Illinois, which is where he taught all his life. He got famous because he was an important figure in the Euripides revival that took place in the earlier part of this, the twentieth century, which should go a long way toward explaining how I happened to get stuck with the middle name I unfortunately possess. I suppose he had visions of me becoming a Greek scholar like himself, and if that had happened, my name would have been a winner: Raymond Euripides Trevitt. But such did not turn out to be the case.

My father didn't have a sense of humor; he never laughed much, and there was hardly a thing about him you could call amusing. Except maybe the bedtime stories he used to tell me. Whereas most kids got Mother Goose or along those lines, I got the Greek tragedies. "Go to bed now,

1

Raymond, and I'll tell you the story of Medea." Or Antigone. Or Hippoly-tus. Before I was seven, I knew the plots to all those Greek plays. And if you happen to, then you know that they're not for kiddies, being crammed full of sex, blood, murder, etc. Well, those were my bedtime stories, but the way my father told them, with his careful, very clipped way of speaking, they never came out dirty at all.

As I said, he was a scholar and so were his friends, also teachers from the college and nice enough, I suppose, in their own way. We never had big parties at our house, but only small gatherings of three or four cou-ples who sat around, chatting softly and sipping dry wine. At the start, when I was very little, my father used to trot me down for a visit, which always ended with me telling the plot of one of the Greek plays. " 'Gweat heavens,' Œdipus scweamed. 'My wife is my muvver.' " And I guess it was pretty cute at that, what with me being so young, because they'd always applaud before shipping me back upstairs.

All that ended, though, when I was six or seven, seeing as by that time they had heard me say all the plots and I hadn't advanced much in my studies. I never was a scholar, especially about Greek plays, and it was at this time that my father and I parted company. For he was wise enough to know that I could never follow in his footsteps, so he just let me try to make my own.

But, of course, the thing for which I'll always remember my father was what happened with the guppies.

Which isn't fair, I know, since it wasn't typical of him at all. I should think of him sitting in his study at his big brown desk, sucking on a pipe, his head almost lost behind the wall of books that was always piled up there. I should, but I don't. I think life works that way, though. We are not remembered for what we are, not for an action that portrays us truly, but more often for some little thing, some one-time wonder when we crossed, just for a minute, outside of the natural orbit of our lives.

And so, I always remember my father and the guppies.

They were his guppies. There was never any question about that. He bought them for himself and he kept them in his study along with all the books. He put them against the wall in front of his desk and many is the time I walked by his open study door and saw him, sitting quiet, just staring off at something I knew to be them.

A guppy, and I haven't seen one in fifteen years so therefore this is strictly from memory, is a fish. A little fish, I suppose tropical, and you keep them in a big rectangular bowl. They are beautiful, guppies are, being more than one color and sort of shiny when they happen to swim through a sunbeam.

And if my father loved those guppies, I know I did too. I loved them as much as I loved my first dog, Baxter—all my dogs I have named Baxter after that first one—but I couldn't tell you why. Because there's nothing you can do with a guppy but just sit there and watch it. Which is what I'd do on rainy afternoons when my father was away at the college. I'd go into his study, pull myself up in his big chair, rest my chin in my hands, and stare at them. And if they knew I was there, they made no show of it, for all they ever did was just swim around and around and around in their own little glass world.

In the years that have passed since it happened I have wondered and thought many times about why I loved them so much. The only answer I can come up with is this: they seemed so goddam happy just swimming around and around. I suppose a guppy knows what he is and never did one die of *hubris* which, by the way, is a Greek word that you can't translate into English except by saying that it sort of means pride. Wanting too much. It's the reason Œdipus got into all that trouble and why Antigone got hers. *Hubris*. That's why. You could put guppies in a huge pool or in a little dish and they'd still swim around and around, happy, I think, and never complaining. They'd found the handle. Which is more than most of us can say.

And one hot, rainy afternoon I was sitting in my father's chair, watching them. Having just eaten lunch I was feeling pretty at peace with the world when, for some reason, I got to wondering if guppies ever were hungry. I clambered down from the chair, walked over, and stuck my nose against the glass, staring at them cross-eyed. Then I ran and asked my mother, who was sipping tea with Mrs. O'Brien, a neighbor from a couple of houses down. When I asked her, my mother smiled at me, and I'll never forget what she said: "Why of course they do, Raymond. Just like people, they have to be fed. Now run along."

So I ran along, back to the study. And a little later, when I saw that big jar sitting high on a bookshelf, I knew, just as sure as God made green apples, that it was guppy food. So I took it down, looked at it and, after a while, I sprinkled some on top of the water.

Those guppies went wild, swimming around, zooming up to the water top, opening their mouths, zooming down, then up again. They were so cute I almost wanted to cry. I sprinkled some more food. They ate that too. So I took the lid off the jar and poured the whole thing on top of the water where it lay like a roof. And even now, the idea of living in a house where the roof's made of food is pretty close to my idea of heaven. They were still eating away when I tossed the empty jar into the wastebasket, closed the study door, and left them.

Along about five that afternoon I was playing in my room when my father came home and a little later I heard him talking with my mother. After which I heard him coming upstairs, and then there he was, standing in the doorway, looking like he'd never looked before.

"Did you feed the guppies?" he asked, and he didn't purse his lips or do anything to his forehead. The words just shot right out.

"Yes," I answered. "Yes sir."

Then he had me by the arm, dragging me down the stairs while my mother stood at the top yelling: "Be careful! Be careful! Be careful!" and then we were in the study with my father yelling: "Look! Look!" and pointing. I looked.

The guppies were dead. Bloated, they lay motionless on top of the water.

"You see!" my father yelled. "You see! You did that! That's your work!"

I was about to answer, but I couldn't, because right then I started to cry as he grabbed my arm again, pulling me down to the basement.

Water was hanging in big drops from all the pipes down there, it was so hot. My father took off his coat, dropped it on the floor. Then his vest, and tie, and shirt. Then he stood up, pale as snow.

I was crying when he took me over his knee and gave me my first and only beating. He kept slapping down hard and at first it only stung, but then that gave way to pain. It hurt like hell but he kept on, and with each blow he swore at me: "Damn you. Damn you. Damn you. Damn you!" I couldn't twist away he was holding me so tight, but once I managed to turn and see him. He was wet all over. It was the only time I ever saw him perspire; even on the hottest summer day, his skin was dry.

The rest of it is pretty hazy. I suppose I got hysterical, and then it was over with me lying on the cold stone floor of the basement, not crying tears any more, because they were gone. Used up. My mother took me to my room, cared for me some, and after a few tense days, the status quo set in. Nothing was ever said of it again.

Except once, long after. I knocked at the door of his study, which was now always closed, and when he said to come in, I did.

"What is it, Raymond?" he asked me.

I blurted it out. "I just wanted you to know I loved those guppies too," I said.

He took the pipe from his mouth and stared at me for a long time. Then he pursed his lips; wrinkled up his forehead. "Guppies?" he said. "What guppies?"

My Grandmother Rae was my father's mother who was almost dead when she came to live with us, she was that old. Small and skinny, she was practically bald, so she always wore a black hairnet to disguise it, which did the trick about as well as an "I am bald" sign would have done. She came to our house when I was seven and went immediately to the maid's room, which was empty, seeing as we never had one. Once she got inside that room she never, never left it, except maybe for an occasional trip to the bathroom. But even that wasn't a sure thing.

I always saw her at mealtime. Since she never left her room, food had to be brought to her and, not surprisingly, I was elected. So, three times a day, I made the trek up from the kitchen with her meal and then, when she was done, I'd carry the empty tray down again. It all went smoothly the first few weeks. Then one night, after supper, she held out her hand.

"Here, boy," she said, handing me a dime. I asked her what for. She pointed to the tray. "I always pay my share," was her answer.

Which confused me, so I had a chat with my mother about it. Naturally, she told me it was just the old lady's way of being nice and I should be the same and accept it graciously. But it still didn't seem right; you just don't take money from an old woman living alone up in your maid's room. So the next morning I gave the dime back to my mother and told her to return it to Grandmother Rae. Which worked out fine, since I found out later that my mother had given her the money in the first place, because the old lady didn't have a penny in the world to her name.

And that was how the round robin was established.

Every evening my mother gave her a dime and the next night I'd get it back and give it to my mother. That was the way it went and it turned out to be one of the greatest games I ever played. We kept one dime—dated 1919—in circulation for over two months and the only reason it wasn't longer was because my mother slipped up one morning and gave the dime to the milkman. I was really sorry when it got away and even now I still think I'd give a lot more than ten cents to get it back.

I always remember my Grandmother Rae as a cripple. She wasn't. She could walk as well as anyone. But I still remember her as such, a crotchety old crippled lady living out her days in the back room of my house. And she was crotchety. She didn't like anyone, including my father, who was her own son. Sometimes he'd go back to visit her, but not often, and my mother even less. I was her main connection with the world beyond the door, and I know she didn't like me. I know that because she was a mutterer. She kept up a steady stream of conversation all day long. It didn't matter if someone was in the room or not, she'd just talk away, about how dumb the boy was (being me), or how slow the boy was, or how the bathroom pipes leaked so she couldn't hear herself think, or whatever else came into her head. She was old and gray and full of sleep—Zock taught me that one—and I think only one thing in the world made her happy.

Reading to me.

She loved that. The only books she'd ever read were the Winnie-the-Pooh stories. After supper, after she'd given me the dime, I'd pull her chair over to the lamp, or the window if it was summer, and she'd read me a chapter from one of the books, which secretly I believe she knew by heart. And it's a shame there are only two of them, because if there'd been more, she probably would have lived awhile longer.

So I'd sit there on the floor, listening to the adventures of Pooh and Piglet and Christopher Robin and all the things that went on in the Hundred Acre Wood. And if Grandmother Rae couldn't do much else, she could read those books—her head bent over, her lips moving slowly, her voice full of excitement. It was beautiful. Because she believed in the Hundred Acre Wood. She had been there. It was real. So it wasn't that she was reading to me as much as she was telling me about what had happened to her. As if she had been present at Eeyore's birthday party, had sat up in the tree when Pooh rescued Piglet with the honey jar.

And I believed it too. I knew the Hundred Acre Wood like I knew the cracks in the ceiling over my own bed. And I'd think—as I listened to her reading, I'd think: "That's a nice place, that Hundred Acre Wood. That's a place for me. You can take me to that place any time."

Naturally, I never got there. And even my visiting stopped, because one day, the old lady died. I suppose I have known more than my share of death, but hers was the smallest. Nobody cried. Nobody said, "What a tragedy." She just was, and then one day, she wasn't any more. Like a pebble thrown far out in a pond when you're not looking. You hear the sound, but later, when you turn slowly to look, the ripples are gone and the top of the pond is smooth again. . . .

As I remember my father for what he once did, I most remember my mother for what she once did not do. Again, this isn't fair, since she was a fine woman, loving wife, good mother, etc. But memories are often like that.

She was a pretty girl whose parents were religious missionaries in India. They died of some plague, both at the same time, which, although it shook her up when it happened, isn't half as bad as it might have been. Together is a good way to go. She attended Athens College and when she was a sophomore she had a class in Greek Literature taught by my father; when she was a junior they got married; the year she would have been a senior, I was born.

I have already said how my father was a famous scholar. Once I went to a speech he gave and heard him introduced as "America's leading expert on Euripides," a pretty silly way of introducing anyone, but still I believe it to have been the truth. And my mother, with the zeal probably inherited from her missionary parents, threw herself into the job of being the wife of America's leading expert on you-know-who. She was a pillar of society, my mother, and I say that without malice or scorn, because if you don't have pillars, then society would fall down on your head, and my mother just happened to be one.

And if it was my father who gave up on me, it was me, in turn, who gave up on my mother. There was never any clean break. We kept arguing about the usual things, such as would I or would I not wear long underwear in the wintertime or rubbers in the rain. We always spoke to each other, her trying to guide me as a mother should and me obeying, more often than not, as a son. But still, after what happened with Baxter, nothing was ever the same.

Giving credit where it's due, I freely admit that had it not been for my mother, I never would have gotten him in the first place, as my father was against it from the start, mainly because he didn't like dogs. You couldn't help liking Baxter though, since he was far and away the greatest animal ever to walk on four feet, a thoroughbred cocker spaniel, small and golden brown. Once I got Baxter—which happens to be my father's middle name, proving I was no moron even then—I was almost never home, but rather out in the ravine or running around the neighborhood or down at the beach.

All of which secretly suited my mother, I think, because she was at that time challenging for the lead in the faculty wives' league and the local PTA. There were always meetings going on at my house, three and more per week. My father took to coming home later than usual, for he and I shared a very strong dislike for anything resembling a faculty wife.

The day it happened there was a big PTA meeting at our house, so I obviously planned to be absent. Which I was. I went down to the beach and skipped stones awhile. Then I threw sticks for Baxter to fetch, trying to fake him out by pointing one direction and throwing in the other. I didn't fool him once, since he was smarter probably than I was, even though I was more than eight at the time. Finally, I got bored and he was panting some, so we headed for town, and right when we crossed the main street with me watching it all, Baxter was run over and killed by a big gray car.

At first I didn't believe it but just stood there as the car ground to a stop and the driver got out. He came back and looked down at Baxter. Then he prodded him with his shoe. When I saw that I let out a yell and went tearing up, not caring about the people gathering around or the honks from the other cars stymied there on the main street of town. I was screaming blue murder and nothing anybody could do would make me stop, so finally they all stepped back. I bent over Baxter, picked him up, cradling him in my arms, the blood from his body slopping onto my clothes.

Then I started home. Because I was crying, the trees, the grass, the sky, everything melted together and I saw mostly the color green, a long tunnel of green with me in the middle, walking through it, going home. I kept expecting Baxter to come to, so I shook him every so often. We were both drenched with blood and my stomach ached from crying and that walk is the closest I ever expect to come to the march on Calvary.

Kicking the front door open, I went into the living-room. It was set up like an auditorium, with rows of wooden, stiff-backed chairs, an aisle down the middle, and a speaker at the front—who happened to be my mother. When she saw me, she stopped talking and stared. All the others did the same, turning, watching me as I stood there holding Baxter, the both of us covered with blood.

"Baxter's been murdered," I said, and right away the room was full of buzz-buzz-buzz. But nobody moved. "Baxter is dead," I said again, staring straight at my mother.

She just stood there. I was looking right into her eyes, the both of us like statues, and in her eyes I could see it, that she was ashamed. Of me.

I turned and made for the door when I heard Mrs. O'Brien saying: "You girls go on with the meeting. I'll take care of Raymond," and then she had an arm around me, not caring about the blood. She was a fine woman, Mrs. O'Brien; built kind of like a cube, but fine nonetheless.

She talked to me awhile, saying that probably we ought to bury Baxter, seeing as how he was dead. I nodded, and went to get the shovel from the garage. Then we both walked into the ravine. Putting Baxter down gently, I started to dig. When the hole was large enough, I set him inside and began covering him. While I was doing that my mother came down and told me how sorry she was. But she was too late. Even though the next day she bought me a new dog, she was too late. Because soon after-ward Zock moved in next door and that changed everything. So it was that afternoon, during the big PTA meeting, when my mother and me said good-by.

Which takes care of my family.

If I have treated them unfairly, I didn't mean to. They were a good family, as families go, and I have no complaints. What I am, I suppose, I am either because of or in spite of them, which amounts to the same thing. And if they were not the parents I would have picked, had I been given the choice, I know that I am not the son they would have chosen. So it all ended even. And in this world, you can't ask for more.

II .... The Boys

I first heard of Zachary Crowe one night at supper. We were eating, and my mother was talking away to my father about Mrs. Janes, the wife of the English professor who, according to my mother, had practically ruined a meeting that afternoon by arriving "in her cups," as she always put it. My father didn't even look up from his lamb chop as he pursed his lips, wrinkled his forehead and said: "Indeed?"—which was by all odds his favorite word. And then my mother said: "Really, Henry, something ought to be done about it," and he said: "Of course, my dear," and went on sawing at his food.

"And I paid a visit to the new neighbors this afternoon," my mother went on. "She seems like a lovely girl."

"Neighbors?" my father asked, just to keep things alive.

"The new ones," I told him, pointing with my fork. "Next door."

"Raymond," my mother said. "Please don't do that. Yes," she continued. "He is the owner of that new clothing shop."

"Indeed," my father said.

"And Raymond. They have a boy just about your age. He seems like an absolute angel."

"Indeed," I said, immediately not liking him.

"Such fine manners," she went on. "Zachary. His name is Zachary."

"You're kidding," I said. "Nobody's named Zachary."

"I think it's a fine name," my mother said. "And it wouldn't do you any harm to be nice to him. Would it, Henry?"

"Indeed," we both said together.

So the next morning I sauntered over and began playing half in their back yard and half in mine. After a while he came out, started doing the same. When we got to within a few feet of each other, I stopped and gave him the once-over.

Zock was ugly. His eyes were terrible even then; he had black, kinky hair and obviously must have worn braces every day when he was

11

younger. Lots of people are ugly at the start, but then, as they grow, they get more presentable looking. Not Zock. He got uglier all the time. When we went through the pimple stage he was always way out in first place. You've heard of a face only a mother etc. Well, his was it.

"I hear you're an absolute angel," I said to him that morning.

"I hear you're not," he came right back, which threw me, because I didn't know how the news had spread so fast.

"Where'd you hear that?" I asked.

"Around and about," he answered. "Around and about."

"Yeah," I said. "Well." And then I stopped, not being able to think of anything to put after it.

"Well what?"

"So your name's Zachary," I sneered. "That's a good name for a dog." Which got to him, I know, because he really liked his name. One of the things I'm sorry about is that once I got started, nobody called him Zachary again. But only Zock. Even in school, the teachers called him that, which, as I said, is my fault. Because one day I was thinking of nothing in particular when the words "Zichary Zachary Zock" came into my head. I began calling him that, and then just Zock alone. It caught on, and poor Zachary went right out the window.

"Yes sir," I went on. "Zachary is a good name for a pig."

"Glad to meet you, Zachary," he said, which I decided then and there was enough of an insult. So I shoved him, knocking him down, and when he got up, I did it again.

"Let me take off my glasses," he said, which seemed logical, except that without them he was blind as a bat. Zock was never very strong. He was a year and some older than I was on account of having been sick a long time when he was younger, but even so, he wasn't very strong. I let him take off his glasses and then, while he was trying to locate me, I tackled him and jumped on top. I hit him for a while and when I got tired of doing that, I sat on his face. "Give up?" I asked.

"Of course," he answered, so I got off and began dusting myself. He was crying a little, which was understandable, for I had given him a couple good ones, and while I was brushing away, he took a big stick and clobbered me all he had in the middle of my back. So we went to it again, both of us crying now. Then, later, we quit, going our separate ways home.

The first thing that happened to me when I got inside was I ran right into my mother, who just stared. "I tripped," I told her, trying to sneak by.

"You've been fighting with that new boy," she said.

"What new boy?" I asked, smiling.

Which didn't sit too well, as she started drumming her fingers on the wall, a bad sign. "He," I began. "It was his fault. I was only . . ."

"You go upstairs," she ordered. "You go right upstairs this minute and take a bath and then we're going over to apologize."

Which we did, chatting with Mrs. Crowe for a while first, because Zock was up taking his bath. As I sat there I got to thinking about what I should say to him, seeing as it really was all my fault. I just wanted him to like me. I think that's natural enough, but I still couldn't feature myself saying, "Zock, the only reason I did it was I was afraid you wouldn't like me."

He walked in. "Have we something to tell Zachary?" my mother asked, very sweet.

"I'm sorry for sitting on your face," I said.

"Accepted," he said.

"You two run along now," Mrs. Crowe told us. "I want you to get to be pals," an awful thing to say in anybody's book. But I later got to know that she was always talking like that. Antiquated Expressions, Zock called them. As if it was the gay nineties and everybody still drank coffee out of mustache cups.

We ran along, and when we were out of sight Zock said: "I meant to hit you in the head with that stick, but I don't see very well without my glasses."

"I'm glad you missed," I told him.

"The only reason I did it," he said, "was I was afraid you wouldn't like me."

And such was our beginning. . . .

It's a funny thing, but did you ever stop to realize that most of the time, your friends really shouldn't be? For example, if you took a test on what you liked and your friends did the same, the answers wouldn't come very close. Everyone will tell you that your friends are those with the same interests as you, but that's bunk. Zock said a friend was somebody you could tell to go to hell and he wouldn't mind. And that may be true, though to me I think it's more of a feeling, an understanding, that no matter what you do or say or where you go, I'll be there. When you need me, just turn around and I'll be there.

Which is the way it was with Zock and me right from the start. He was a whiz at school, while I was at best barely average. I was outdoorsy and he hated it. He liked poetry and I didn't. So what happened was that we'd go tramping in the woods, and after a while, we'd sit down and he'd read to me out of some book of poetry he'd taken along. All of which is a compromise, I know, but I have yet to be shown what's wrong with them. Because pretty soon Zock got to like tramping around and I got to like poetry, though we never admitted same to each other.

The summer following our graduation from the seventh grade was the hottest in twenty years, according to the radio. Which was not good, since we couldn't go to the beach as Zock had never learned to swim and refused to get near the water. Actually, I think it wasn't the water that bothered him so much as just walking around in a bathing suit. For his build was never too pleasing and already he had terrible red pimples all over his back. So time began to hang heavy on the two of us until one night when, not being able to sleep, I got my idea. Naturally, I told him about it first thing next morning.

"I was thinking of running away," I said.

He nodded. "Any place special?"

"Chicago," I answered, that being the biggest city in the area not to mention the entire state of Illinois, and lying only about fifty miles to the south.

"You have any money?"

"Some," I said. "And I get my allowance Saturday. That ought to see me through."

"I don't know," he began.

"Aw, Zock," I interrupted. "Come on. Let's go. It'll be great. There's nothing like running away. I've done it plenty and it gets better every time."

He looked at me awhile. "Not too much doing around here anyway," he said, finally.

Late Saturday morning we took off. At the edge of town I put a note on Baxter's collar, which was Zock's idea, seeing as he thought it only fair to let the parents in on what we were doing. "Zock and me have run away," the note said. "Not to Chicago." Which was my idea and one I take no particular pride in. I prodded Baxter on his fanny and he went scooting off, while we began the long walk to the big highway outside of town.

We went slowly, it being very hot, chatting about this and that and, almost before we knew it, a car stopped and the driver was asking did we want a lift. Zock asked him where to and he said Chicago so we got in the back seat and began giggling, because everything was working out so well.

The driver was a little man with hairless arms. "You seem like nice boys," he said.

"Oh yes," Zock told him. "We're very nice."

He kept staring at the two of us through the rearview mirror and after a while, he didn't bother with Zock any more, but only me. I wasn't saying much seeing as Zock could do it better. And right then he was talking a blue streak.

"Why doesn't your friend say something?" the man asked.

"I don't think he's too bright," Zock answered. "A very backward boy who was seven before he could crawl." At which I laughed.

"He has a nice smile," the man said.

"Oh, he's a beauty," Zock agreed.

"Why don't you say something?" the man asked me. "Why don't you come up here and say something?"

"O.K.," I said, jumping over into the front seat.

"That's better," the man said. He patted me on the head. Then he felt my arm. "Strong," he said. "Very strong for a blond boy."

"He's hard as nails," Zock told him. "And a terror when aroused."

"You don't say," the man answered. He put his hand on my shoulder, keeping it there, driving slow.

Right then Zock started gagging in the back seat, making horrible sounds, doubled up, his face red.

"What is it?" the man asked.

"I don't know," I answered.

"Phone," Zock gasped. "Get . . . to . . . phone." The man sped up, turned onto the main road, stopping when we got to a gas station.

I jumped out, and so, to my surprise, did Zock. "You all right?" I asked him.

"I better wait here and see," he said. "You go on," he told the man. "Thanks." The man didn't say a word but just roared off down the road.

"You got him mad," I said. "What for?"

"A whim," Zock answered, feeling my arm. "Very strong for a blond boy," he laughed. "My, my, my."

"Why did you get him mad?"

"I'll tell you all about it when you're older," he said, and by then we both were laughing, walking down the highway to Chicago.

Getting picked up a little later by a traveling salesman from Milwaukee who was very fat and jovial and who twice bought us ice cream along the way. His name was Mr. Hardecker and he never stopped laughing. He had eight children and a wife who weighed more than he did, but he still never stopped laughing. And, in the years that have passed since then, I have often thought of trying to locate him again to talk to, because I think Mr. Hardecker had found the handle. But you can never be sure.

When we got to the Loop he let us out, said good-by, and drove away. So there we were. Right smack in the middle of the Loop along with millions of other people. Except that they all knew where they were going. I got scared. Zock was walking down the street and for a minute I lost him in the crowd, but I started running, ducking in and out, finally catching up and grabbing hold.

"Zock," I said. "There's something I got to tell you. I lied before. I've never run away."

"That's all right," he told me. "I have."

So I began to relax and enjoy it.

What we did mostly was look at people and look at movies. In shifts. We'd range around the Loop awhile and when we got tired of that, we'd find a movie to go to. All in all, we saw five movies.

Three of which were *Gunga Din* and to this day it's still my favorite. We sat through it three times straight, which took up all evening. We were pretty tired from the walking we'd done, but *Gunga Din* was tiring too. Because we cried so much, both of us. At the ending.

You see, Gunga Din is a water carrier and, at the end the British troops are about to get ambushed by some natives. And he's wounded very bad in the belly to start with, but even so, he takes a bugle and starts to climb this temple of gold. Inch by inch he makes his way, his pain something awful, the British troops coming closer and closer to getting massacred. But finally he makes it and there he is, high up, standing on the top of the temple of gold. And when he gets there he blows his bugle, warning all the British troops who then mop up the natives in fine style. He stays up there, old Gunga Din does, blowing that bugle until the natives shoot him dead. Now, nobody wants to die, but he knew when he started that climb that he was going to get his, just as sure as God made green apples. But he did it anyway. He didn't have to. He wasn't even a soldier, but only a water carrier. Still, he made that climb and when he started inching his way up I started bawling and so did Zock, not stopping until after the picture was over. All three times we did the same thing. Gunga Din on the temple of gold. It was beautiful.

When the movie house closed, we went out in the street. Neither of us felt much like talking so we didn't, but started moving instead, scuffing our way through the Loop and beyond, heading east toward Lake Michigan. We sacked out, curled up against some big square rocks which aren't hard to sleep on if you're really tired. We were. I yawned a couple of times, looking straight up at the sky full of stars, listening to the sound the waves made. " 'Night," I said.

" 'Night, Euripides," Zock mumbled.

We were quiet for a while. Then I spoke up. "It's a shame he had to die," I said. "Gunga Din. I wish he'd lived longer.

"It doesn't matter," Zock said, very soft. I pushed up on one elbow, looking at him. His eyes were closed, his hands clasped behind his head. "Nothing matters when you know it all. All the answers."

I lay back down and thought for a long time, going over and over what he said. Then I pushed up on one elbow again. "What do you mean?" I asked.

He didn't answer me, didn't even hear; he was asleep. So I thought about it some more, staring at those stars, trying to stay awake. But pretty soon my eyes closed and the last thing I remember was the sound of the waves, slap, slap, slap, against the rocks, and then I was out.

The sun woke us. When we took stock we found we had exactly twenty-six cents between us and nothing to do, so we tried sleeping some more, but now the rocks were hard. After a while, we started walking. Except we were both pretty stiff and sore, and you can't go far when you're like that. Finally, we came to a bench in front of a bus stop. "Pretend you're taking the bus," Zock said, and we did, sitting there, slumped over, peeking up every once in a while just in case anyone, such as a policeman, should wander by.

But it was no policeman who found us on that bench. Instead, it was Kavanaugh. Neither of us heard him coming, though we knew somebody was around because of the smell, probably the worst liquor smell I've ever come in contact with. And it all belonged to Kavanaugh, who was no pleasure to be near the first few minutes. After a while, though, you got used to it, and accepted it, as if it was a part of him.

He sprawled down on the edge of the bench close to me, his head in his hands, moaning and groaning as if he was about to die. Zock and I just looked at each other, too tired to move. But Kavanaugh moved. He got to his feet, staggered to the curb, and threw up all over. Then, when he was finished, he turned to face us. "Thank the Lord I got a weak stomach," he said. And, in the same breath: "The name is Kavanaugh."

Long before, he must have been handsome. Now he was old, fifty or more, and his face was wrinkled. He needed a shave and his clothes were filthy dirty, but his smile was fine, his eyes bright.

He came back to the bench where we shook hands all around, told him who we were, and right away he started talking. In all my life, I have never met or heard a man who could talk as well as Kavanaugh; not my father; not even Zock when he got older. It was as if talk was his religion and he was spreading the gospel.

He asked where we were from and then he told us where he was from, Ireland, where things are more beautiful than any place else in the world. The water shines like green gold, the skies are as blue as the eyes of your mother, and so on. Then he asked what we did. We said we went to school, and that started him off on education. Which is also better in Ireland than anywhere else, although it is a good thing no matter where you find it. Kavanaugh was self-educated and loved Shakespeare more than he loved his dear dead father, in spite of the fact that Shakespeare was English. Finally, he began to quote. From *Hamlet*; from *Romeo and Juliet*; and on. He had a fine voice, Kavanaugh did, deep and rich, and his words echoed down along the empty street.

But right in the middle of Shylock's speech about "Hath not a Jew hands, eyes, etc." his voice dropped. Gradually at first, then more and more. His eyes got dull, his body sagged; he slumped against the bench, his arms dangling loosely at his sides.

We waited, not knowing what to do. When he began to talk again, everything was different. "If I was half a man," he whispered, "just half a man, I'd kill myself." Which sent shivers up me because not ten minutes earlier he had been so obviously in love with life you almost wanted to cry. "I'm an old man, boys," he went on. "With nothing to live for. So you'd be doing me a favor if you'd do the job for me."

"Stop that," I said.

"It's the truth," Kavanaugh whispered. "There was an epidemic in my village when I was a boy. It caught my mother and it caught my sister and I would to God it had caught me too. For there's nothing to this life but suffering and getting old and it's better to be done before it starts."

"Stop," I said again.

"There'll come a day when you'll bless me for what I'm telling you," he said, and we had to strain to hear. "You'll see."

Right then, Zock took over.

Reaching across me, he grabbed Kavanaugh by the shoulder. "Are you hungry?" he asked. "Could you use something to eat?" After a minute, Kavanaugh nodded. Zock stood. "We've got twenty-six cents," he said. "And you're welcome to it." He lifted Kavanaugh, me helping, and carried him along until we found a coffee place. Putting him at a stool by the counter, Zock bought him twenty-six cents worth of food. By the time he was through eating, he was quoting Shakespeare again.

Out on the street, we shook hands. "My mother in heaven will pray for you every night," he said.

"Thank you," Zock said. "We can use it. Good-by."

"Good-by," I echoed.

"Fine lads the both of you," Kavanaugh said, walking away.

"People like that," Zock said. "Just give them a loaf of bread and the sun is shining." The last we saw of him, he was staggering along the street, waving his arms for balance, bowing to each and every person who passed by.

Leaving us stuck in Chicago, hungry, thirsty, and broke. We tried walking, but pretty soon Zock gave out. "I've had enough," he said. "What about you?"

"I suppose."

"Well, then drag me to a telephone."

"Home?"

Zock shook his head. "I've got cousins in Chicago," he answered. We found a phone where he made a call, coming out smiling. "She'll be right down, Euripides."

"Who will?"

"My cousin Sadie," he said. So we sat down on the curb to wait for her.

Even if I could talk like Kavanaugh, I couldn't come close to describing her. Sadie Griffin. That was her name and she came roaring up a little later, driving a white convertible with the top down. Zock waved to her. I was about to do the same, but when I saw her close up, I couldn't. I couldn't do anything but stare.

I have never seen, either on the street or in the movies or any place else, a girl as beautiful as Sadie Griffin. She had long golden hair and from just looking at her you knew that if she'd been around when Paris was fiddling with the Golden Apples, then Helen would have stayed home with Menelaus and there never would have been a Trojan War.

She lived with her folks in a big apartment overlooking Lake Michigan. They fed us, first calling up Athens, and after a while, Sadie Griffin drove us home. I stared at her all the way, hardly ever talking. Toward the end of the trip she began teasing me about it, which only made me clam up more. She was eighteen years old that summer and getting ready to start college. Just eighteen years old, just five more than me, but I couldn't have been more tongue-tied talking to God Almighty Himself.

Back home there was the usual scolding together with some minor punishment, none of which proved too troublesome. And the summer went fast afterward, seeing as we had so much to talk about. There was Kavanaugh and Mr. Hardecker and sometimes Sadie Griffin. But most of all there was Gunga Din, the poor old water carrier who saved the British troops by blowing that bugle from right on top of the temple of gold.

And besides helping the summer to pass, that trip also made us the leaders of the eighth grade. News of it spread, naturally, which we really couldn't object to, since we did most of the spreading ourselves. And when people came for more details, they got them from the both of us, together. We were always together, me and Zock. We were our own gang. We were a foundation and the others were alone. And when you're alone you look for something to be with, something solid. So they all came to us. Zock was a sort of silent partner, because things worked out better that way, him not being much good at sports, whereas I was. And I already described how he looked, being ugly, while I was more the All-American-boy type—good build, blue eyes, nice smile. Even Zock's smile was crooked, and I often thought that God should have given him something decent looking on the outside, instead of putting it all in, hiding it, so that nobody could ever see it at first glance.

But make no mistake, we were the head, the two of us, walking side by side. And behind us came "Buttons" Dooley, a very nice kid and so called because one day he came to school unbuttoned in exactly the wrong place, which was pretty funny at the time. And Johnny Hunkley, the strongest boy in school but such a slob that nobody cared. Plus nine or ten others. We did the things gangs usually do, such as switching street signs or scaring Miss Blaul, the old virgin librarian, by hooting outside her window at night. And other juvenile activities which I am not particularly proud of but which did nobody any lasting harm that I can see.

So eighth grade went by, as did the summer following, and when it was almost gone, Zock took to acting funny for a while, and I didn't see him much. I went swimming with the gang, horsing around, the bunch of us just killing time until the shift into high.

Then one evening, right after supper, I was sitting on the front porch reading a magazine when Zock sauntered over. "Have we met?" I asked him as he came. "Your face certainly looks familiar, because nobody could forget a face like that. Do you have a name? What do people call you?" And I chattered on and on. He didn't answer, but just sat down in a rocker and began going back and forth, back and forth. "Cat got your tongue?" I asked, using one of his mother's favorite expressions.

He looked at me. "Want to read a poem?" When I said sure, he handed me a sheet of paper. "Let me know what you think," he said. "Come right over when you're done." Then he ran off.

I opened the paper. It read:

So seize the moment
While there is a moment yet to seize.

Take it now.
Else faceless Time
Creep in on little cat's feet
To take it.
While I love you; while my love falls
Like love shaken from a petal.
Take me now.

I must have read that poem over about twenty times right then, I thought it was so beautiful. I studied every word until I knew what the whole thing meant. After which I tore over to his house. He was sitting in his room.

"Well?" he said.

"What the hell is it?" I asked, very serious.

"It's supposed to be a poem."

"I know that. But what's it mean? Exactly."

"Whatever you want it to mean. That's the wonderful thing about poetry."

"Who do you want to take you, Zock? Who are you in love with?"

"Jesus," he said. "I'm not in love. It's a poem."

"And what about those cat's feet?"

"I stole that," he admitted.

"What for?"

"It's legal. In poetry it's legal. Everybody does it."

"And what about this 'love falling like love' part? Is that what you meant? Shouldn't it be love falling like water? Or dew. How about dew?"

"It's an image," Zock yelled and I saw I'd gone too far, so I stopped. But it was too late. He snatched the paper out of my hand, ripping it. "Goddam you," he shouted. "Goddam you to hell!" And then he swung on me, something he hadn't done since that very first day.

I ducked easy enough and dove at him, pinning his arm behind him, yelling right back. "I-loved-that-poem! I-was-only-kidding. I-loved-it. I-think-it's-beautiful. Honest-but-I-think-it's-the-prettiest-goddam-poem-I-ever-read. Now-will-you-stop?" He was swearing at me but my voice was louder so that he had to listen. And he knew I meant it. Every word.

"You do?" he said. "You really do?"

I nodded, letting him go.

"Euripides," he said. "You are the smartest guy and the best critic in the whole world."

"Naturally," I said. "But let's cut out this fol-de-rol and go do something useful. Let's go scare Miss Blaul."

Now I'm not the smartest guy or the best critic in the whole world, and I'm the first to admit it. But just the same, Zock showed me every poem he ever wrote after that. They got better all the time, except I still liked that first one best, with love dropping like love. I know they got better because when Zock was sixteen, he won a national poetry contest and by the time he was seventeen, he'd had several poems published. He would have been a fine poet, maybe even a great one, if only I'd given him the chance.

High school was a disappointment at first, as it wasn't much different from grammar school which I had eight years of, nine counting kindergarten. We stayed within our own gang, not meeting many new people. We did the same thing as before, but now nobody cared. The work wasn't any more interesting, only harder, and although I stunk at algebra, Zock pushed me through.

So by the time spring came around, there wasn't much to show. Then, on the night of the third of April, something happened and I'm not sure yet for better or worse. But I date my high school career, such as it was, from that night, for to all intents and purposes, it began then.

Spring vacation it was, with me living at Zock's house since my parents were up East someplace where my father had been invited to give a couple lectures dealing with Symbolism in Euripides which, I must admit, doesn't sound any too racy. Zock's folks were off at a party and there we were, a soft warm night, both of us feeling itchy, and nothing to do. Just who got the idea first I don't remember. It doesn't matter though, for we both wanted to and, almost before we knew it, we were standing in front of his old man's liquor cabinet. At this time, neither of us knew for beans about alcohol. There never was any at my house, only dry wine, and Zock had never cared much, one way or the other.

"Well, Zocker," I said. "How do we start?"

"I don't know," he admitted.

"And how do we know when we get there?"

"I don't know that either."

"Then you must be pretty stupid," I told him, grabbing a nearly full bottle of rum and pouring myself a glass. Zock took out a bottle of Scotch, a wise move and one that accounted for his better condition through the night and next day or two.

We started swilling it down, sitting in two easy chairs, facing each other and laughing. I drained the first glass pretty fast. It didn't affect me at all, but halfway into the second, I began feeling rocky.

"Yes sir," I said. "You can say that again."

Zock looked across at me. "I didn't say anything."

"Well, don't say it again if you want to. I'm a liberal."

Which confused him, I think, so we didn't talk for a long time but concentrated instead on our drinking, gulping it down. And I must admit that, pretty soon, I was in my cups, as my mother would say.

"My mother would say I'm in my cups now. How about that. In my cups. Isn't that the stupidest expression?"

"Isn't what the stupidest expression?"

"Aren't you listening to me?"

"I'm trying," Zock said. "But you're not coming through very clear."

"If my father knows so much about Euripides, why isn't he rich?"

"Who's Euripides?" Zock asked, which stumped me awhile.

"I am," I said finally. "That's who."

"Well, if you're Euripides," Zock said. "Why aren't you rich?"

"Maybe I am," I told him. "Maybe I'm the richest guy in the world. Maybe I'm so rich I can't stand it."

"I don't believe you," Zock said.

"It's the truth," I said. "I am so rich I can't stand it. Do you know what I blow my nose on?"

"Ten-dollar bills?" I shook my head. "Twenty-dollar bills?"

"Wrong."

"What, then?"

"My shirtsleeves," I said. Which I still think, considering the conditions and all, was pretty funny. But not so funny that you'd fall off your chair laughing at it. I did, though. I hit the floor and stayed there, waving that empty bottle.

"Rise," Zock said.

"I could if I wanted to," I said. "I just don't want to."

"Here," Zock said. "I'll help."

Well, he tried. That much you have to say for him. He did try. He even made it out of his chair. But crossing the floor beat him and he fell down on top of me.

"That's a helluva thing to do," I told him. "Falling on one of your own guests." We rested there awhile, our heads spinning around. Then Zock spoke up.

"You know what, Euripides?" he said. "I think we made it." Which was the truth. For if ever two people were drunk, it was us.

"What'll we do now?" I asked.

"I don't know," he answered. "Something."

"Great idea," I told him and we tried getting up. Neither of us could, alone, but together we somehow managed to make it and stagger out of the house into the street.

"Well," I said when we got there. "What now?" He didn't answer me right away so I waved my hand in front of his face. "What now?" I said again. "Answer my question."

He waved his hand in front of my face. "Beats me," he said.

"Well, you sure aren't very bright. Nothing but a moron."

"I was about to say the same of you."

We were both about to say a lot more when suddenly somebody had us by the shoulders and there was a policeman. Not smiling.

"Good evening to you, officer," I said.

"What's the fight about?" he asked.

"Fight?" I said, really confused.

"I saw you," he said. "And if you don't stop, I'll have to take the both of you in."

"But we weren't fighting," I insisted.

"All right," he sighed.

"Absurd, officer, absurd!" Zock broke in strong. "We are the best of friends."

"Then go home," he told us, letting go. We started back for the house but I don't think Jesse Owens could have made it, because we hadn't taken more than a step or two when he grabbed us again and herded us into his police car.

The trip down wasn't too eventful except that I managed to throw up all over the back seat, which didn't strike him very funny. Zock and I laughed though, all the way there. At the station it got pretty confusing. The man behind the desk kept asking us our names and Zock kept asking him what he wanted to know for, since it wasn't any of his business.

"Please, boys," he said over and over. "Please. Co-operate."

"Absurd," Zock said over and over. "We are the best of friends."

Then he began standing on his rights as a citizen and finally he started quoting poetry while I tossed in a couple baseball statistics I had handy.

The upshot of it all was that we spent the night in jail.

Which, as I said earlier, made my reputation. Because, when we finally did get back to school, we were famous. Zock preferred not to capitalize on it and wouldn't even answer any questions. So everybody came to me and the more I told the story, the better it got. And in less time than it takes to tell, I was the school character. I was voted class clown when I graduated and it can all be traced back to that warm April night when Zock and I got drunk, both for the very first time.

So our gang became the most talked about in the school, even though we were only freshmen, and got the reputation of being the wildest, which we weren't. I really basked in glory that spring and summer and early fall. Time went zipping by, one day much like the next, and the only thing I remember plain was what happened that summer afternoon.

I was out in the back yard throwing rocks at the big trees on the far side of the ravine, connecting three times out of four, which is better than most can do. Zock came over and stood around awhile, watching.

"If only there was some way of making money out of this," I said, "I'd be rich." He didn't answer but just stood there, watching me throw, listening to the thud of the rocks as they lambasted those tree trunks.

"Don't be shy," I said. "I'm really nice enough, once you get to know me."

He cleared his throat. I waited. Then he started talking. "This isn't my idea," he began. "I want you to know that my mother put me up to it. But the thing is, you're supposed to come to a party at my house a week from Sunday. Two in the afternoon. And wear a necktie."

"Ridiculous," I answered, hitting a big oak across the ravine. "I won't come."

"My mother may never get over it," Zock said. And then: "What if we forget about the necktie?"

"I might," I told him. "You going to be there?"

"Unfortunately, yes."

"If you can take it," I said. "Then so can I."

"Fine." Zock laughed. "You just won me a double allowance."

"What's the party for?"

"My cousin Sadie," he answered. "She's getting married." I didn't say anything. "To some yokel from Michigan Law School," he went on. "She's getting married in three weeks. And you will come?"

"Naturally," I said, throwing a handful of rocks all at once. "I'll be there."

Naturally, I wasn't. I decided it that afternoon out by the ravine where I stayed, throwing rocks, until dusk set in. At dinner my mother gabbed about the party, since she and my father were invited too, and what should I wear and did I have a summer jacket that looked decent? I went along with her, nodding when she said what a wonderful party it was going to be and wasn't I lucky to get an invitation. There was no point in telling her then. So I waited.

Until the day before. That afternoon I ran around, getting red and sweaty, after which I dashed home and told her I didn't feel so well. She bit, felt my forehead, told me to go right up to bed. I grumbled, as was expected, but wild horses couldn't have kept me from the sack right then. I moaned a lot during the evening and listened to the White Sox on the radio. When it was time for sleep she gave me a couple aspirin and turned out the light.

"You've got to be all right for tomorrow, Raymond," she said. "It's not every day you get invited to a party."

"Gosh, no," I told her. "I'll feel fine tomorrow. I wouldn't miss that party for the world."

The next morning I really hammed it up. I snuck an extra blanket under my bedspread, making sure I'd sweat plenty, splashed water in my eyes, getting them good and red, plus various other tactics. When the afternoon rolled around, I knew my mother wouldn't have let me out of bed even if the house had been burning down. So I fought the good fight, moaned about how much I wanted to go, and in general earned the Academy Award for malingering. Finally, when I thought I couldn't stand it much longer, she and my father left, and I was alone.

I turned the radio on, threw the covers off, and lay there, staring at the cracks in the ceiling. Then I started to swear, but that never does much good. So I snuck downstairs to the living-room, to the big window that faced out on Zock's house.

I saw it all, from first to last, standing there in my pajamas that hot summer afternoon. About the only time I missed was once when I heard my mother coming up the walk so I had to beat it back to bed, barely making it, smiling bravely until she left again.

It was a garden party Mrs. Crowe gave. With punch. There was a big bowl of it set on a table in the back yard. When I started looking just a few were present; Zock, my folks and his, plus some I didn't know, probably other cousins who made the trip out for the occasion. It appeared about as dull as you would expect Mrs. Crowe's parties to be, what with that big cut-glass punch bowl right smack in the middle of the lawn and other goodies spread around, little sandwiches, etc. Nothing much happened until suddenly everyone hurried around to the front of the house because of the honking from the convertible that had just driven up.

And Sadie Griffin got out. Dressed all in white with her golden hair tumbling down her back, her skin tanned from the summer sun. She smiled and started kissing everybody, throwing her arms around them, so I dashed to the kitchen for a glass of water, hurrying back in time to see her half turn, hold out her hand. And there he was.

He was tall and dark-haired and even from my distance you could tell that a giant size bottle of hair oil would last him about three days. If he went easy. And he was wearing a blazer, complete with crest and gold buttons. On a hot summer day the son of a bitch was wearing a blazer. With gray pants and white bucks and a red striped tie. His name, I found out later, was Alvin. Everyone called him Al, but you can bet if I'd ever met him, it would have been Alvin right down the line. He took her by the hand, Old Hair Oil did, and together they walked around to where the punch was, smiling at each other all the time.

More people came, lots of them, some of them wives from the college dragging their husbands. They all just stood around gassing, except for Zock's father, who kept going inside for liquor, bringing out drinks for the menfolk, as Mrs. Crowe called them, and thank God for that. Everyone looked pretty stupid from where I was, like actors in the old silent movies who gestured with their arms, raised their eyebrows, moved their lips but you couldn't hear a thing they were saying.

After a while I got tired standing, so I brought a chair up to the window, out of sight, staying there for hours, sitting and watching, my chin in my hands. And I was like that when I heard my mother again, close by, coming up the walk. Shoving the chair back, I ran for the stairs.

I made it only to the halfway landing when she spoke to me. And this time it wasn't my mother. It was her.

"I'm sorry you couldn't come to the party," she opened, and I turned, stared down, said nothing. She was standing in the middle of the foyer, away from any windows, almost in shadow, but not quite.

"It's really a wonderful party," she went on. "And I am sorry you couldn't come. I asked for you especially."

"That's the breaks," I said.

"Your mother told me you weren't feeling well."

"She told you right," I said. "I'm sick."

Sadie Griffin started coming up the stairs.

"I'm sick," I said again. "So you better not come close."

"I'm not afraid," she said.

"You might catch something," I told her, backing up the rest of the stairs. "You'd have to postpone your wedding." She kept on. "You wouldn't want to have to postpone your wedding."

She got to the halfway landing but by then I was at the top, away from the railing by the wall.

"I've told Al about you," she said. "He was very anxious . . ."

"I'll bet," I cut in.

"You'd like him," she went on. "He's"—and she threw her arms out wide—"wonderful."

"He'd be more wonderful if only he'd use a little grease on his hair. That'd probably make him perfect."

At which she laughed and started talking softly up to me. "When I was fourteen," she whispered. "I had an algebra teacher named Mr. Dillon. He was short and not very handsome, but . . ."

"Can the crap!" I said which, vulgar as it was, did the trick, for right after, she turned to leave.

"I only came over to say hello," she finished. "And to hope you feel better soon."

"Thank you," I said.

"Good-by, Euripides." She waved, and she was gone.

As soon as I heard the front door close I went to my room, switched on the ball game, got under the covers, and lay there sweating until my parents came back. The next week Sadie Griffin got married. Neither Zock nor I ever mentioned her again.

The rest of the summer went fast, me spending most of my days with the gang. Just wasting time, for want of something better to do. And I probably would have gone on like that indefinitely, if Felix Brown hadn't come to school that rainy fall day which now seems so long ago.

I was standing by the main door of school with some of the others, watching for any new faces that might wander past. All of a sudden "Buttons" Dooley, standing behind me, said: "Jesus Christ, I don't believe it." I turned around and when I saw what he was looking at, I just stared.

Because Felix Brown came walking in, big as a mountain.

At the age of sixteen, which is what he was then, Felix Brown stood over six feet five and weighed close to 250 pounds. When he took off his black raincoat you could almost see those muscles rippling under his shirt and I thought that if there was anyone I never wanted to meet in a dark alley, I was looking at him.

He walked over and asked "Buttons" where to go to register. "Buttons" kind of gaped, pointed, and said: "Over there, sir. Through that door."

"How about that, Rip," he asked me after Felix had walked away, "did you see the size of that nigger?" I nodded.

"He's not so damn big," said Johnny Hunkley, who weighed about the same as Felix but was, as has been pointed out, a slob.

"Then I don't know who is," I answered, and I walked away.

I already said how I became a wheel at school by spending one night in jail. Felix didn't even have to do that. He just strolled around school that day, wearing a dark-red corduroy shirt and Army pants, and by the end of classes, he was a legend. Boys flocked up to him, introducing themselves. Girls followed him with their eyes as he moved along. For Felix was a very handsome boy. With fine features and really beautiful skin, not black, but kind of cocoa-colored. He was built the way everybody wants to be but never is; shoulders a yard wide, slim hips, no waist at all. And he moved with a terrific rhythmic walk, graceful, like a panther.

By the end of his first week in school, Felix was a very popular guy. Those that knew him said he wasn't dumb at all, like you'd expect, and they almost bragged when they said it. As if it was a gold star for them just because they happened to sit next to him in geometry. Which is understandable, I suppose, for I have noted that people like a chance to show they aren't prejudiced, even when they are. So that later they can say: "I had a good buddy once in college who was a Catholic," or "I once went out with a Jewish girl and she was a real lady." I'm not trying to turn this into a sermon so I won't say any more, and besides, being a white Protestant, no one has ever said such things of me. Still, I have no doubt but that I am correct in my observation.

Getting back to Felix. Everyone expected him to go out for the football team, which stunk, excepting Johnny Hunkley, who was probably the best tackle in the whole state of Illinois. But Felix didn't. Until one day in Assembly Coach Haggerty got up and made a big speech about how we needed players as Johnny Hunkley couldn't do it alone, and anyone who was big enough to play and didn't was chicken. After that, the pressure was really on, so one afternoon Felix went out for football. But only for one afternoon. Because they put him at fullback and in the course of a single scrimmage he accidentally injured two players and also got into a hassle with the coach, an easy thing to do, for Haggerty was something of a moron.

Before I can explain what happened next, I have to put in a word about Athens High School, which is very small, being made up of people from two grammar schools in the area, Athens itself, and Crystal City. Naturally, these groups stayed mostly to themselves and a rivalry grew up to see which one Felix was going to be a part of. That sounds pretty juvenile, I know, but we were in those days. Anyhow, the bunch from Crystal City was paying a lot of attention to Felix and it looked like he was going to join them. Nobody in our gang was particularly pleased by this, except Zock and me, who didn't care, and Johnny Hunkley, who disliked Felix anyway, for obvious reasons. But "Buttons" and the rest were a little worried as, if anything ever did happen between us and Crystal City, they would be a cinch to mop up, since Felix alone could have done the job. So pressure was put on me to do something, and I gave in to it, for I freely admit I enjoyed being high muckamuck and did whatever I could to maintain my position.

I talked it over with Zock and he agreed to come along that night as we took the walk from my place to where Felix lived. Which was on the college grounds, as his old man was a new janitor there and also, I later found out, something of a lush. Anyhow, we walked over on that beautiful October night, not saying much since I was rehearsing in my mind what I was going to tell Felix. I rang the bell and his old man answered, reeking as usual, and said that Felix was in the back room, lying down.

He was. Wearing only underwear shorts. That being the first time I had ever seen him in the flesh, it shook me, for the room was small, the ceiling low, and he seemed to fill it as he lay there on the bed. He sat up when we came in, the muscles rippling under his cocoa skin, and I remember thinking that he just had to end up as heavyweight champion of the world or as king of some South Sea island.

He looked at us and said: "Well?"

Zock nodded to me but I couldn't say much, having forgotten all I'd rehearsed. We sort of stammered around for a while, not getting anywhere, and then I said that it was such a beautiful night Zock and I decided to take a walk. Felix Brown's answer is something I'll never forget as long as I live.

He said: " 'Pale amber sunlight falls across the reddening October trees.' "

Zock right away replied: " 'That hardly sway before breeze as soft as Summer.' "

Which might sound like gibberish to the general public, but I knew what they were talking about. Those were the first lines of a poem by Ernest Dowson, a rummy English poet and Zock's favorite at the time. I liked him too, although to my mind, he could never hold a candle to Kipling.

Well, Zock followed it up with more Dowson. " 'You would have understood me had you waited.' " And Felix said: " 'I could have loved you dear as well as he.' "

Which started things off.

They went all through Dowson, me throwing in my favorite lines from "I have been faithful to you, Cynara, in my fashion."

I have forgot much, Cynara. Gone with the wind.
Flung roses, roses, riotously with the throng.

After Dowson came William Butler Yeats: "But I being poor have only my dreams. I have spread my dreams under your feet. Tread soft, for you tread on my dreams." Then Eliot with his hollow men, and I put forth the first paragraph of "Danny Deever." Followed by "I weep for Adonaïs, he is dead," and even, "Jenny kissed me."

After about an hour, Felix went to the icebox, got some beer, and we took it out in back, sitting on the grass, drinking. We did some more poetry, me listening and swilling down the beer as I was just then acquiring the taste. I was pretty looped before too much longer and so was Zock. But not Felix.

And when the poetry wore thin, we started talking. I couldn't possibly explain what happened out there on the grass that night. I think it had a lot to do maybe with the weather, which was perfect, for you almost had the feeling you were floating, so that when you turned your head you could feel the air shifting around you, making a new place for you in the scheme of things. Or maybe again it had to do with the fact that we were getting drunk. But that still doesn't come close to explaining it.

For we talked about ourselves, free and open, like a Catholic at confession, not hiding anything but just speaking our minds. I found out some things about Zock that night, such as that he wasn't too pleased with the way he looked, being ugly and all. And I suppose he found out some things about me he'd never known before. And we both learned a lot about Felix Brown. Such as that, like Zock, he too wanted to be a poet; he had written poetry that I never saw but Zock did and said it was much better than anything he had written, which must have ranked Felix pretty high up on the list. And how he hated being a Negro. And how he wished he were smaller, normal-sized, so that people wouldn't always be staring at him like a freak. Plus a lot more.

And the upshot of it all was that Felix didn't join the gang from Crystal City. Or my own. Because, after that night, Zock and me left the gang ourselves, left it to Johnny Hunkley for whatever he could make of it. So we walked together for a while then, the three of us, probably a funny sight when you think about it. Big Felix and little Zock and me, with me in the middle and a poet on either side.

I don't want to give the impression that all we ever did was sit around, telling each other our innermost thoughts. It's just that it never made any real difference what we were doing. There was always so much to talk about, our coming from different backgrounds, Zock's being sort of sickly and Fee's just the opposite, on account of his having been brought up in one of the worst slum areas in the entire city of Chicago. Fee was very smart though, not quite as good as Zock, who was tops in the school, but close, and my grades picked up considerable, what with having two people to help me instead of Zock alone. But I have to admit that even school work wasn't bad when we did it together. Such as the Saturday afternoon over at Fee's house when we were boning up for a big Monday test on *Hamlet*, a play I didn't like, though it is sacrilege to say so, mainly because it is so damn long.

"The way I see it," I said that afternoon, "Hamlet had the hots for his mother."

Fee, lying on his bed, began singing "It Ain't Necessarily So" in his deep bass voice. Zock just shook his head. "What makes you think that?" he asked.

"I read it some place," I admitted. "Or maybe somebody told me." And I took a swig from a can of beer, one of many we had taken from Felix's old man's icebox.

"Well, forget it," Zock said.

"Then give me something to remember," I said right back.

"O.K.," Zock began. "How about this? Why don't we say that in this play we have Man coming to grips . . ." stopped then, because Fee had snuck behind him and lifted him high into the air, so that his nose was almost rubbing against the ceiling.

"Must you do this?" Zock asked Felix.

"Somehow it satisfies me," Fee answered.

Zock sighed. "All right," he said down to me. "Where was I?"

"Man was just coming to grips," I told him.

"Quite right," Zock said. "Yes. We have Man coming to grips with the one force he is unable to combat."

"What force is that?" Fee asked.

"The Air Force," I butted in, slapping my knee. "Get it? The . . ."

They ignored me. "You see," Zock went on, "Hamlet is equipped to handle almost any situation. He is brave; he is strong; he is brilliant. But then, whammo, comes this one problem he can't handle, and he's done for. How's that?"

"Great," I said. "Marvelous. It stinks."

"What's wrong with it?"

"Jesus Christ," I told him. "If you believe that, who do you put the blame on?"

"Set me down," Zock said. Fee did. "Now," he continued. "Why do you have to blame somebody?"

"Forty people are murdered in this play, for chrisakes. That's why."

"No, you don't," Fee cut in. "Here. How about this," and he closed his eyes a second, thinking. "Let's say that when somebody was a kid, his father beat him. And this guy goes to jail for beating somebody else. But this guy's father only beat him because his old man whaled him when he was a kid. Who do you blame?"

"The grandfather," I said.

"But what if the grandfather only beat the father because his father beat him. And the grandfather's father was brought up by an old biddy of an aunt who was cruel to him. And she was cruel because she never got married. You can't blame the world because nobody ever married the aunt."

"Why didn't they marry her?" I asked.

"Because she was ugly. Now, whose fault is that?"

I was about to answer when Fee's father staggered by. "Don't mind me, boys," he said as he went past the door.

"Afternoon, Mr. Brown," Zock and I both said.

"Afternoon, is it?" he answered, and then he was out of sight but we could still hear him staggering along. Then we heard the icebox door opening. Then a bellow. Then he was back.

"Someone's been stealing me blind," he said.

" 'Afternoon, Pa," Fee said.

"Someone's been stealing me blind," Mr. Brown said again.

"You mean about the beer?" Fee asked. Mr. Brown nodded. Fee looked very serious. "A bunch of beggars came by a little earlier on their way to Kankakee for a convention. They asked for a beer so I gave them one each. Plus one more for the road."

"A beggars' convention in Kankakee," Mr. Brown muttered, letting it sink in. "Well, I'm damned. Didn't know they had them."

"Every year," Fee told him. "In a big vacant lot just outside of Kankakee."

"Well, I'm damned," Mr. Brown said again. Then he smiled, turned, heading back for bed. "Don't mind me, boys," he called as he disappeared.

"All right, Euripides," Fee said when we were alone again. "Now. Whose fault is it? Who's to blame?"

"Hamlet," I answered.

"Why?" they both asked at once.

"Because the way I see it," I told them, swilling down my beer, "he had the hots for his mother . . ."

We began, the three of us, on that wonderful October night, and we went right through the winter, always together, into early spring. When things started going wrong.

The first indication was that Zock's father, Old Crowe, which I thought up and have never been ashamed for doing so, found that business at his clothing store was dropping off. Something I still believe was his own fault, since he was never what you might term a J. P. Morgan. But naturally he said it was on account of the company Zock was keeping.

And then one night after supper, my father called me into his study for a talk. "Scuddahoo, Scuddahay," he began, an old Greek proverb he never bothered translating but which I knew went something like this: "Don't pal around with niggers because I am America's leading expert on Euripides and I don't like it." He said some more Greek, threw in a little English, all of it going over my head. He never got to the point. Teachers and politicians never do. They just say some crap that doesn't mean much, but you know what they're really talking about. And I knew what my father meant so I said: "Yes sir, you bet." He smiled, did you-know-what to his lips and forehead, muttered, "Indeed? Fine," and told me to run along.

I did. Over to Fee's where we talked all about it. So after that the three of us started meeting secretly. Or staying late around school. Or lying about where we were. I suppose we saw each other almost as much as before.

But it wasn't the same. And we all knew it. What happened next was obvious: we drifted apart. Or rather Fee did, away from us. We hated seeing him go, but there just wasn't much we could do about it.

So when we saw each other in school we smiled and chatted a bit, but that was all. Before we knew it, Fee had taken up with the gang from Crystal City. They weren't a bad bunch of people, when you got to know them. Except that right then, they weren't people at all, but just so many flies, buzzing around Felix Brown. They worshipped him. And what they worshipped him for was not his mind, and not the fact that maybe he was going to be a fine poet. But his strength. I suppose you can't really blame them for that, since it is a natural thing to do. Besides, if you wanted to pray at the font of the mighty, you couldn't have picked anyone better than Fee. He was so strong it was frightening. He could lift me with one hand, hold me out at arm's length without the least sign of strain. And he wasn't brute power either; Fee was controlled, co-ordinated, catlike.

Soon after we split up he began going downhill. He took to drinking too much and sometimes arrived at school smelling like he'd just walked out of a beer keg. Which bothered us plenty until finally one day, when Fee looked and smelled particularly bad, we went up to him.

"Gee," Zock said. "I've never seen you looking better."

"Leave me alone," Fee told him.

"I just wanted you to know how nice we thought you looked," Zock went on. "And what a swell reputation you're making for yourself. And how proud we both are of you." And then Zock really let him have it. He stepped right up to big Fee and shattered him. Fee just stood there, staring out over Zock's head. Finished, Zock waited for an answer.

"I want to leave town," Fee said.

"Leave," Zock told him.

"I want to go to San Francisco," Fee went on. "I want to get away."

"There's nothing keeping you here," Zock said.

"I haven't got the guts," Fee muttered, and then we were all three quiet for a while. Finally he started talking again, talking very low. "They treat me real nice out in Crystal City," he said. "I got a lot of friends out there. I'm like a god out in Crystal City, Zock. You ever been one? It's nice." He began moving off. "You ought to try it sometime."

Which didn't make much sense to me at the time, but Zock understood it all. Because he wasn't surprised at what happened after, when Fee really went to pieces. He got in trouble twice with the police, didn't show up much at school and was drunk when he did come. And surly. With nothing to say to anyone, especially Zock and me. We never talked about it, as whenever I started to, Zock cut me off, telling me to wait, to wait and see. So I waited.

Until that night in early summer, with school about to stop for the year. It was Friday, and we were standing in the main corridor after classes when Fee came up.

"Be at the Palace in Crystal City tonight," he said. That was all.

The Palace is an auditorium where they hold dances, and roller skating on Mondays, and town meetings, and whatever else you can think of that goes on in a little place like Crystal City. Friday night was an "open dance." That was what it was called, but actually it was just a place to go to pick up girls, who always appeared from somewhere, most likely the woodwork, judging from their looks. They had what I suppose you've got to call a three-piece band playing on the stage. It was hot and crowded inside. Most of the people from school were there. Johnny Hunkley with our old gang; lots of girls; and, of course, the bunch from Crystal City. Zock and I arrived early, went over to one corner, and waited.

Finally Fee came in. About nine o'clock. He walked to where the Crystal City crowd was located and they all bunched around him, which was pretty sickening I thought, but Zock kept saying: "Wait, wait," again and again, very excited. Then Fee started showing off, jumping around, stamping on the floor, shouting, picking people up, holding them at arm's length, making a fool of himself. The room got noisier and noisier until finally it seemed that all hell just had to break loose.

And it did.

Because Fee suddenly raised his giant arms. Everything quieted. Even the music stopped. Then he pointed across the floor, pointed right at Johnny Hunkley, who was standing there, scowling.

"Don't you like it?" Fee asked.

There wasn't a sound.

Then Johnny Hunkley said: "What if I don't?"

"I guess you better do something about it," Fee told him. "Do something, or get out."

They both stepped into the middle of the floor. The musicians grabbed their instruments. Fee and Johnny Hunkley started circling each other.

It might seem as if Johnny Hunkley was a boy with a lot of guts, standing up to Fee like that. But I don't think so. It was more his being stupid than brave. For he might have gotten himself killed that night and ought to be thanking God to this day that he's still alive.

They circled for a while, Fee on his toes, the other flat-footed. Then Fee snaked out a long left that stung alongside Johnny Hunkley's cheek. And with that slapping sound, the Palace came to life. From all over people crept up, whispering at first, getting louder and louder.

Then Johnny Hunkley charged like a bull, head down. Fee stepped aside easily, driving his fist down at Johnny Hunkley's neck as he went by. Johnny Hunkley went down hard, got up slowly, charged again, and again the same thing happened. And this time, when he got up, you could see the fear showing plain in his eyes.

But, as I said, he was stupid, so, head down, legs churning, he charged. He did it six, seven, eight times, and by then his neck was swelling and blood was streaming down his face. Felix, fresh and smiling, waited out in the middle, balanced on his toes, light and fast as a featherweight boxer.

But Johnny Hunkley was tiring. Panting terribly, gasping, he was gulping down air, filling his lungs with it, and the sound of his breathing echoed in the room, over all the other noise. Pushing himself to his feet, he charged one more time.

Felix just stood there.

Johnny Hunkley's 250 pounds caught him right in the pit of the stomach. Everyone started screaming, closing in tight, watching as Johnny Hunkley rolled over on top and began swinging down at Fee's face with everything he had. When Fee wasn't moving any more, Johnny Hunkley stood up, swaying, covered with blood, and the Palace went wild.

Somebody yelled something about the cops so they all rushed for the door, Johnny Hunkley in the middle, being carried along by the crowd. Fee was trying to get up when Zock and I reached him. "Meet me out in back," he said. So, without another word, we went there and waited. Nobody else came up to Fee. The gang from Crystal City had already gone, probably with Johnny Hunkley, although I never knew for sure.

Zock and I waited a long time before we heard footsteps. It was Fee, walking quickly toward us, carrying a satchel in his hand. He came up and stood there smiling, big as God.

"California, here I come," he said.

"You burned your bridges," Zock said, shaking hands good-by.

"I did that," Fee laughed. "I did that very thing." He turned to me. "So long, Euripides," he said. Then he was gone. In a minute, the night had swallowed him up, and all that was left was the click of his heels on the pavement, the sound of his humming in the air.

So Zock and I got drunk, which was our way of wishing him bon voyage, good luck, and God be with you. Zock never saw Felix Brown again. I did. But that comes later and right now I've said all I want about the boys I knew at the time. Not that there weren't others, for there were, lots of them, and more as the years went by. But that summer something happened to me and it changed my whole life. What happened, naturally, was just this:

Girls.

III . . . . The Girls

I have to start this with Helen Twilly.

Who was a freshman in the college when I first knew her, and a very easy person to describe. Helen Twilly had huge cans. Now ordinarily, in this day and age, that should be enough to make a girl reasonably popular. But not Helen. For her face wasn't much and neither was her figure, her butt also being very large. Her cans were so big, though, that it made you forget most of the rest. Zock and I used to refer to other girls' with her name. "Twillies," we called them. But that was later.

The reason I met her at all was because of my mother. I was in the seventh grade at the time, when, out of the blue, my mother decided that I should have piano lessons. It was, I suppose, a last-ditch attempt on her part to bring some culture into my life. Culture, even today, is not one of my strongest points and I had less of it then. Anyway, my mother had a long talk with me one night at supper, beating around the bush, going on about the importance of the arts, especially music. Finally, she came out with it: I was to take piano lessons. My father had asked at the college for someone who might give them to me and had come up with Miss Twilly. So, in spite of anything I could do, the lessons began.

The first one was the worst. Mainly because my mother insisted on staying in the room while Miss Twilly gave me the business about scales. They were as far as I ever got, scales, but nobody knew it then. I sat there, sweating, pounding away on our little upright piano with Miss Twilly beside me, smiling over at my mother who smiled back, and I don't know how. For my ear has never been very good as far as music is concerned. The reason I stopped taking piano was because it turned out I was tone deaf. This has never been a heavy cross for me to bear, but it did come as a blow to my mother who, I think, honestly had visions of me being a child prodigy and knocking them dead at Carnegie Hall.

"You must cup your hands, Raymond," Miss Twilly said to me that day. "Cup them over the keyboard."

"Sure thing," I said, doing as I was told. Which didn't make the scales sound any better since, being tone deaf, I was never sure when I did something right or not.

"Do, re, mi, fa, sol, la, ti, do," Miss Twilly sang along. "No, Raymond. La. La." And she hit the correct note.

"La," I said. "La, la, la." And I pounded away on that poor key.

"Not so hard, Raymond," Miss Twilly pleaded, smiling at my mother. "Gently. We must learn to caress the keys. As though they were our friends."

And that was how it went for the first lesson. I wasn't as unhappy about it as I might have been, for I knew from the start that I was never going to play at Carnegie Hall or any place else. Some things you take to right away, but to the piano I never did. It was all a joke, my only worry being that the news might spread around school. Which never happened, since Zock was always a good man at keeping a secret.

I told him right after it was over. Mother and Miss Twilly were having a whispered conversation so I slipped on by them to Zock's house. He was waiting to hear, but what I talked about was not so much the music as Miss Twilly's cans. I was so expressive that he asked if he could see them.

And the next time she came, the following Tuesday, he was there, waiting. She walked in and smiled at me. He just stared. Then, before the lesson started, he got up to go.

"They're big all right," Zock said, and he took off.

Which threw Miss Twilly. "What are big?" she asked me.

"I don't know," I answered. "Sometimes it's very hard to figure just what he's talking about."

But all the same, she knew. She was a little flustered during the lesson. Not really embarrassed, just flustered. She kind of hunched her shoulders forward, trying to make them seem not so noticeable, which in her case was an impossibility.

After that, I began to like her. I think she knew about my being tone deaf from the start but said nothing of it to anyone because she needed the money. At any rate, from then on we played the piano less and talked more, about all kinds of things. She had a way of patting me on top of the head which, with most people, you don't like, seeing as it makes you feel as though you are a dog and they are petting you. But with Miss Twilly it was all right. She was such a sweet girl. Very shy and kind, with a soft, gentle voice. She was so shy she blushed all the time, even in front of me, which should show the kind of person she was.

But the music part never got anywhere. I stayed with those scales the whole eight weeks I took piano lessons. And I did try. Each time before she came I'd practice half an hour, trying to cup my hands and sit up straight, trying to make those notes come out right. But some people can do some things and others can't, and playing the piano was not my forte, a pun Zock thought up one day.

So, finally, Miss Twilly had a long talk with my mother and told her the truth. About my being tone deaf and how this kind of hurts your chances of ever making it as a piano player. And my mother stopped the lessons right after. At the last one, Miss Twilly and I talked and laughed, having a gay old time. But when she got up to go, I think we both felt sad.

"Well, good-by, Raymond," she said, patting me on the head.

"So long, Miss Twilly," I answered, walking her to the door. "I sure hope you can make it to Carnegie Hall." Which of course she never did, but just the same it was what she wanted more than anything else in the world. "Maybe I'll see you around sometime."

"Maybe," she said, patting my head once more. "Let's hope so."

And I did see her. Often, during the next couple of years. Uptown or around the campus I'd see her walking alone or with some other girls. Whenever that happened, I'd wave and shout: "Hello there, Miss Twilly." And she'd blush and wave back. She was never with a boy, at least none I ever saw. And that was a shame, her being such a fine girl, shy and gentle and all.

Then, in June of my sophomore year in high school, her class graduated, her along with it. Graduation day at Athens was something I never cared for. All those caps and gowns and crying mothers. I had already made up my mind that when I graduated from college, I was going to skip the whole business. But of course, the way things worked out, I never had to miss much sleep on that score.

Anyhow, I was puttering around the house, waiting for it to get over. Zock used to like to watch, so he was up by the college auditorium taking it in. My father was there, too, being as he was such a big deal at the school he had to go. And my mother wouldn't have missed it for the world. About the time I figured it was done, I started getting ready for the trip to Zock's house, when there was a buzz at the front door. I went down to answer. It was her.

"Hi, Miss Twilly," I said, opening it.

"Hello, Raymond," she said, walking in. It was a hot day and she was perspiring so she took off her cap and gown, smiling at me. She was wearing a big skirt and a very thin white blouse you could see through. "I thought I'd come over and say good-by," she told me. "I'm leaving this afternoon."

"That was real nice of you, Miss Twilly," I said. "I'm glad you did." She put her hand on my shoulder and we walked into the living-room where the little upright piano was. We started laughing.

"I suppose," she began. "You don't. I mean. Any more, do you?" She was very nervous on account of just having graduated, but I got what she meant.

"Practice?" I answered. "I'd rather be strung up by my thumbs."

It was very hot and stuffy and we both laughed at what I said, even though it wasn't funny. That is something I'm not much good at. Being funny. Once in a while, alone with Zock, I could do all right, but not often. He said not to worry about it since I had a fine sense of humor and could appreciate a joke as well as anyone. And that, he explained, was every bit as important, for if there was nobody around to laugh, where would the funny men be? True enough, I suppose, although I suspect he was just trying to make me feel better at the time. Which he did.

So we laughed at my joke, standing there in that stuffy room. We laughed for a long time, giggling away, and the next thing I knew she had her arms around me and was kissing me on the mouth, something that had never happened to me before. She pulled me in close and held me tight, kissing me over and over. First I tried to get away. But I stopped that quick.

Then she turned my head and began blowing in my ear, which has never made me turn cartwheels. Actually, I believe it really doesn't do anything to anybody, but long ago the idea started that it did, and it's kept on ever since because no one has had the guts to stop it. Well, she was blowing away at my ear, tickling me, though I never in this world would have laughed, as it would have hurt her feelings. Then she started to talk.

"Raymond," she said. "Raymond. Raymond. Raymond."

"What?" I asked her.

She didn't answer but just kept saying my name again and again as she horsed with my ear. And I knew that sure as God made green apples, I wasn't keeping my part of the bargain.

So finally, I suppose by instinct, I started doing something which I now know was a good thing, being what she wanted. Except then it was pure luck that I did it.

I started unbuttoning her blouse. It took me about an hour, since my hands were shaking, but I finally managed it. After which I pulled her blouse out from her skirt. A woman's brassière is something I can now work with my eyes closed, and frequently have. But right then, I couldn't find the handle. I tugged and pulled and sweated over it, but the goddam thing stayed put. I tried lifting it up, pushing it down, yanking on it every which way, getting no place. Then she gave that soft laugh of hers, put her hands behind her back for just a second, and it was loose. I lifted it, gently I think, and there they were.

"My God, Miss Twilly," I said. "They're huge."

She blushed, tried to cover herself. "I know," she whispered. "I'm sorry."

"No," I told her, pushing her hands away. "It's O.K. with me."

She put her arm around me and began walking me toward the stairs. "Come on, Raymond," she said. "Come on." And she started up with me following.

I have walked those stairs many times in my life, both before and since, but never has it seemed as hard or taken as long. Because halfway up I started sweating and shivering so that I could barely move. We got to my bedroom where she pulled down all the shades, one by one, and when she did that I could tell her hands were none too steady either. Then she closed the door. It wasn't very dark; we could still see each other plain. As I watched, Miss Twilly started taking off her clothes.

"You too, Raymond," she said.

But I didn't move. I couldn't. So when she was done she came over and tried pulling off my shirt.

"I can do it," I whispered, my throat very dry.

"All right," she said. "Show me you can."

I turned my back and she laughed softly at that, so I turned to face her again. I took off my shirt and pants. Finally I stood there, wearing just my sneakers.

"Finish it up," she said.

"Even my shoes?"

"Even your shoes."

I kicked them off. She sat down on the bed, smiling, and then she lay all the way back, stretching her arms toward me. I didn't move. She sat up again, reached out her hands, taking me gently, guiding me over to the bed. Pretty soon everything was warm and soft and neither of us was shaking any more.

Anyway, that was the first time.

After we'd said good-by at the front door, her patting me on the head, sort of crying, I ran over to Zock's house and told him all about it. Not in a boasting way but mainly because I was confused and he, being older, knew more of such things than I did.

He listened very carefully, pulling at his lower lip, a way he had when he was concentrating.

"That's it," I finished up. "She was crying and we went downstairs to say good-by. What do you think?"

"You bastard," Zock said, laughing.

"Come on," I said. "Don't kid around."

"A toast," he shouted. "A toast is definitely called for," and he took off, running to Old Crowe's liquor cabinet, me in hot pursuit. I watched as he filled two glasses, handed me one, smiling.

"And now we need a toast," he said. "But to what?"

"To Miss Twilly," I suggested, raising my glass.

"No," he said. "No good. She's over and done with. A thing of the past." He pulled at his lip awhile. "Wait. How about this? How about: a toast to those to come."

Which sounded fine to me and we drank to it.

So, at the age of sixteen, I had lost my virginity but had never been out with a girl. A state of affairs that I think might have continued for many years had it not been for Bunny Gustavson, whose real name was Eleanor.

It was the summer before we were juniors, the summer when Fee lost his fight to Johnny Hunkley and left Athens singing to make his mark in San Francisco. Like all summers, this one was stifling, with a lot of rain and a lot of time hanging heavy on your hands. It was that way for me, at least. But not for Zock. He took to acting strange, sneaking off during the day, not telling me where he was going. I never asked him either, since it couldn't really have been called my business.

But one night after supper, I wandered over to his house looking for him. "Zachary is upstairs," Mrs. Crowe said. Then she giggled for a while.

"O.K.," I said, starting to walk by.

"He would prefer you didn't, Raymond," she told me, kind of blocking my way. "He said that he would see you tomorrow. So toodle-oo," which was her way of saying good-by.

I toodle-ooed back and went outside, thinking. And the more I thought, the more I didn't know. So naturally, I snuck in the rear door and crept up the stairs to Zock's room.

He was standing in front of his mirror, practicing smiling, which was understandable, since I have already described how his smile twisted, with one side going up and the other, unfortunately, down. He didn't see me until I said: "Toodle-oo. Zachary's upstairs getting dressed."

He spun around, red as a beet. "What are you doing here?" he asked. "Why did you come?"

"A whim," I answered, using one of his favorite expressions, flopping down on his sack. "Just call it that. A whim."

"Get out, Ripper," he said. "Please."

"In due time, perhaps," I said, imitating him. "But there's something I'd like to know first. Zock, what the hell's going on?"

"Nothing," he mumbled.

"In that case," I told him. "I'll just stick around."

"Please," he said again.

"Tell me. Then maybe I will."

"No," he said.

"Fine," I said. "I like it here anyway."

Zock sighed. "All right, Ripper. I'm going to the movies."

I pointed to the necktie he was wearing. And to his hair, which was combed. "Continue," I said.

"I'm taking a girl," he choked. "Now get out."

I fell back on the bed, laughing and kicking my heels, him watching me all the time, getting redder and redder. I laughed and roared and kicked and then I sat up like a shot.

"You're kidding."

"No. I'm not."

"Zock," I pleaded. "You got to be kidding."

He shook his head and pointed to the door.

"Who's the girl, Zock? Do I know her? Is she from around here? Who's the girl? You're not really going. You're kidding. Aren't you, Zock? Who's the girl? Naw. There's no girl. You're only kidding."

While I was going on he went to the closet and took out a sport jacket I didn't know he owned. Then he walked past me to the doorway.

"Bunny Gustavson," he said. After which he ran.

I went home, puttering around the rest of the night, not doing much but just thinking about Bunny Gustavson. Who was the smartest girl in our class and also probably the ugliest. She was uglier than Zock, I thought then, but later, when I got to know her well, I judged them as being about the same. She was a fine girl, Bunny was, as fine as any I've ever known, bright and lots of fun. She had an awful figure though, completely without shape, and very bad eyes and skin. But she always looked clean. That was probably her most attractive feature; you had the feeling you could eat right off her, she was so clean.

The next morning I went over and woke Zock. "How was it?" I asked.

"How was what?" he mumbled.

I shook him. "Cut that," I said. "How was it?"

"It was all right, I suppose."

"You going to take her out again?"

"Maybe. Maybe not."

I started pulling him out of bed. "Did you really ask her out last night, Zock? Really? Honest to God?"

"Of course I did," he snapped back, landing on the floor.

Which was a lie, as I later found. She asked him out that first time. And for the next ones too, until he got the hang of it. She had set her cap for Zock, as Mrs. Crowe put it, and had begun following him around. Which was where they were during those days, walking around town, Zock first, Bunny right behind, gradually closing the gap as the days went by. I think she was in love with him from the start. And I know he never took out any other girl, for when he went to Harvard, she chose Wellesley, which is close by, so they could be together. Just when Zock fell in love with her I don't exactly know, but he was on the night that he died.

And, that summer, it got so he was with her practically every evening. After the first few times I went along and I don't believe anybody minded much, for Bunny and I hit it off well from the start. We'd go to the movies together, then have a soda, then walk her home. Where they would neck awhile on the porch, with me waiting out by the street for them to finish.

Sometimes, though, I used to turn around and watch. They'd both take off their glasses and put them carefully somewhere, a slow process, for without them they were blind. Then, eyes open, they'd grope for each other, their hands moving slowly until they made contact. And to this day I have yet to see anything more tender than that, the two of them blind as bats, reaching softly for each other in the dark.

But naturally, such an arrangement couldn't go on forever. It was me who first brought the subject up.

"Something has got to be done," I said.

"What," asked Zock, "did you have in mind?"

"Well," I told him. "I don't know."

"Sally Farmer's back from camp," Bunny said. "How would you like to go out with Sally Farmer?"

"Don't be ridiculous," I answered. "That is probably the most ridiculous thing I have ever heard."

It wasn't, actually, and after a little, they talked me into it. Bunny went over to Sally's house to ask her for me, they being best friends, while Zock and I waited on his front porch. I just sat there, sweating, not saying a word until, finally, Bunny came back.

"Well?" I said.

Bunny closed her eyes and began reciting. "Sally says: 'The answer is absolutely no. If he wants to take me out let him ask me himself. Besides, he has the worst reputation in the whole school.' " She opened her eyes. "Verbatim."

"Well," Zock said. "I guess you'll just have to call her up, Euripides."

"Ho, ho, ho," I said. "I'm not going to do it."

"Suit yourself," Zock told me.

"What would I say to her, Zock? I could never think of anything to say to her."

"Try it now," Zock said.

I took a deep breath. "Hello, Sally," I tried. "This here is Ray Trevitt. What the hell are you doing on Saturday?"

"I'm afraid that's not quite it," Bunny said.

"A trifle blunt," Zock agreed, shaking his head.

"Well. It's the best I can do."

"Women have to be coaxed, Ripper. They're funny about that. But you have to play by their rules or they'll pick up their baseball and go home."

"Zock," I said. "Help me."

"All right." He nodded. "It's the least I can do. We'll call her this afternoon. At five o'clock."

"What if she's not home?"

"Bunny will pay her a visit at half past four. Right?" Bunny nodded. "So she'll be there." And with that they both disappeared into his house, leaving me alone.

I didn't see him again until late that afternoon. He came in grinning, waving some sheets of paper.

"I've got it right here," he said.

"You've got what right where?"

He shook the papers in my face. "Here. Here in my hands at this very moment is a copy of the conversation you are going to have with Sally Farmer. All you have to do is read it."

I grabbed the papers. It was just what he had said, a conversation, written like a play with two parts, marked Sally and Euripides.

"Better run through it first," Zock said.

"Well, I don't know," I answered.

"You've nothing to lose," he told me. "So begin at the top."

I sighed, took a deep breath, and started reading. "Hello," I read. "Is this Sally Farmer?"

"Yes," Zock replied, his voice very high. "This is she."

"Well, this is Ray Trevitt."

"Oh, hello, Ray," Zock said. "I'm so glad you called."

"How the hell do you know she's going to say that?" I asked Zock.

"It's only polite," he answered. "And Sally's a very polite girl. Bunny says so. She helped me write this."

"O.K.," I said and went on reading. "I heard you were back from camp and I thought I'd just ring up to say hello."

"That was awfully considerate of you, Ray," Zock said.

"You have a good time at camp this year? I understand you were a junior counselor."

"That's right," Zock said. "I had four seven-year-olds in my cabin."

"Gee," I read. "That sounds like a lot of fun."

"Oh, it was," Zock said. "I loved every minute of it."

"Jesus Christ, Zock," I said, putting down the paper, "this is terrible. She's going to think I'm a moron."

"All right," Zock said, throwing up his hands. "If you don't like it, don't use it. It's no skin off my nose. I don't care. The fact that Bunny and I spent hours writing it shouldn't enter in. If you don't like it, don't use it. For all I care, you can contact her by semaphore."

"I'm sorry," I said. "Please. I'll use it. I'm proud to use it. I'm honored. I just hope it gets better later on."

It did. We went all the way through it, and Zock had actually written a fifteen-minute conversation for the two of us, it took that long to read. And toward the end it got very clever, especially the asking-out part, which was put in such a way that she couldn't possibly refuse.

"Zocker," I said when we were done, "you're a genius."

"Naturally." He looked at his watch. "It's five o'clock. Make the call."

"Sure thing," I said, and I dialed the number. When the receiver got picked up, I put my finger under the first speech and started reading. "Hello," I said. "Is this Sally Farmer?"

"No," came the answer. "This here is Ingebord."

"Who's Ingebord?" I whispered to Zock. It beat him. "Well," I ad-libbed. "Is Sally there?"

"I'll see," was the reply.

"What if she's not there?" I said to Zock. "For chrisakes . . ."

"Hello," came a voice on the other end.

I grabbed up the papers. "Hello," I said, reading away. "Is this Sally Farmer?"

"Yes. Who is this?"

"Well," I read. "This is Ray Trevitt."

"Who?" she asked me.

I panicked. "Zock," I whispered. "She says 'who?' What do I say?"

"Tell her who you are," he whispered back.

"Well," I said again. "This is Ray Trevitt."

"I don't know any Ray Trevitt," she said. "You must have the wrong number."

"Cut the crap, Sally Farmer," I yelled into the phone. Zock smacked his forehead and fell on the floor.

"What did you say?" she asked.

"This here is Ray Trevitt," I answered, trying to get calm. "You know. Ray Trevitt."

"Oh yes," she said, sounding very haughty. "Perhaps I remember."

"You must have the mind of a minnow," I told her. "Seeing as I sat behind you all last year in geometry."

"Oh," she said. "That Ray Trevitt."

"The same," I said, starting to read again. "I heard you were back from camp and I thought I'd just ring up to say hello."

"How did you know I was at camp?"

"You have a good time at camp this year? I under—"

"That's really none of your business," she told me.

I went right on reading, mainly because I couldn't think of anything else to do. "I understand you were a junior counselor. Gee. That sounds like a lot of fun."

"What in the world are you talking about?"

"I'm talking," I screamed into the phone, "about your seven lousy four-year-olds. I mean your four lousy seven-year-olds. Sally Farmer," I said, throwing the papers away, "do you know what you can do? You can take—"

"If you called to ask me out," she interrupted. "The answer is no."

"Ho, ho, ho," I said. "Who would want to ask you out anyway? Not me. Not under any conditions."

"In that case," she said, "I accept." Then she hung up.

And so it was arranged.

We double-dated, a term I hate but what else can you call it, on Saturday evening, the 29th of August. Zock drove and we headed out to the Palace in Crystal City to dance. Which Zock told me not to worry about, since Bunny had been giving us dancing lessons every day in her living-room, first taking one of us, then the other. But I was no Fred Astaire then, and even today the resemblance is slight.

We drove out in absolute silence. Zock made a few stabs at conversation but they didn't go over. I couldn't think of a thing to say, and besides, I was pretty tired from just getting ready. All in all, it took me four hours to do same, what with having my hair cut, shaving, which I didn't need to do but did anyway, managing to gash my chin good in the process, two showers, one bath, shining my shoes, plus all the rest. So I was not exactly calm, and Sally Farmer's looking the way she did wasn't much of a help.

Sally Farmer was cute. She had short hair and a great smile but under no conditions could she be called anything but cute. There are a lot of girls that look just like her, and they all have short hair and great smiles, with never a pimple or blemish of any kind. They all look healthy, as if from the day they were born they have eaten nothing but yogurt.

We got to the Palace and right away Zock went dancing off with Bunny, a terrible thing to do. And there we were.

"I don't suppose you dance," Sally Farmer said.

"You suppose wrong," I came right back, and we started. Conversation while dancing is a gift, one I never received, so we stumbled around in silence for a while.

"You certainly don't dance very well," she said.

"I was about to say the same of you," I replied. Which was a lie, for she danced as well as anyone I ever knew. Beautifully, in fact. We stopped there, in the middle of the floor.

"I don't know why I came," she said. "Pity, I suppose."

"Listen," I began, trying to pull out a cigarette. I had practiced smoking in my room at night and although I was still gagging some, I figured she wouldn't know the difference. But right then I was all thumbs, and the pack dropped out of my hands. I started swearing.

"Maybe I ought to go home," Sally Farmer said.

I stood up. "Listen, Miss High-and-Mighty," I told her. "I have screwed many a woman in my time, so you are nothing special to me."

At which she ran away.

I don't know why I said it, seeing as it was an exaggeration. But I had to say something and that was what came out. Sally Farmer tore over to Bunny and they talked. Then Zock came walking up to me.

"What did you do, Euripides?"

"I should have hit her, but I didn't."

"You did pretty well without that," he said. "She wants to go home."

But they calmed her down, and all that happened was we changed partners, so that I was dancing with Bunny. Who was very mad at me, seeing as Sally was her best friend. In spite of that, though, I liked dancing with her, for she knew everything I did wrong before I did it, and therefore not once did I step on her feet.

About half an hour later she excused herself to go to the ladies'-room, and Sally did too. When Bunny came out, she said to me: "Sally is outside and would like to speak to you."

Which she was. Standing alone at the edge of a grove of trees that ran along one side of the Palace. "Bunny says you want to speak to me," I said. But that is not at all what Bunny meant. What Bunny meant was: "Get out there and apologize for being such a booby," booby being one of her favorite words. And I would have, if only she'd told me. At that time, though, I was not too strong on what Mrs. Crowe calls the social graces.

"That's a lie," Sally Farmer said, turning, walking deeper into the trees, me following. "I bet everything you say is a lie."

"Not on your tin-type, sister," I answered, but blushing anyway, for I knew what she meant and also that I had stretched the truth considerable. But I had to keep going. "Yes sir," I said. "I have screwed so many women as almost to lose count."

"You just don't have any manners, do you?" she said, stopping, turning around, waiting for me to catch up to her. "Do you?" she said, softer.

"Do I what?" I answered, starting to crumble. Because right then, standing there among those trees, half in shadow, Sally Farmer was as cute as any girl I have ever seen.

"Do you?" she whispered, closing her eyes.

Which completely threw me. Not being able to say anything, I took the other road. I did something. I grabbed Sally Farmer and kissed her as hard as I could. Then, when I was about to let her go, she began kicking and screaming as if I'd practically raped her.

"For chrisakes, Sally," I said. "Take it easy." She didn't answer but just ran into the Palace, leaving me standing there, shaking my head. A minute later, Zock came tearing up.

"What happened?" he asked.

"Zock," I told him, "I don't know. I honest to God do not know."

"You didn't hit her?" I shook my head. "Well," he said. "At least that's something."

They came out in a little, Sally with tears in her eyes. At the car there was a scene, because Sally said she didn't want to ride home with me, seeing as I was a monster and there was no telling what I might do. But Bunny calmed her down so we finally got in, the girls sitting in the back seat, Zock and me in the front, with Sally's sniffling the only sound heard all the way. . . .

That was not, however, the end of me and Sally Farmer. Quite the contrary, in fact. For the next day she happened to accompany Bunny over to Zock's house where I naturally happened to be. Of course she didn't speak to me, but every so often I caught her looking over in my direction. And the day after that we bumped into each other not far from my house, where I took the bull by the horns and apologized. Once I did that, I couldn't get rid of her until she had to go home for supper.

Sally's old man, Elias P. Farmer, had more money than God and lived in a great white house with pillars, overlooking the college. Old Elias had never gone there, but instead went into the clothing business where he made his bundle. He was very famous, since he was always giving money to somebody, usually Athens College, and so had his picture in the Chicago papers all the time. Actually, he wasn't as bad as you might imagine, and he was a Cub fan, which you would never expect. Since I was a Cub fan too, we always had a lot to talk about whenever we got together, and that was pretty often, for I took Sally out for a long time. Practically a year. So Elias P. had plenty of opportunity to moon with me over the good old days when Billy Herman was covering second and Cavarretta skipped like a dancer around first. At the start, Sally and I used to double-date with Zock and Bunny. But later we drove in my mother's car or in the Cadillac convertible that Sally's old man had given her.

I cannot say too much in favor of Sally Farmer, in that all I know as far as manners are concerned, she taught me. I think I was sort of a project with her. She improved my dancing and got me in the habit of opening doors for her, lighting her cigarette first, plus all the other little things women are brought up to expect.

It might be thought, from the above, that Sally was what Mrs. Crowe called an "old-fashioned girl." And I suppose she was, because all during that year we would horse around, me trying to get her clothes off, but never succeeding. For each and every time things started rolling, she'd grab me by the shoulders, look me in the eyes and say: "Ray. We mustn't." I suppose I heard her say "Ray. We mustn't" upwards of ten thousand times in the course of that year. I always knew exactly when she was going to come out with it, so, sometimes, I said it right along with her. She never thought that was funny. But then, Sally was not a girl who could be accused of having a sense of humor.

Then, one night in the early summer after our junior year, we went to a beach party where she got pretty smashed, what with not eating and drinking too much. So I took her home and when I did, it turned out that Elias P. was away and no one was in save the maid, a fine old deaf lady named Ingebord. We snuck upstairs to Sally's room, flopped on the bed and, in the course of time, I managed to get her clothes off.

"Ray," she said. "We mustn't."

"Sally," I said. "We're going to."

"No," she said.

"Yes," I said.

We didn't. Mainly because she started whimpering, something I've never been able to take. So I got up, thanked her for the evening, said good night, and left her there.

And soon, Sally and I began to go our separate ways. There were no scenes, nothing violent like what was going to come later with Annabelle. But gradually at first, then more and more, she began staying with the country club set, seeing less and less of me. I was never broken-hearted over the turn of events, since I wasn't too nuts about her. I liked her, I suppose. But that was all.

And after Sally there came a whole procession of girls, some smart, some stupid, some pretty, some not. There was Bobby Pope, and Nancy Heimerdinger, who was all right except for her name, and Jayne Stein, a real phony, and Alice Blair, with even a couple of college girls thrown in here and there, a feather in my cap seeing as I was still only in high school. But I don't want this to turn into either a catalogue or a boasting contest, so I'll say no more about the girls I knew up until I graduated. For none of them ever meant so much as a hill of beans to me. Not in the long run.

But what I do want to talk about now is college, and Zock's departure to it. He wanted to go to Harvard, so, naturally, they accepted him. Since not only was he a great guy but was also the number-one student in our class, going through the entire four years without getting anything lower than an A.

College was never a real problem for me, as there wasn't any doubt but that I would go to Athens. There were reasons, many of them financial. But mainly it was because my grades were not very good, being low Cs, those of a gentleman. To tell the truth, I'm lucky I got accepted anywhere, as none of my teachers were for me. And probably Athens would have given me the thumbs-down too, had it not been for my father being such a big deal, not to mention America's leading etc., etc., etc. So Athens it was, and there an end.

The night before Zock left for Harvard, we doubled-dated for the last time. He was with Bunny, naturally, which irritated me, seeing as it wasn't a tragic parting, what with her leaving for Wellesley in three days. And so, probably for spite, I took out Marjorie Bluestone, a college freshman at Athens who did the trick. She was sort of a slob, Marjorie was, with absolutely nothing else to recommend her, but still, I had been keeping company with her, off and on, for some time.

We went to the Palace, strictly for old times' sake, the three of us and Marjorie, who thought it was corny. We danced a little, then drove out in separate cars to the Crib, a little bar some miles from town.

As I said, I was pretty peeved to start with. And Marjorie didn't help things any, for she kept gassing on about sociology, her way of showing that she was in college while we, as yet, were not. Every time Zock or Bunny said anything, Marjorie jumped right in and put her foot in her mouth, which probably accounts for the peculiar shape it had.

Finally, I told her. "Why don't you shut up," I said.

She laughed, thinking I was kidding.

"I mean it," I said. "Shut up."

So she did. Which only made things worse. We sat around drinking beer, not talking. The jukebox there played nothing but loud brassy saxophone music, and right then it was going full blast. I began getting itchy. Zock, too.

"I think maybe Bunny and I will move on," he said.

"What's the matter? We bore you?"

"Intensely," he answered.

"Run along then," I told him. They got up. "See you at Christmas," I called.

Zock turned. "Fine," he said. Nodding once to Marjorie, he took off.

"Thank God," Marjorie said, the minute they were gone. "Where did you dig them up from? I've never seen such rude, unpleasant people."

"Take a look in the mirror," I told her. "You're no rose."

Naturally, being drunk, she started to cry. Sniffles at first, then the real thing, with tears running down her face, streaking her make-up.

"Cut it," I said. "Cut it out right now or we go home."

And with that, she started. I was Cruel, she said. And Heartless. And Totally Without Understanding. Not to mention Sympathy. Her voice got louder and louder and people turned to watch as she pointed at me with a stubby finger.

"Let's go," I said, grabbing her by the arm. "I told you once and once is plenty." I pulled her outside, shoved her in the car, and began the drive home.

As we passed Half Day Bridge, she reached over, switched off the ignition, grabbed the key, opened the door, and stepped out.

"Marjorie," I said. "Cut the act and give me the key."

"Make me," she said, half laughing, half crying. "Make me. Come on, you son of a bitch. Come on."

So I got out of the car and started wrestling with her. She bit me and clawed and the next thing I knew, there we were, half naked, sprawled on the warm, muddy ground. Which was, I figured, just a perfect way to end a perfect evening.

Afterward I drove her back, said good night from the car, and went home to bed.

But not to sleep. Tossing, turning, swearing out loud, I lay there watching the clock. Then, about three, I threw on some clothes and went over to Zock's house. I hit his window with a couple of pebbles and right away he was there, looking down.

"That you?"

"The same," I answered.

"What's up, Ripper?"

"Nothing. I just thought we might take a drive. Or a walk. It's nice out."

"Be right down," he said, and a minute later, he was. "Well," he asked. "Walk or drive?"

"Walk," I said, and he headed for the beach.

"That Marjorie's a fine girl," he began. "You've really got something there."

"I know it," I told him. "I already married her in secret. For fear she might get away."

"Good move," Zock said. And then: "Did you?"

I nodded. "In the mud near Half Day Bridge."

"Why?" Zock asked.

Which stumped me. "I don't know. Why not?"

"I guess you must be state champion by now," he said. "Why don't you retire and rest on your laurels?"

"Gee, thanks," I told him. "I wanted to ask you for advice only I was too shy to come right out with it."

"Free," Zock said. "Tonight everything's for free."

"Just don't tell me to find a nice girl and settle down. Please."

"I won't," he said. "But why don't you find yourself a nice girl and settle down?"

I didn't bother to answer because by then we were on the beach, walking slow along the sand. It was a beautiful night, with just a sliver of moon shining down on the smooth top of Lake Michigan. Way off in the east you could almost feel the sun, stretching, about to make its move. Peaceful. That's probably as good a word as any. With everything exactly right in place, right where it ought to be. And you just knew, as sure as God made green apples, that nothing wrong was ever going to happen; that come flood or war or famine or anything else, we were going to make it, Zock and me; come what may, we were going to live forever.

So we walked along, not speaking but just walking quiet on the sand, under that sliver of moon. We walked for miles, hours, never once saying a word. Because right then, we didn't have to. We knew all there was to know; ourselves, the world, each other, everything. Then, before dawn, we sacked out on the beach, like we had done that night in Chicago years ago. And, as I was slipping away, all I heard was the slap, slap, slap of the waves against the shore. . . .

Those hours are the happiest I have ever had in all my life. And they are mine. Mine alone, now. And I don't give a shit what anybody says or what anybody thinks or what anybody does. Nothing, nothing in this world is ever going to take them away from me. . . .

We woke in the early morning and made our way home, jabbering like jaybirds. Throwing stones, joking, wrestling, singing, jumping around in the sand as if we were crazy. We were pretty tired when we got to Zock's house, but we kept right on horsing, standing there in the middle of the yard.

"So they're actually letting you into Athens," Zock said.

"In three days I start. They had to accept me. Because, and this may come as a surprise to you, my old man happens to be America's leading expert on Euripides."

"Do tell," Zock said. "Now I wonder who is America's second leading expert on Euripides? Just think of him. 'Here I am,' he probably says to himself each morning over tea. 'America's second leading expert on Euripides. Now, when is that lousy Trevitt going to die?'"

"A sad tale," I said.

"Tragic," Zock nodded. Then we were both quiet.

"Well, Zocker," I said, belting him one on the arm. "Don't take any wooden nickels."

"My mother has already warned me."

"And stay loose."

"I shall," he said. "I shall endeavor to try."

"Do endeavor so," I said, imitating him.

We shook hands. "Good-by," I said.

"Good-by, Euripides."

"Good-by."

But neither of us moved.

"I hear you're an absolute angel," I said finally.

"I hear you're not," he said.

Then we both ran.

IV .... The College

The town of Athens is separated from the college by Patriot's Square, which is so called because of two students, Mark Dawes and Philip Morgan, who left during the Civil War and got blown up by mistake on their way to Shiloh. The town itself lies along Lake Michigan, with the college stretching inland for a couple of miles. Most of the school buildings face onto the square, and behind them the college owns a few hundred acres of woods and swamp that they have been trying to raise money to fix up ever since I can remember. It is a sort of constant battle between the two, the college and the swamp, to see which is going to swallow up the other.

If you believed the brochures, you would probably think that as far as beauty is concerned, right after the Taj Mahal comes Athens College. This is not true. For it is an ugly school, being made up almost entirely of buildings that are eyesores and which they would like to tear down, except they haven't got the money. If it wasn't for Elias P. Farmer, plus a few graduates who were lucky enough to make good, it is my opinion that the swamp would have won out long ago. But instead of admitting that their school is ugly, the old graduates speak of it as being "quaint." Talk to anyone who ever went to Athens and that word is sure to pop up. Quaint. And more than that, they'll tell you they like it the way it is and wouldn't change it for the world. Because Athens is a school that is strong on tradition.

There is, naturally, Patriot's Square. And Kissing Rock. And the Ancient Oak, a huge tree which Elmer Houston, a legendary goofball, tried valiantly to poison in the spring of 1927. Plus about half a dozen other places that the mere mention of makes old graduates misty-eyed. Athens was founded by missionaries, and their spirit still hangs over the place like a rain cloud. The girls are mostly muscular and unattractive but interested in "things"; the boys are pipe-smokers who love to sit around and gas about what's happened to the Monroe Doctrine. Social life at Athens is based on talk, since there isn't much else you can do. It is one of those co-educational-white-Protestant-no-drinking-no-driving-no-swearing-no-especially-not-THAT-schools where mothers can send their kiddies in complete confidence that nothing awful is ever going to happen.

And if my memories of Athens do not center on Kissing Rock, a name I really hate, this is not to say that I don't have my memories too. The greased pole I remember. And of course the two girls, Harriet and Annabelle. And most of all what happened that beautiful night on Half Day Bridge. But none of these have much to do with the college itself, which is as it ought to be, I suppose, for I was never much of a part of it.

I knew that, the first day of school, as I walked from my house to classes. I could almost feel myself moving from the one world, the town's, to the other, ruled by the college. And as I walked I guess I realized that even though I was a member of both, I really didn't belong to either of them.

But being the only town boy in the freshman class, as well as the son of a famous professor, I was something of a curiosity. Many were nice to me, out-of-their-way nice, for people, as I have already noted, like to show they are open-minded, particularly when such is not the case. So the first days went pleasantly enough, if you don't count the classes, which I disliked, especially chemistry with Professor O'Brien, whose wife had helped me bury Baxter in the ravine that day years before.

The second week at Athens is officially known as Frosh-Soph Week. There is a good deal of harassing that goes on, one class against the other, all designed to forge school spirit, which is ridiculous. But naturally, during that week, I was outstanding. I managed to black the eye of the sophomore class president during a scuffle in Patriot's Square; I threw three dozen firecrackers into the biggest sophomore dorm, not once getting caught and keeping most everyone awake all night long. And I climaxed it on Friday afternoon on the football field, during the climbing of the greased pole.

There were hundreds of people out there that day, faculty and students, sitting in the grandstand. Probably more than half the school, all of them cheering, waving banners. In the very center of the field was the greased pole, stuck solid in the ground. And ringed around it were about fifty sophomore boys wearing khakis or jeans and T shirts, waiting. We were in a bigger circle around them, also waiting, looking up every so often to the top of the pole where there was set a blue beanie, the object of it all. If a freshman got to that blue beanie, then they won; if the sophomores kept anyone from climbing, they carried the day. Old Man Higgins, the football coach, came out and gave us a brief talk on sportsmanship, by which he meant: "No eye-gouging, boys, and keep your knees where they ought to be." Then he stepped back, took a last look around, and shouted: "Go get it!"

Everybody charged, and immediately there were fifty small fights going on, people scuffling, shoving, rolling on the ground, while those in the stands blew horns, whistled, and cheered like mad. Boys were getting thrown all over, this way and that, and I watched them, hanging back, waiting until I saw my chance.

Finally it came.

After about five minutes when they all were tired from the wrestling, the action began to ease up, like a camera suddenly switched to slow motion. Right then I saw it, a path, leading straight to the greased pole.

I tore along that path yelling like a maniac, spilling people right and left and then there I was, by the pole, alone. I jumped up as high as I could. It was slippery, but I held on, digging in with my fingers, kicking down at the hands trying to grab me. Then, after a second, I was safe, over their heads, with nothing left to do but just climb that pole right up to the top, up to that blue beanie.

Clamping my legs around the pole, holding tight, I scraped with my hands, going an inch at a time, making my way. The crowd hushed suddenly and when I looked out all I saw was hundreds of faces, tense with excitement, staring at me. One time I slipped and the people in the stands groaned, but I cursed, caught myself, held on for dear life. By then I was really tired, so I set to work, clawing away, using my legs as a brace. And at last, with one final push, I cupped my hand over the smooth rounded top of the pole, grabbed the blue beanie and waved it high over the crowd.

They all went wild. Shot, I slid down, holding onto that blue beanie for all I was worth, and when I got to the ground I was dazed. But still, I can't say I minded when people began pounding me on the back, laughing like crazy. Because no one had climbed the greased pole in years, more than ten, until me. Then a bunch of boys hoisted me up atop their shoulders and carried me all the way back to the center of campus that way, shoulder high, as the poem says, with hundreds of others crowding around, waving flags, jingling cowbells, screaming. And I sat above them, covered with grease, smiling like a fool, that blue beanie perched on my head every step of the way.

From that day on, I was the best-known freshman in the school, a distinction I maintained throughout the year. For I was the one who had done it, had climbed the greased pole, and so was a celebrity, at least as far as the students were concerned. But such, unfortunately, did not also apply to the teachers, and in a few days the glory faded and was forgotten in the rush of school work. At which, as I said, I did not excel. English was dull, history duller, and chemistry got so bad I didn't bother going.

And one afternoon as I cut chem lab and started across Patriot's Square on the way to town, a girl appeared from somewhere and began following me. I walked slowly and so did she, about ten feet behind me, right through the Square into town. When I reached Harold's Drug Store on the corner, I turned.

"Are you following me?" I asked.

She stopped, several feet away. "Pardon?" she said.

"What are you following me for?"

She came right up then and stared me in the eye. "Because I think you're the greatest thing since sliced bread," she answered, after which she whipped on by me into Harold's, where she was headed all the time.

A little flustered, I waited for her to come out. Finally, she did, carrying some pads of paper and eating an ice-cream cone. "Hey," I called, but she didn't stop, so I hurried up and walked along beside her.

"I guess you weren't following me," I said.

"Oh, you're a bright one," she came right back. "That's plain to see."

"I'm sorry," I told her.

"No need," she said, not looking at me but instead licking away at her ice-cream cone. "It was a simple error. One any moron might make."

"Listen. I'm trying to apologize."

"Keep at it," she said. "It might do you some good."

It went on like that all the way to her dorm. Every time I said something, she made an insult out of it. So pretty soon I stopped talking and watched her. She was little and dark and not very pretty. But she had a fine body for a small girl and a voice as deep as mine. Which was cute enough almost to make you forget that her nose was too big and her eyes too close together.

She was about to go into her dorm when I took her by the arm and spun her around. "I'll pick you up tomorrow afternoon," I said.

"Somehow I doubt it," she said.

I ignored her. "Listen. Bring a bathing suit. Tomorrow. Three. I'll pick you up. Right here. We'll go swimming." She didn't say anything. "Please," I said.

"Don't be ridiculous," she answered. "It is to laugh." Then she dashed inside and I started walking away. I was already on the sidewalk when she stuck her head out of the parlor window.

"Make it four," she yelled. "And my name is Harriet."

"Raymond Euripides Trevitt," I yelled back, bowing. "And the pleasure is mine."

So the next afternoon we went to the beach. It was cool, but we went anyway, which was a good thing, since we were the only people down there. We chatted awhile, lying next to each other on the sand, Harriet apologizing for the way she looked, as she had to borrow the bathing suit and it was too big. I told her I wouldn't hold it against her and she went zipping off into the water, horsing around at first, splashing, getting used to it, then swimming out. She was a good swimmer and she went on until her head was practically out of sight. Then she turned back.

"Come on," she said, when she got to shore.

"Later," I told her.

"Now," she told me, starting to throw sand in my direction. Which got no results so she ran back in the Lake and kicked water at me, but she wasn't too accurate. Finally, she bent over, scooping it out with her hands, me rolling around on the sand, laughing, trying to dodge. She bent all the way over, scooping the water, giggling, and right then her bathing suit slipped a little but enough, so that when she stood up, her twillies were showing.

"Hey," I yelled, almost hysterical. "You're cross-eyed."

"What?" she said, not understanding, trying to smile.

I pointed. "You're cross-eyed," I said again.

At which she sort of looked down. And when she saw she gasped, blushed, threw her arms across herself, broke out crying, and tore off to hide behind a sand mound at the back of the beach.

I waited a couple of minutes, then sauntered up atop the sand mound and looked down at her.

"Hi, Harriet," I said. "What's new?"

"Go away," she said.

I sat next to her. "Don't be a baby," I said. "And please. Don't start crying again."

"I won't," she promised.

"Why did you have to cry in the first place?"

She looked at me awhile. "Because I'm a lady, goddam it. That's why."

"I believe it," I told her.

Shivering, she threw her arms around me. "And yesterday," she whispered. "Yesterday. I was following you."

"I believe that too," I said, holding her tight.

The minute I got home I sat down and dashed off a note to Zock. "Have found a nice girl and am settling down," it said. That was all.

A week later I got his answer, which is the only letter I ever received from him. It went like this:

Euripides:

Harvard is a wonderful place. I use wonderful in the old sense. Let me explain. Everyone here is smart and a number are more than that. As you walk to class, you can almost feel all those minds generating full blast behind all those horn-rimmed glasses. Perhaps we should have our I.Q.'s tattooed on our foreheads. Then, instead of saying, "Good morning," we could just point and say, "162. What's yours?" It would relieve a lot of tension.

Courses thus far are bearable, but Bunny is already behind, so I have time to myself. Most of it has been spent touring the streets of Boston, which is a strange city, full of age and tradition almost thick enough to eat.

My roommate is named Clarence. I am not certain yet if he is human or otherwise, for at the age of 18, he has written three epic poems, one of which I glanced at. It won't make Homer worry, but still, to have written three epic poems while still a virgin (he confides in me) is a trifle frightening. As to your letter, it took me several hours to read it all, but I feel it was time well spent. You were a trifle skimpy on specifics concerning Her, but I assume she has large Twillies, the wisdom of Solomon, and the patience of Job. Those, I think, are the minimum requirements. I advise you to hang on tight, for such people are rare.

And so to bed. Toodle-oo.

Zock

And if Harriet wasn't all that Zock said, she didn't miss by much, being without doubt the finest girl with whom I have ever come in contact. Much smarter than I was, she tried not to show it, which was considerate, but impossible. Like Zock, she had been the best student in her high-school class, and why she chose to come to Athens, I'll never know. She had a million interests, being president of her dorm and already having made a big splash at *The Athenian*, the college literary magazine. Also, she was an actress, a good one, as I later found out. But while we went together she threw all that away in the hope of bringing me in line. She forced me into going back to chemistry, which I did, although it was useless and I knew it at the time. She dragged me off to the library every day to study, which I also did, although that was useless too, and we both knew it. She was wonderful, Harriet was, sweet, gentle, and kind, with, to quote Mrs. Crowe, a heart as big as all outdoors.

We went together that semester and for the first month or so of the next. Zock came back at Christmas, but they never met, since she was home in Rhode Island visiting her father who sold insurance and I guess did all right. I was sorry for that, because the two of them would have got on so well, Harriet and Zock.

At the end of the first semester, Professor O'Brien flunked me in chemistry, something for which I bear no grudge, as I well deserved it. The rest of my grades being less than average, I was put on probation, which was also fair and which I expected from the first day of school. This humiliated my father, I suppose, assuming that he cared enough, which I doubt, for he never once mentioned it to me.

Right after the start of the second semester, Harriet tried out for a big part in the spring play, a sad one called *Uncle Vanya* by Chekhov. Naturally, she won it and soon was spending much time in rehearsal. To this day she probably thinks that had a lot to do with our breaking up. But it didn't. We actually broke up the first time I ever laid eyes on Annabelle, who had transferred into Athens from some junior college up East. Because once I saw her, then everything else just had to follow.

It is very hard to describe Annabelle. As far as looks are concerned, she ranked right up at the top of the list, having long black hair, slanting green eyes, and without a doubt the greatest body in the world. She always wore make-up, but she wore it well. She never laughed much and her smile was slight, being just a quick turn up at the edges of her mouth.

Another thing that should be mentioned about Annabelle is this: she was crazy. I don't mean strange and I don't mean troubled. I mean crazy. Nuts. She had a nervous breakdown at the age of fourteen, which is pretty fast work in anyone's league. For two years after that she saw a psychiatrist three times a week, and why she stopped, I'll never know. Because if ever a girl needed one, it was her. As a kid, she was afraid to call up her own house when she was out, for fear that she might answer. She sort of smiled when she told me that, as if it was all a thing of the past and now she was Miss-Stability-in-the-Flesh. But later, when I thought about it, I realized I'd never seen her once use the phone.

All this and more I knew about her at the time. I walked into what happened with my eyes open, so I haven't got anyone to blame. No matter how hard I try to twist the facts, the fault always comes back and points straight at me.

My first contact with her, if you can call it that, was one afternoon in the Open Shelf room of the library. That was where we always studied, Harriet and me, it being a big place with two round tables, all the bestsellers, and usually some townspeople. I arrived on schedule to meet Harriet, who was to come later, being in rehearsal. It was our usual procedure, her arriving a little after me, then quizzing me on the work I was supposed to have done in her absence.

I clumped in and sprawled at the first table, dropping my books with a crash, also a procedure, for it rattled Miss Blaul, the librarian in charge. She glanced over, gave me the usual dirty look and I smiled right back at her, showing all my teeth. In her own way she was O.K., Miss Blaul, wacky of course, but all librarians get like that after a while. She'd known me for years, since the days when I wailed outside her window at night to scare her, and also my family, especially my mother, who devoured bestsellers as fast as they became one. I looked around the room and, seeing no one of interest, I opened a book, cracked the binding, and began to read.

Right then Annabelle came in.

Wearing a black cashmere sweater, open at the throat, a strand of pearls around her neck. She walked very stiff and fast, carrying a book in one hand, sitting down erect in a chair at the other table. I watched her as she walked, and when she sat down I watched her too, just stared at her, trying to think of some way to make an introduction.

It was after a few minutes, with me getting nowhere, that she stood up and left the room. Once she was gone, I quick dashed over, grabbed her book, checked the title and ran to Miss Blaul.

"Gimme *Remembrances of Things Past*, by Proust," I said.

At which Miss Blaul started laughing.

"Please," I said, half whispering. "I'm in a hurry."

"You won't like it, Raymond," she told me, giggling away. "But why don't you try this?" She pulled out a book. "It's called *Murder on the Mesa* and I just know—"

"Miss Blaul," I interrupted. "Get me that book." Still laughing, she walked to one corner of the room, searched around a second, picked it out, came back and handed it to me.

"Let me know how you like it," she said. "I can hardly wait."

"Very funny," I muttered, filling out the card, sailing it back at her. I took the book and sat down at the table where Annabelle had been. I opened it, cracked the binding, put my head about six inches from the print, and waited.

She returned, walking very fast, with quick, sharp movements, sat in the chair again, starting to read, never once looking in my direction. I fiddled around some and then, when I couldn't stand it any longer, I cleared my throat.

"Pardon me," I said, "but is that Proust you're reading?"

Startled, she stared in my direction. But not at me. Over my shoulder. She nodded. Once. That was all.

"It's a coincidence is why I ask," I went on. "Because I'm reading Proust too." I held up the book. "You know, I bet we're the only people in the whole state of Illinois that are reading Proust right now." This time she didn't even look up. I should have stopped then, since it was pretty obvious she wasn't being swept off her feet. But I kept on. "Do you like Proust?" I asked her.

She shrugged and went on reading.

"Do you like Athens?" I said, game to the core. "You're new this semester, aren't you? Do you like it much? Some do. Some don't. I don't. It's probably the worst college I've ever been to. Of course"—and I forced a laugh—"it's the only college I've ever been to, which puts me in a position to talk. I mean, if the whole place floated away one morning, I wouldn't shed a tear." I stopped to catch my breath and looked at her. On her face was one of those "Well, it's time I got out of here" expressions.

"Matter of fact," I hurried, "I don't care much for Proust either. Matter of fact, I don't like him at all. Not this book, anyway. I don't like *Remembrances of Things Past* one bit." She began sitting up. "Of course, some of his other books. Those are fine. I like some of them a lot."

"He never wrote any other books," Annabelle said, talking for the first time. And with that, she grabbed old Proust and whizzed on out of the Open Shelf room, leaving me there, shaking my head.

"Hooray for our sex," I heard somebody say, and turning, I saw Harriet sitting at the other table, laughing.

"What are you doing here?" I asked her.

"Just watching a seduction," was her answer. "Shall I tell you about it? It seems there was this boy . . ."

"How long you been here?" I interrupted.

"And he said to this girl: 'Pardon me, but is that Proust you're reading?' "

"The whole thing, Harriet. You saw the whole thing."

"Unfortunately, yes."

I got up and walked over to Miss Blaul. "Here," I told her, handing her the book. "It stinks."

"I knew you'd like it," she said.

I went back to Harriet. "Come on," I told her. "I'll buy you some coffee."

"You know," she whispered, making her low voice even lower, "we're probably the only people in the whole state of Illinois that are going for coffee right now." She started laughing again. "Honestly. I wouldn't have missed that for the world. 'Pardon me, but is that Proust you're reading?' "

"Not too good?"

"Awful, Euripides. Just terrible." She sighed. "But I'll give you credit for one thing. She is beautiful."

"Maybe so," I said. "But you should have seen Sadie Griffin." Then we left the library and headed downtown for coffee, Harriet giggling every step of the way.

Two afternoons later we were in Harold's when Annabelle came in and sat down by herself.

"There's your pen pal," Harriet said.

"Who?" I asked, all innocence. "Where?"

"How would you like to waltz right over and apologize to her?"

"For what?"

Harriet began counting the reasons off on her fingers. "For making a fool of yourself. For probably frightening her half to death. For driving her out of the library. Enough?" She started shoving me.

"Ridiculous," I told her. "I won't do it."

"I suspect otherwise," Harriet answered, giving me one final push. I stood up. "Go on," she whispered. "Before you lose your courage."

Annabelle was staring down into her coffee cup when I got there, her head resting in her hands. She didn't look up.

"I'm sorry for bothering you in the library," I broke in. "I apologize." I walked away.

"You didn't bother me," she called. I turned and faced her. She tried to smile, but smiling was never one of Annabelle's strong points, so she didn't quite bring it off.

"Anyway," I said. "I'm sorry."

"It's all right," she answered, sitting erect, staring past me. She always did that, stared past people. Never at them. As though there was some third person around and it was him she was looking in the eye and not you.

"That makes everything even," I said.

"I don't like Athens much either," Annabelle said. And then, softer: "Can you sit down?"

"Sure," I said, and I did. I sat there for about ten minutes while she finished her coffee, talking about not much of anything. I could see Harriet across the way, watching me, applauding and laughing, but every time I made the move to go, Annabelle started off on something else. So there wasn't a thing I could do but wait until finally she got up and left, trying that smile again, nodding good-by. I walked back to Harriet.

"Her name is Annabelle," I said, sitting down. "And she doesn't like Athens. She wants to major in philosophy and the coffee here is weak."

"And she lives in Connecticut," Harriet said, taking up where I left off. "Her family is very rich. This is her third college. She's five foot eight, has insomnia, and never wears a girdle." She giggled. "Want more? I have spies."

"No," I said.

"And I'm proud of you," Harriet finished, patting me on the head. "For being so polite."

Which I may have been, but Annabelle sure wasn't. Because the next day, when we passed her in Patriot's Square, she didn't even nod to me.

"Well, goddamn," I said, turning to watch as she hurried away.

"She's trapping you," Harriet explained.

"Yeah," I answered. "Well, she better watch it. It looks like I'm getting away."

"Nonsense," Harriet said. "Admit it. Your curiosity is aroused."

"Not mine," I told her, and we walked on.

But it was. And I made it a point to find her, which I did, the next afternoon, while Harriet was rehearsing. She was hurrying back from town through Patriot's Square, going very fast, as was usual. I called out to her. She didn't stop so I took off, cutting through the square, finally catching up.

"Why didn't you talk to me yesterday?" I said right off.

"When?"

"You know damn well when. Yesterday."

"I didn't see you," she answered, staring off at her third man.

"Why don't you look at me?" I said.

She turned then, began walking away. I grabbed her by the arm. She shook free. The March wind was blowing strong through the square and she shivered with the cold. We were both quiet for a while.

"I'm sorry," I said finally.

"There's no need to apologize," she answered. "There's no need even to talk to me."

"Sure there is."

"What?"

"I'm curious."

"Be curious with somebody else, then," she said, starting to walk again.

"Hey," I called out. She stopped. "What are you doing tonight?"

"What do you care?"

"I told you once. I'm curious."

"What about the other one?"

"You let me worry about that. What are you doing tonight?"

"Not a thing," she answered. Then she left me there.

I told Harriet the whole story a little later and whether she was mad or not I never knew, because all she did was smile, congratulate me, and head me toward the coffee shop. We didn't talk much, mainly because I was nervous, wondering what I was going to say that night to make conversation. I thought about it all through supper, not even listening to my mother and father as they buzzed away. And when I got dressed, I thought about it too. I thought about it so much that by the time I picked Annabelle up to take her to the movies, I was as tense as she was. The way things turned out, though, it was time well wasted.

Because we didn't say anything.

Hardly a word. I tried, at the start, on the walk downtown, to make chitchat. She never answered, but only nodded, shook her head, or shrugged as the occasion demanded. We walked very fast, and inside of a couple minutes we were at the theater. We sat down, her rigid, me slumped, and gazed at the silver screen while Gregory Peck followed that girl around Rome. Then, after the shorts, the cartoon, and the previews, we left.

Stopping for a minute out on the sidewalk. "Some coffee?" I asked. She shook her head. "Hungry?" Again the shake. "What would you like to do?"

"Go home," she answered.

"You got it," I said and we started off, walking even faster than before. We walked through Patriot's Square, passed the college buildings, right up to her dorm, without a word.

" 'Night," I said at the door and walked away.

"Wait," she called. I stopped, turning. "What day is today?"

"Blue Monday," I answered.

"I'll go out with you again next Monday," she said.

I couldn't help laughing. "What makes you think I'll ask you?"

"Oh, you'll ask me," she said, and hurried inside.

It being still early, I headed for a bar and stayed there, drinking until it closed. Then I went home and had a few glasses of dry wine. Then, finally, to bed. But sleep was a long time coming, because I kept thinking of Annabelle, seeing her face, her throat, the way her sweater quivered when she breathed. For like Harriet had said, Annabelle was a beautiful girl.

The next day, I gave Harriet a blow-by-blow as we walked down for lunch. "And the hell of it is," I finished up, "that I'm going to take her out next Monday."

"It's understandable," Harriet said.

"But we can't even talk to each other."

"A very old story, Euripides. You're just being torn between the flesh and the spirit. I," and she curtsied, "represent the spirit."

"Who wins?" I asked her.

"The spirit hasn't got a chance," she answered, and with that we went in for lunch.

So things went along as usual for the next few weeks. With just one exception. Monday nights I took out Annabelle, and I still don't know why, exactly, seeing as our evenings together weren't too hot. As a matter of fact, they were awful, with little talk and much tension. I took her to the movies twice and dancing once, which was really bad, seeing as she wore high heels that night and consequently was taller than I was. But I kept on, losing interest in her I suppose, though you can never be sure.

Then, toward the end of March, something special happened. Harriet had a birthday. That was the beginning. After a lot of talk, we decided not to make a big deal but just to spend a quiet evening, maybe having a decent dinner in one of the restaurants outside of town. I was to pick her up at seven, wearing a necktie, and please, would I shine my shoes. That was all she asked. Everything was set.

At about 6:30 I was getting dressed, alone in the house, when the front doorbell rang. I went to the landing and yelled that it was open and to come in. A second later, Annabelle was standing in the hallway.

"What's up?" I asked her.

"It's Monday," she answered, walking up the stairs, stopping close by me, on the landing.

I fidgeted awhile. "Jesus, Annabelle," I said finally. "I'm sorry. I'm busy."

"But it's Monday night," she said again.

"I told you I was sorry."

"Busy how?" she asked.

"Harriet's birthday. We're going out."

"I suppose that takes precedence?"

"It sure does," I said, starting back to my room. "If you want to wait around a little, I'll drive you home."

"If she won't mind," Annabelle said, following me up. The first thing she did when she got to my room was to take off her camel's-hair coat and fling it across the bed, tucking her sweater inside her skirt. I watched. Then she hurried across to my dresser and picked up the stuffed dog I'd bought as a present for Harriet. Which are good things to give women, stuffed animals, being cheap, but sentimental, and therefore much appreciated.

"For me?" Annabelle asked.

"Fat chance," I told her.

"I bet it's a present for Harriet. For her birthday."

I nodded.

"Sweet," Annabelle said. "No one can deny that."

"Listen," I told her. "If you don't like it, walk home."

That shut her up for a while, so I went on getting dressed, which took me longer than it should have. I was nervous, shaking some, because for once she was looking right at me, watching me close. I didn't stare back, but whenever I passed the mirror above my dresser, I glanced in. Our eyes met in that mirror every time.

I was brushing my hair before she spoke again. "You look very nice," she said. "Just like a gentleman."

"Thanks."

"But then, you're a handsome boy, aren't you, Trevitt?"

"Sure," I said. "I'm a beauty."

"Don't go," Annabelle whispered, out of the blue.

I turned and stared back at her.

"I don't want you to go."

I turned away, not answering. She came up behind me, put her arms around me, running her hands over my body, barely touching. I just stood there. She went to the door, flicked out the light. "And you won't, either," she whispered. "Not for a while." We waited in the darkness, neither of us moving, getting accustomed to it. All I could hear was the sound of my own breathing.

Then she was on me.

I don't know why or because or what or anything else. It just happened. But I do know I'll die before I ever find anyone like her again. And it wasn't the sex alone, though I have no complaint whatever on that score. It was what came after. That was the important thing.

Because, suddenly, all her tenseness was gone.

We were lying there, me with my eyes closed, holding her, when for no reason, she started to talk. About her family; their home in Connecticut, their summer place in Maine. About her past, her future. About what a good and faithful wife she was going to be. About her trips to Europe; about her room at home. On and on she went, whispering, sometimes almost laughing, sometimes serious. And then, after a while, she started humming a song I'd never heard. It was her bed song, she told me, and she'd made it up herself, long before.

I opened my eyes and looked at her as she lay there, beautiful, pale-white, her long black hair outlined around her face like a dented halo. And as I watched, she raised one of her perfect legs straight up into the air, pointing her toes. She ran her hands along that leg, just as high as she could reach, touching it gently, skimming it, humming all the time, almost smiling.

Annabelle belonged there, in bed. She was always happiest then, and I sometimes thought it was a shame she couldn't stay there, live out her life there, from first to last.

I wasn't exactly miserable either. Even if I'd wanted, I couldn't have stopped looking at her, she was that lovely, pale-skinned and naked in the moonlight. I felt like taking a deep breath and hollering Hallelujah! For I'd had more than my share of women by that time, except that with the others, as soon as it was over, I only wanted to tuck in my shirt, zip up my pants, and run. But not with Annabelle. Beautiful she had always been. But carefree, calm; that was my doing. I had done that for her. And right then I just knew I could take on the whole civilized world single-handed and come out smelling like a rose.

I had no idea what the time was, but when I finally did force a look at the clock, it was way past when I told Harriet I'd meet her.

"Annabelle," I whispered. "I've got to go."

She shook her head.

"Please. I've got to. I'm late now."

I could feel her starting to tense. After a few seconds, she nodded. We got dressed fast. By the time we were in the car, she was staring at that third man again.

Ten minutes later I parked outside Harriet's dorm and ran up the walk, holding that stuffed dog behind my back. She was downstairs in the parlor, waiting.

"I'm sorry," I said right off. She didn't answer but just looked at me. "I had to get a book from the library," I explained. "For my father."

She smiled. "That was nice of you."

"Sure. I'm a regular prince."

"Tell me then, prince. What was the name of the book?"

Which took me by surprise. "I don't know," I said. "I forget. But listen, Harriet . . ."

"No," she interrupted. "You listen. I've been sitting here over an hour. But that's all right. I don't mind that. It's your lying I mind. I don't like being lied to. Not by you or anyone else. I don't—"

I quick grabbed her, pulled her to her feet. "You shut up," I said. "You shut up and listen. There's just one thing. One thing I want to know. Do you love me?"

And now it was her turn to be surprised. "I can't say," she answered after a while.

"Sure you can. Yes or no?"

She was quiet for a long time, looking straight at me. "I guess no, then," she said.

"O.K.," I said. "All right. Fine. Then you got no strings on me. Here," and I tossed her the stuffed dog. "Happy birthday."

She held onto that dog for all she was worth. I put my arm around her, whispered in her ear. "Come on, baby," I said. "Come on now. Let's go. It's time to eat." I led her out.

The next morning I phoned Annabelle and asked to see her that night. She hemmed and hawed awhile, finally accepting. And that night again we went to bed, the two of us, up in my room. Then afterward, after she'd talked some and hummed her song, she pulled me close.

"No more Mondays," she whispered. "From here on, it's every night. You'll see me every night, starting now."

"Is that so?" I answered, going along with her.

"Yes. And you won't see her any more."

I sat up in bed. "You're kidding."

"I never do," she whispered.

"Well, you got the wrong guy, Annabelle."

"Oh, you don't have to," she said. "But it's going to be one of us or the other."

It was Harriet that went.

Actually, I let her break off with me, which she did one terrible night full of tears and parting, her crying, calling me about every name in the book, staring at me, never taking her eyes from my face. I didn't say a word, seeing as most of what she called me I deserved, but only stared back at her since I felt at least I owed her that much. And when she ran away from me, I figured it was over. But it wasn't. For she took to follow-ing me around campus, whether I was alone or not, it didn't matter, because wherever I went, there, half-a-block behind, would come Harriet. Eventually, though, she got hold of herself and we had a pleasant chat, laughing and talking. Then I didn't see her for a while, since she was always at *The Athenian* or rehearsing in the theater, getting ready for the spring play.

But I was busy, too. Because, when you went out with Annabelle, you were with her all the time. I took her to classes, met her after them, walked her everywhere, was with her every night. And mostly it was just the two of us, for she wasn't the kind of girl you liked being with in company.

So I began checking up on what my folks did. Which was funny, because all my life until then, I hadn't cared how they came and went. Now I followed their every move. My father was never home during the day, so he was no problem. Sometimes my mother stuck around the house, but more often she had meetings to go to. I got so I knew her schedule by heart and even today I can still quote the hours the PTA met, and the teachers' wives, and the Red Cross. And when my mother left the house by the front door, Annabelle and I would sneak in the back.

Which was all right with me. Even though being with her was usually pretty dull, seeing as she was most always tense and quiet. But the times in bed made up for all that. I never knew when it would happen and I suppose I liked it that way, for it was the same as a year-round birthday party, with presents being showered on you when you least expected. And up in my room, it was perfect. For when she'd start to hum, raising one of her long legs straight into the air, I knew there couldn't be a canary left alive in this world, because I'd swallowed them all.

So everything went along fine, until the night of the opening of Harriet's play. First we had an argument. She didn't want to go. I told her she didn't have to. Then it turned out she didn't want me to go. I told her I was going whether she liked it or not. Finally, she came along, being late when I picked her up and nasty all the way over.

Once we got there, though, I didn't mind. Because of Harriet. I'm not a judge of acting and don't pretend to be, but just the same, I know that Harriet was an actress that night. Her part called for her to be in love with a doctor, a nice enough guy but who didn't care a hill of beans for her. It was so sad watching her eating her heart out that I wanted to jump right up on that stage and make him propose. And that night, in spite of her too-big nose and her too-close-together eyes, Harriet was beautiful. On the stage, she was something to see.

But Annabelle didn't think so. During intermissions, all she said was how terrible the ugly girl was playing the daughter. She knew Harriet's name all right, but she never used it, never called her anything but "the ugly girl." I just let her talk, not answering. With Annabelle, it was the best way.

Then afterward, I pulled her off to a corner of the lobby. "I'm going back to see Harriet a second," I told her. "Wait for me here."

"Don't," Annabelle said.

"I won't take long, I promise."

"I don't want you to," she said. "I forbid it."

Which was a little too much, even for her. "Come again?" I said.

"You heard me," she whispered. "If you go, I won't be here when you get back."

"I may never get over it," I said, walking away. Which sounds as though I was pretty sure of myself. Actually, I just knew Annabelle well enough to realize she could never bring herself to walk home alone.

There were a lot of others crowded around Harriet when I got there, so I stood off in a corner until they were gone. She didn't see me come in and when she started for the dressing-rooms, I called to her. "I think you're the greatest thing since sliced bread."

She didn't turn but only muttered thanks and kept on walking.

"Hey," I said, running up and grabbing her. "This is me."

"What do you want, Euripides?"

"To tell you how wonderful you were," I began. "To—"

"You just told me," she cut in. "Now—"

"Be a nice girl," I whispered. "Or I'll tell the whole world you're cross-eyed."

With that she slapped me hard across the face. And ran.

After a couple of minutes of just standing around, I walked back to the lobby. Annabelle was there all right. Talking and laughing with Professor Janes, who taught English, and his dipsomaniac wife, who looked to be pretty in her cups right then. I came up, said hello, and the four of us chatted until Mrs. Janes began twitching some, losing control. He excused himself, smiling as if nothing in the world was the matter.

"I suppose he must be used to that," I said.

"Who?" Annabelle asked, staring off some place.

"Him. Professor Janes." She nodded. "Thanks for waiting," I said.

At which Annabelle laughed out loud. "The pleasure," she told me, "was mine."

She was in a good mood that night and the days following. Spring was starting to make its move, so we went on long walks in the woods or along the beach, me talking with sometimes her joining in, but more often just nodding, a half-smile turning up the corners of her mouth. She wasn't as tense as she'd been before and once in a while she almost got playful, skipping on ahead of me as we moved along.

Then one night, the second week of April, we were up in my room, lying together, talking quiet. All of a sudden, the front door opened.

"I wonder who that can be?" Annabelle said, as calm as you please.

"Shhh," I whispered. "They'll go away."

Somebody yelled my name. "Euripides!"

And before I knew it, I answered back. "Zock! Zock! Hello."

He started coming up the stairs.

"Why don't you wait in the living-room?" I called out to him.

"Why should I?" he asked, his footsteps getting close.

"Zock," I yelled. "For chrisakes go wait in the living-room."

"Nonsense," he said, walking right in, switching on the light.

Nobody said anything. He looked at me. Then he looked at Annabelle. Then back at me. Then at her. It was like a five-set tennis match watching him as he stared, his mouth wide open, from one of us to the other, beet-red. Some things though, once you've started, you just have to finish. So he went on with it.

"Hi," he said.

"Zock," I said. "This here is Annabelle. Annabelle, meet Zock."

"Hi," he said.

She didn't answer, but nodded politely, the covers pulled up to her neck.

"I've told Annabelle all about you."

"Hi," Zock said.

"What's new?" I asked.

"Not much. What's new with you?"

"Not much. What are you doing home?"

"Spring vacation."

"How's Harvard?"

"Can't complain."

"Zock goes to Harvard," I said to Annabelle. She nodded again.

"I thought I'd stop over to say hello. I just got in a few minutes ago."

"Glad you did."

"I guess I'll wander home," he said. "Stop over sometime."

"Conceivably," I answered, imitating him.

"A pleasure to have met you," he said to Annabelle, and with that he took off down the stairs out of the house.

The minute he was gone I grabbed hold of her and squeezed her as hard as I could. "Annabelle," I said. "You were just great."

She squirmed free. "It's time I went home," she said.

"Did you like him?"

"It really doesn't matter," she answered. I hugged her a few more times, then we got dressed and I walked her home.

Zock was waiting in the living-room of his house when I got there. The minute he saw me, he started to laugh. I fought it as best I could, but it beat me. So in a second we were both laughing, tears rolling down our faces. He went on and on, still going strong long after I'd stopped, my stomach aching. I went over and poured us each a drink.

"Well," I said, when he'd finally calmed down. "How do you like her?"

"She's gorgeous all right," he answered.

"I know that. But how do you like her?"

"I assume she speaks English."

"She's shy is all," I said.

He looked at me. "That wasn't quite the word I had in mind."

"Well, she is. Very shy. Honest to God."

"I believe you on faith," Zock said.

"Wasn't she great up there?" I went on. "I mean, wasn't she just great?"

"Experience, Euripides. It's probably happened before."

"Not to Annabelle," I said.

"Again, on faith."

"Dammit—" I began.

"Take care, Euripides," Zock said.

"I will," I told him, laughing. "Next time I'll lock the front door."

With that we toasted each other, and drank.

Which made it pretty obvious to me that the two of them were not cut out to become bosom buddies. And which also put me in a somewhat uncomfortable position, what with wanting to be with Zock during his stay home, and having to be with Annabelle at the same time. I worried about it awhile that night, but I needn't have. Because everything was solved the next day, much to my amazement, by Annabelle. Who, it turned out, had a big paper due and would I mind if we didn't see each other the rest of the week. Naturally I protested, fought the good fight, losing with honor. So Zock's stay went very fast, with no new complications showing up. Bunny was home, too, and the three of us went out some, but just as often it was Zock and me alone. We talked, horsed around, doing one thing and another. I saw Annabelle twice for coffee that week and she was in a good mood, as her paper was coming along fine.

Zock left for Harvard on a Sunday night, flying from the airport in Chicago. I drove him and afterward, on the way back, I stopped off at Annabelle's dorm. She wasn't in, though, being at the library. I didn't see her at all Monday, but Tuesday afternoon we had an appointment to meet in Harold's at four.

She never showed.

So, when I got tired of waiting, I wandered over to her dorm and asked was she in. The girl at the desk buzzed her room. She buzzed back. I waited. There were quite a few others milling around and I sort of watched them. Waiters were zipping in and out, setting up for the evening meal; some clown was trying to play the piano; the living-room was full of hand-holders. Finally Annabelle appeared, wearing a man's white shirt, her black hair loose along her back. She walked down the stairs very fast, stopping a few feet above me.

I smiled at her. "Where were you?" I asked. She didn't say anything. "Cat got your tongue? What gives? I'm a busy man. I've got better things to do than just sit around waiting for girls not to meet me."

"Don't wait any more then," she said, turning, starting away.

I grabbed her, pulled her down. "Where were you?"

"Busy," she answered, staring off some place. She tried twisting loose but I wouldn't let her, holding on tight to her arms, digging in with my fingers.

"You might as well know," she whispered. "I won't be seeing you any more."

"What's the joke?" I said. "Come on, tell me, let me in on it." And by now my voice was louder and I knew everyone was staring at us. But I didn't care.

"Joke?" she said. "I told you once. I never joke. Now let me go."

I did. For a second. Then I grabbed her again and started shaking her hard, talking to her, my voice suddenly the only sound on the whole floor. "Annabelle," I said. "This is me. For Christ's sake, snap out of it." A buzz-buzz-buzz began behind me and I got louder and louder until I suppose I was yelling. "Please. Come on. Goddammit! Look at me!" I twisted her head so she had to. "This is me, Annabelle. Trevitt. Remember? The house? The stairs? The bed, Annabelle. The bed. For Christ's sake remember that."

She stared past me. "Bed?" she murmured, as if in all her life she'd never heard of it.

I sagged against the banister and she tore loose, running up the stairs, away from me. I didn't move for I don't know how long, and when I did, they all watched me, those whispers following me on out the door.

I got drunk that night. I thumbed my way to the Crib and was squiffed by suppertime. But I kept on, drinking, mumbling into my glass, swearing, until they wouldn't serve me any more. I staggered home, which took many hours, and when I got there I walked right by my folks who said not one word to me. I made it to my room, flopped on the bed, and, in a minute, I was out.

I suppose it was near four in the morning when I woke, groggy, thirsty. Stumbling to the bathroom I turned on the faucet, bent over, pressed my lips against the spout, and let the water run down inside me until I was bloated and my stomach bulged. Then I went back to bed. But I couldn't sleep. I couldn't do anything but think of Annabelle and swear, cursing her as well as I knew how. Every time I thought I was all right, I'd feel her lying next to me, hear her humming her song, see her as she lifted one of those perfect legs straight up into the air.

I tried to cry but I couldn't. I hated her but I didn't. My stomach hurt, felt hollow for all the water I had drunk. I thought about killing her, watching her die. I thought about killing myself. I listened for the phone to ring but it never did. I waited for sleep but it never came. I just lay there, wide awake, rolling and twisting, my stomach aching like hell.

It was just before dawn that I realized I was in love with her.

The next morning I got down to her dorm early, waiting for her, standing by a tree on the far side of the street. After nine, she came out and as soon as I saw her I bolted across, calling to her. She didn't stop. "Annabelle!" I yelled, running up beside her. "Listen. I've got to talk to you. Please. Stop. Will you listen to me? There's something I have to say. Annabelle, will you for chrisakes stop and listen?" She stopped.

"I love you."

She didn't answer but started walking again.

I grabbed her, spun her around. "Didn't you hear me? I said I love you. I swear to God, Annabelle. I do."

"I'm sorry," she whispered. "You're too late."

Which shook me. Because all the time I'd been waiting for her I just knew that as soon as she found out how I felt, everything was going to be all right; that before the day was over we'd be back in my room, on my bed, her humming soft beside me, relaxed and happy.

I couldn't say anything more then. She walked away from me. I watched her go.

But later, when I got to thinking about it, it all came clear. There was somebody else. There had to be. So I took to following her around campus, like Harriet had done with me, only now the river had changed. Wherever she went I kept her in sight, stopping when she stopped, hurrying when she hurried.

Professor Janes turned out to be the man.

Which I should have guessed from the start, but didn't. She visited him in the afternoons, with me following and her knowing it but visiting him all the same. After she'd go inside I'd creep up to the house and press against the wall underneath the bedroom window. And once, on a warm day, they left that window open and I could hear her humming her bed song, the sound of it drifting down to me.

We had a lot of scenes after that, about every day for a while. They were always the same. I'd start pleading with her, then I'd yell, and finally go back to begging again. She never listened much to what I said but only looked off somewhere, nervous and tense, anxious to get away.

The last one was a real whopper in which I told her I was going to tell the school authorities and then both her and Professor Janes would be canned. I guess it must have been pretty funny, but I didn't think so, not then. So when she laughed at me I lost control and shoved her. She fell into what happened to be a mud puddle, ruining her dress, ripping it. After she'd gone I jumped up and down on that mud puddle like a crazy man, splashing the water away, soaking my own clothes. When there wasn't any water left, I went home.

What was so terrible was that I knew exactly when she'd be with him, because Mrs. Janes belonged to the same organizations as my mother, had the same meeting schedule. So I could tell, almost to the minute, what was going on, except there wasn't a thing I could do to stop it. Once, when Mrs. Janes was at my house I almost broke up the meeting I wanted so badly to run down and tell her to get the hell home, to hurry because right that second her husband was in bed with the girl I loved, to catch them because then everything would be fine again. I didn't, of course. Instead I started throwing things around my room; books, shoes, whatever I could lay my hands on. When there was nothing left to throw I tore out of the house to the Crib and got drunk.

I tried a couple other women, among them the college dietician, an excitable woman of forty. But it didn't help. So finally I called Harriet, telling her to come over right away, hanging up before she had a chance to say no.

I went to my room and waited, lying on my bed, all the shades down.

It was a beautiful day outside and the sun slanted in at the edges of the windows, striping the room. I stared at those golden stripes, riveted my eyes on them, wishing for Harriet to hurry, trying not to think. Which is always a mistake. Because by the time she did ring the doorbell, I was so tense I wasn't in shape to see anyone.

I yelled down to her, letting her know where I was. Then I heard her hopping up the stairs.

"What a cheery place," she announced, walking in. She went to the shades, starting to fiddle with them.

"Leave them down," I told her.

"Sure," she said. And with that she raised them all, one by one, pulling at the string, letting them fly, watching as they snapped around and around at the top. Then she sat down, drummed her fingers awhile, looking over at me. I didn't say anything, but just blinked, staring back.

"It's been swell talking to you," she said, standing, heading for the door.

"Jesus, Harriet," I muttered. "Quit acting like that."

"How could any maiden resist you?" she answered, coming over to the bed. "How would you like me to act? Sweet and demure? Bursting with sympathy? Really, Euripides. Lying here in the dark. All you need is 'Hearts and Flowers' playing in the background."

"Maybe you better go," I said. "Now."

"A young man asked me over for a chat," she answered. "And I'm not leaving until we've had one." She sat down beside me on the bed. "I know all about it, Euripides. You don't have to bother explaining. I know you've been bedding with her. And that she dropped you. And about that wing-ding you had in her dorm. The freshman class talked of little else for a week." She looked at me. "That pleases you, doesn't it? Admit it, you feel better already."

"I love her," I said.

"Oh, baby, you don't love her. It's just being dropped that upsets you. 'How can she do it to a great guy like me?' Isn't that the truth?"

"Let's skip it," I said, knowing she was trying to be nice, acting clinical and all. As if it was just something minor, like a skin rash, and tomorrow it would be gone. But right then I wasn't buying.

"No," she said. "Let's not skip it."

"Harriet," I warned. "Shut up."

"Sure. 'Shut up, Harriet, and cry on my shoulder.' And you know something? I probably would, if it was somebody else. But I won't weep for her, not for Annabelle. Do you know what she is?"

I turned on her then, yelling. "Do you know what you are? You're jealous! Green as grass jealous. So don't go around calling other people names when you're not so goddam perfect yourself. Because I'd drop you for her again in a minute if I had the chance and don't you ever think I wouldn't!"

She bolted.

Running out of the room, down the stairs, while I just lay there, listening to the sound of her footsteps. Finally I went to the window on the landing, opened it, and called after her, yelling for her to come back, that I was sorry. But she was too far away; she never heard me. So I stayed there, leaning out the window, watching her as she ran, as fast as she could, until she was out of sight.

That's the last I saw of Harriet for more than a year. We didn't talk again during that time so I don't know what happened to her. But I do know what happened to me. I did just what any normal, red-blooded American boy would do.

I went to pot.

By drinking. Every night for more than a month I drank myself blind. I took money from my father's wallet and my mother's purse. I snuck into Zock's house and stole bottles from his old man's liquor cabinet. I lied to everyone, never went to classes, but instead, to the Crib, which opened at noon, running as much of the way as I could, just trying to get there. For the month was May, the weather fine, clear and warm, with maybe a hint of wind blowing in off the Lake. That wind was what I hated most on those walks. It knotted my stomach so that I had to stop and scream at the top of my lungs to get some release. I didn't eat during those weeks nor did I sleep much. I didn't do a thing but drink, coming in late, sometimes making it to my room, but more often not, spending the night on the lawn, the floor, the stairs; wherever I happened to fall.

My mother tried to help and my father even called me into his study for a talk, which was sad, for I think he really wanted to help. But all he did was sputter around in Greek awhile. I didn't listen to him and I didn't listen when President Atkins called me in to tell me I was in danger of flunking out and "think of your family." I just went right on, making a fool of myself, I know, but there wasn't anything else I could do.

And then, late one morning in the first week of June, I was awakened by someone shaking me. I fought free and turned over. The next thing I knew, water was being poured on me. I came out swinging and there, standing over me, peering down, was the ugly face of Zachary Crowe.

"Zock," I yelled.

"Morning, Euripides," he said cheerfully. "Time to rise and shine."

"What are you doing home?"

"School's out," he answered.

I nodded and started getting up, but still being dizzy from the night before, I couldn't quite find the handle.

"You seem in fine shape," he said to me, sniffing. "And you smell nice too." I didn't say anything. He began hitting me on the arm. "Want to go a few rounds?"

"No," I told him. "I don't."

"And I loved your letters," he went on. "Nothing like letters to keep things alive. Boy. That last one of yours was a riot."

"Cut it out," I said.

"No, Euripides. You cut it out."

"I'm trying, Zock," I answered. "Believe me. That's just what I'm trying to do." And right then I told him. Everything that had happened since he'd left. About the shaft, Professor Janes, my drinking, the works.

"That Annabelle sounds like a terrific girl," he said when I was quiet again. "Great. Somehow, though, I think I prefer Marjorie Bluestone."

And when I heard her name I started laughing. It wasn't funny but that didn't matter. I fell back on the bed, rolling around, kicking my heels, tears streaming down my face. It was the first time I'd laughed in a month so I kept at it, forcing it until I ached.

"Who died?" Zoch said, watching me. And then: "Come on over and let's have lunch. Move."

So I did. Bunny was there and we yacked it up, laughing at all the dumb things Mrs. Crowe said, finally driving her out. Then just the three of us talked, about this and that, nothing in particular, but mostly the old times, and it really made me feel good, sitting there. It was middle afternoon when Bunny stood up.

"I have to go change," she said.

Zock nodded. "We're all going for dinner tonight," he explained.

"You're busy then?"

"Come along," he said. "You know you're welcome."

"No. Thanks anyway."

"What will you do?"

"The Crib," I said.

"When are you going?"

"Now," I told him. "Before the rush-hour traffic."

"Stop being melodramatic," Zock snapped. He pulled at his lip awhile. "Tell you what. I'll go along. I'll get dressed now and go on out there with you. Pick you up around seven?" he asked Bunny. She didn't say anything. "O.K.? You mind? Look, I can't let Euripides drink alone when I'm around. You don't mind."

Bunny hesitated a long time. "Just be sure you're sober at seven," she answered, finally. Then, kissing him once, she skipped on out.

It took a while for Zock to get ready. He chose a white shirt and a dark-gray suit and a striped tie. I gave him trouble all along the line, horsing with him, hiding his shoes, mussing his hair, and like that. He made it though, and then we drove out to the Crib.

"What a great place," he said as we walked in. "I'd forgotten. You could live and die in here and never know the sun was shining."

"Darkness gives atmosphere," I explained. "And charm. And also hides how dirty the glasses are."

We sat over in a corner and started drinking, Zock taking Scotch, nursing it along slow, while I had double whiskies. Pretty soon I began to relax, for liquor soothes me, it always has, though I suppose that is more of a curse than a blessing. I leaned back in my chair and listened as he talked about Harvard. And the way he did it, it seemed like a wonderful place.

"So how were your grades?" I asked.

"I got one B," he answered. "But in the others I did all right."

"Well, you're not so goddam smart," I told him. "Because I got one B, too. In gym. So don't try telling me anything."

"You always were outstanding in academics," he said. "You'll probably end up a college professor too, before it's all over."

"Indeed," I said, imitating my father. "The sex symbol in Euripides," I started off, "symbolizes, naturally, sex. There is the bull symbol, which symbolizes male sex. And there is the cow symbol, which symbolizes female sex. And then there is the calf symbol, which symbolizes carelessness. All together, there are nine calf symbols in *Medea*, seven of them in the chorus. All of which leads us to the conclusion that . . ." and I went on for a while longer.

"You'll cause a sensation," Zock said, nursing his Scotch.

"Gimme," I said, grabbing his glass. "It's refill time."

"You know, you could always stop."

"I suppose so," I answered. "But I'm not about to." I said that very slow and carefully, as I was pretty far gone already. I went to the bar, snuck an extra one, then came back with our refills. He was looking at his watch when I got there.

"I have to leave in fifteen minutes," he said. "You come too."

"Why don't you skip it, Zock? Look, you can see Bunny all summer, so why don't you skip it?"

"Because we're both leaving in fifteen minutes," he answered. "And I mean that."

We didn't talk for a while then, but just sat quietly over in that corner. Finally, I couldn't stand it any longer. "Zock," I said. "For chrisakes. How could she do it to me?"

"Who?"

"Don't be funny. Annabelle."

"Be happy she did," Zock said. "Now. We're going in five minutes."

I managed to make it back to the bar for another, but it was getting tougher each time. I crashed down in the chair and stared across at him. "That girl is a no-good bitch," I said. "Do you know that?"

"Very likely," he answered.

"But I love her. She's a no-good bitch and I love her. Why is that?"

"Beats me," Zock said. "It probably has to do with your metabolism."

"I really love her," I said again. "Isn't that amazing?"

"My mother tells me time heals all wounds."

"Crap!" I said.

"Nicely put," he said. "It has a ring to it. Crap. I must remember that word." He stood up. "Let's go."

I shook my head. "I'm not leaving."

"You just think you're not leaving," he answered, pulling at me. I shook free and swallowed my drink. "We're going home to beddy-bye, Euripides. Whether you like it or not."

"This is my home."

"I told you once to stop being melodramatic. I've got a weak stomach." Then, somehow, me fighting all the way, he got me outside. The cooler air hit me and I sagged against him. "Get in the car," he said.

I broke loose and sat on the ground. "I'm not going anywhere unless I drive," I said. "I'm staying right here unless I drive."

"You're not driving," he said, trying to lift me. "You couldn't."

"I can drive as well as you. Better. I can drive as well as anybody. I'm probably the best driver in the whole state of Illinois."

"Very likely," Zock said. "But tonight you're not going to. So get up." I didn't move. He got in the car. "I'm leaving," he said. "Right now. I'm not kidding, Euripides." I still didn't move. "This is your last chance," he told me. "I'm leaving." Then he drove off.

But he came back, naturally. About two minutes later he pulled up in front of me. "O.K.," he said. "You win. You can drive."

"Now you're using the old bean," I said, getting in the car. We started off, creeping down the center of the highway.

"You're doing fine," Zock said. "Keep it up."

"I'll do finer," I told him, pressing down a little on the gas pedal and singing. " 'Nothing could be finer than to be in Carolina in the morning. Nothing could be sweeter than my sweetie when I meet her in the morning.' "

"No faster," he said. "Don't forget."

" 'I have forgot much, Cynara. Gone with the wind. Flung roses, roses riotously with the throng.' Zock? Why is it 'roses, roses'? Why are there two of them? Why wouldn't just the one rose be enough?"

"Well," he began, staring out the window at the sun, which was starting to head on down. "Maybe so people like you would ask questions. Or maybe . . ."

He stopped talking then and tried grabbing at my leg as I pushed down on the gas pedal. I pushed it farther and farther and when I felt it touch the floor I kept it there, the motor roaring in our ears. I don't know how fast we were going, but pretty soon we were out of control.

Just before it happened, Zock looked at me and said something.

Then we hit.

We smashed into Half Day Bridge going full speed and I guess the door on my side must have sprung open, because the next thing I knew I was lying twisted on the edge, watching as the car roared down into the ravine, rolling over and over, bending, buckling, scraping, until it hit the bottom with a crash and rested there, upside down, the four wheels still spinning around and around and around.

I made it to my feet. "Zock," I whispered. "Can you hear me? Are you all right?" I began losing control. "Zock! Can you hear me? Say something. Answer me. Zock!" I started down the ravine but lost my footing and crashed the rest of the way, rolling over and over, like the car. "Zock!!!" and I guess I was screaming, for by then, I was next to it. The first thing I did was to stop those wheels from turning. I walked around the car, very slow, carefully putting my hands up on the wheels, stopping them. Then, when I was all done with that, I reached inside and pulled him out.

There was nothing to him. Covered with blood, he looked like a rag doll smeared with jam. His arms bent the wrong way. His ribs stuck out through his white shirt. Blood was still streaming from his mouth.

I stood up and the last thing I remember was staring at that beautiful sunset and thinking: "Not like this. There's been a mistake made somewhere. It just couldn't happen on a night like this."

Then I crumbled. . . .

When I came to, somebody was poking away at my cheek and I looked up to find myself in an ambulance with a doctor staring down at me. I blinked a couple of times.

"How do you feel?" he asked.

"Where are we?"

"Parked along the bridge. How do you feel?"

"How's Zock?" He didn't answer. I sat up slowly. "How's Zock?" I asked again.

"You've got a nasty cut along your cheek," he said. I put my hand up and felt it. It went all the way from my temple to my chin. I pulled my fingers away, red.

"But you won't need stitches," he told me.

"He's dead?"

"Yes," he mumbled, his back to me, fiddling with something. "In a few weeks, it won't even show."

"I want it to show," I said. His back was still to me as I reached up with my fingers and placed them in the cut. Then I pushed it open, stretching the skin, digging in with my fingers until I could almost hear the skin as it split, farther and farther. Blood started streaming down my face, almost blinding me. I blinked it away.

He turned, and when he saw what I was doing he came at me, grabbing for my fingers. But I pushed him off, threw open the door to the ambulance, and stepped out.

They were all there, standing quietly on Half Day Bridge, with the sun almost down and just the last red rays slicing in, hitting them, making them look like a band of silent Indians. My folks, and Zock's, and Bunny with hers, all dressed up for the dinner celebration. They were staring down the ravine at the half-dozen men—police and white-coated doctors—who were crowded around Zock's body like so many flies.

"Get away from him," I yelled. "Leave him alone."

"There he is," Mrs. Crowe shouted when she heard me. "There he is. There he is." She came running up. I started to say something but before I could she was slapping me, crying hysterically and slapping me, saying: "Kill him! Kill him! Kill him!" over and over. I didn't move but just stood there, letting her hit me, the blood pouring down my face and dripping onto her clothes, spotting them. Mr. Crowe came up, tried to pull her away, and out of the corner of my eye I saw the doctor from the ambulance standing there, waiting.

"Don't stop her," I said to Mr. Crowe. "It's all right."

But he pulled her away and when I was free I took off down the ravine to where Zock was. They had moved him, had tried to straighten him out, but it didn't do any good. His bones still stuck out through the cloth of his bloody white shirt.

Then Bunny was holding me, crying and pale.

"Bunny, I'm sorry," I said.

"At the end," she whispered. "At the end. Did he say anything?"

I nodded: "He said: 'Tell Bunny I love her.' " Which wasn't what he'd said at all, but I figured I'd done enough to her already that night. One lie more or less wasn't going to change anything.

She let me go and started back up the ravine. I could hear Mrs. Crowe crying and screaming, "Kill him! Kill him! Kill him!" and her words echoed there, in the ravine, with the sun going down.

I knelt beside Zock. "I'm sorry," I said. "Zock, I'm sorry. I'm sorry. Honest to God, Zock, I'm sorry. I'm sorry. I'm sorry," chanting it over and over, trying to drown out the echoes of Mrs. Crowe.

"Shock," I heard a doctor say, and then he slapped a needle into my arm. I got dizzy and fell over on top of Zock, grabbing him, clutching what was left of him. Just before I went out I heard the doctor telling somebody, I suppose my father, not to worry, as I would be O.K. again in three days. And he was right.

Because four days later I enlisted.

V . . . . The Army

I never liked the Army; I never hated it. I don't think you can. It's just something you have to accept, like the law of gravity, since it was here before you were and it'll be here when you're gone. It's ridiculous to go around thinking: "That goddam law of gravity, I'll fix its wagon." How are you going to do it? Answer: you can't. It would be nice, on a hot summer day, to float up a couple hundred feet and cool off. But that's impossible, so why worry about it. The law of gravity has its points, good and bad.

So does the Army. Everybody talks about its bad points, but the good ones are there too. It doesn't ask you a bunch of questions when you join up, such as what you're running away from and why. All it cares is that you can breathe and sign your name, and if you can't even do that, it'll teach you. Which is as fair, I think, as anything you're apt to find, in this world at least. No, the Army isn't all bad; it just seems that way.

And what happens, when you're in it for a while, is that you forget about it. Like everything else that rules you from way off. You don't walk the streets thinking: "I am walking the streets because the goddam law of gravity keeps me here." If you do, you'll go nuts in no time. And so it is with the Army.

What you remember, long after, aren't the marches, but who marched next to you; not the barracks, but who lived inside. And so I remember Ulysses S. Kelly, whom I have not seen for a long time now, but I doubt if the day will ever come when I'll scratch my head and say: "Ulysses S. Kelly? Who's that?" As he is apt to be with me until Armageddon, and who can know for sure when that will be?

We met on my third day in the Army. I was on KP, the first time, at Camp Scott, a big post down South where I had my basic training. But this was before, and what I was doing mostly was processing and pulling details. Which I didn't mind, not even KP, for it kept you busy, your mind occupied, so you didn't have much chance to think about things. Such as Zock's funeral, which I missed, being in the hospital, but at which Mrs.

Crowe went crazy for a while, throwing herself on top of his coffin right in front of everyone, having to be dragged away, crying and screaming, out of control.

I was on garbage detail that third day, and after breakfast when I wandered out, I saw another kid was already there and I walked up behind him.

" 'Morning," I said.

"Knock it off," he answered, not turning. " 'Cause there's a lot of shaping up to be done."

Then he got back to work. I watched him. He was a big kid, and if his mother had been describing him, she'd have said he hadn't lost his baby fat yet, whereas, actually, he was a slob, with pudgy hands and soft, short fingers. It wasn't his looks, though, that made me stare, but how he'd talked. As if he'd been in the Army thirty years so far and had just re-enlisted for six. The truth was, I later found, he'd been in five days total, two more than me.

And as I watched him work, I saw he wasn't doing anything. From a distance it might have seemed he'd die of heat prostration if he kept on sixty seconds longer. But all he was really doing was lifting one garbage-can lid, putting it back, lifting another, switching it with a third, and like that. Busy looking busy.

"The way you're going," I said, "things'll get shaped up the day after never."

"Can the chatter," he answered.

"Glad to meet you," I said, turning him around. "Ray Trevitt."

"Ulysses S. Kelly," he said. We shook hands and it was right then I first realized he was scared half to death.

"Take it easy," I told him. "We got all day."

"We've talked enough," he answered. "Let's snap to."

So we did.

Breakfast that morning had consisted mostly of dehydrated egg, no delicacy, and there was a lot left over. A whole garbage-canful, to be exact, which felt like it must have weighed half a ton. After breakfast a truck came up to haul away the garbage and we were given the job of hoisting that canful of dehydrated egg onto the back of the truck.

We bent down, the two of us, and started lifting that garbage can. The first couple of inches went fine, but then he gave a grunt, pooping out, letting go, and the can dropped with a crash, slopping egg over everything in sight.

Naturally I started to laugh, looking at that layer of yellow mess spreading around. But Kelly didn't. He was too scared. He just stood there, his eyes darting like bumblebees, this way and that, wondering if anyone had seen.

"Get a mop," I told him. "Unless you're hungry." He didn't move. "Get a mop," I said again.

"You did that," he whispered to me. "It was your fault."

"Come again?" I said.

"You dropped it," he went on. "You. Not me."

"I could have sworn it was the other way around," I answered, laughing.

"Now get a mop and clean it up," he whispered. "And don't make me tell you again."

I bowed low, not moving.

"Get a mop," he said, and by this time he was shaking. I stared at him awhile.

"O.K.," I told him finally. "Maybe I better."

About fifteen minutes later, when we were finishing up with the egg, a jeep came roaring toward us. I took one look and jabbed Kelly in the ribs. "Watch it," I whispered. "That's the Chief of Staff." Kelly just nodded.

A Colonel jumped out of the jeep and came walking in our direction. I watched him. Maybe forty years old, he looked to be thirty, short, trim. He was carrying a swagger stick and he flicked it constantly against his pressed trouser leg as he came, walking straight as a ramrod, right up to us. We snapped to attention, Kelly and I, saluting while he gave us the once-over.

"How's it going, men?" he said, biting the words out sharp and clean, those eagles shining on his shoulders.

"Fine, sir," I said.

He looked at what was left of the egg. "What happened here?"

"Accident, sir," I said.

"Accident?" I looked at him, then out of the corner of my eye at Kelly, who was really shaking now, gnawing hard at his lower lip.

"It was my fault," I said. "I dropped a garbage can."

He smiled quickly, flicked us both on the shoulder with his swagger stick, jumped back into his jeep, muttered something to his driver, and sped away.

"Smoking-lamp is lit," I said, pulling out a cigarette, slapping at the flies feasting on my fatigues. Kelly was still shaking. "It's O.K.," I told him. "Relax. He's gone."

"That's my father," Kelly muttered. "He was a war hero. He won the Silver Star on D-Day."

. . .

At that time, there were 25,000 men taking basic training at Camp Scott, a subject I will not linger on, for if you haven't been through it, nothing could be duller, and if you have, you don't want to hear about it again. All I will say is that there couldn't have been many better than me. I was as Gung Ho as you can get, working every second, volunteering for jobs, keeping busy, always being the first one up in the morning, always having the shiniest boots in the company, the neatest uniform, etc., etc. And because of that—my attitude, plus the fact that I had enlisted whereas practically everyone else had been dragged in by the draft—I was supposed to be made platoon leader. All the others thought so, and Master Sergeant Muldoon, the first sergeant of the company, even called me into the orderly room the morning before training began to talk it over.

But I never got it.

Kelly did. Because that afternoon the Colonel appeared, straight and shiny from out of nowhere, and the next morning, when the platoon had reveille, Ulysses S. was put in charge.

And from then on, our platoon was always last. Mainly because Kelly was undoubtedly the worst platoon leader since the freeze at Valley Forge. Everything he did was wrong. When he was supposed to call right face, he called left; when he was supposed to call left face, he called right; when instructions were given, he never understood; when questions were asked, he couldn't answer.

But rather than admit his mistakes, he gave excuses. He had more excuses than Carter had pills. When things went wrong, it wasn't his fault.

It was mine.

I was his whipping boy and he yelled at me all the time, reveille to taps, sunrise to sunset. Which didn't bother me particularly, seeing as I figured I knew why he was doing it, so I just let him go.

And the days went by, one pretty much like the one before, until late Wednesday afternoon in the third week of training. As we broke formation to get cleaned up, the first sergeant called my name.

"What is it, Sergeant Muldoon?" I said, going up to him.

"Someone's in the orderly room to see you," he answered.

"Who?"

"Can't rightly say, Trevitt," he shrugged. "He just asked for you."

I hurried to the orderly room and went in. Someone was waiting for me all right. Zock's father. Standing there by himself, five hundred miles from home. It was still bright in the orderly room but I had to take a couple steps forward, close, before I was sure. He'd changed that much. He looked older, but that wasn't it. Not all.

"Hello, Mr. Crowe," I said.

"Hello, Ray," he said. Then we were both quiet for a while. It was the first time I'd seen him since the night on Half Day Bridge. Five and a half weeks was all it had been. Thirty-nine days.

"How are you, Mr. Crowe?" I said finally.

He put his arm around my shoulder, gently. "Fine, Ray," he answered. "I've been fine."

"You look it," I said.

He nodded.

"How's the clothing store, Mr. Crowe? You still swindling those college kids?"

"Store?" he said. Then he tried smiling. "I sold it. I thought maybe you'd heard. I still work there, of course. But it got to be too much responsibility."

"I guess so," I said.

"Too much responsibility," he went on. "Too much work. When a man gets to be my age, he wants time to rest. So now the other fellow has the headaches while I have the fun." We moved toward the door, slowly, him with his arm still around me. "Say," he said. "I talked to your sergeant. It's O.K. with him if we go into town. Maybe have a good meal. Something like that. How's it sound?"

"What did you come for, Mr. Crowe?"

"I was just driving by," he said. "I thought I might stop in and take you for a good meal. The two of us."

"What did you come for?" I said again. "Why did you come to see me?"

"I guess I don't know," he answered, very soft.

"I'm not hungry," I said. "I don't want a meal."

He nodded. "I'm not hungry either."

"Why don't we go for a walk then? Walk and talk. That suit you, Mr. Crowe?"

He nodded again. "I guess that's what I came for anyway," he said. "To talk."

We left the orderly room and walked on down the noisy company street, the dust rising in clouds around our shoes. Then we turned, neither of us saying anything, and headed out toward the fields and the ranges beyond. After a while, he put his arm around my shoulder again, keeping it there as we scuffed our way, kicking up dust with every step, the sun going down in front of us as we walked West, still silent. After a long time, with the sun almost gone, the heat of the day going, he stopped. I stopped too. He turned to me.

"Why did it happen, Ray?" he said then.

"I don't know why, Mr. Crowe," I said. "But it was my fault. I know that much."

He sat down on the edge of the dusty road, me alongside him, our arms around our knees. "I don't care about the fault, Ray. I just want to know why it happened. I've thought and I've thought and I've thought and I can't understand it. Why did it happen? Maybe it was my fault. Maybe I brought him up wrong."

"No," I said. "That isn't true."

"My wife thinks it was."

"How is she, Mr. Crowe?"

"She's fine," he said. "Fine."

"How is she?" I asked again.

He looked away, staring off at the rim of the setting sun. "You heard about the funeral? What happened?"

"Yes," I said. "I heard."

"She took it hard," he muttered. "Very hard."

"Is she all right, Mr. Crowe? Better?"

"She'll be fine," he answered.

"What do you mean, Mr. Crowe? Will be?"

"They sent her off," he whispered. "The doctors. She'll be back in a little while. I still have the house. In Athens. And then, when she gets back, I thought we might head for California, Mrs. Crowe and I. It's supposed to be wonderful in California. Warm. Lots of sunshine. She'll like it. I think maybe I'll open a new store. There's opportunity in California. New people moving in all the time. New people need new clothes."

"Sure they do, Mr. Crowe."

"And I can sell clothes. I can sell clothes with the best of them."

"I know," I said.

And then all of a sudden he was crying, the sobs deep in his throat, trying not to, trying to force them back, only making it worse. They came out like screams.

"Don't," I said. "Come on, Mr. Crowe. That's not going to help anything."

"It's thirty-nine days since he died, Ray. Just thirty-nine days."

"Is that right?" I said.

He nodded, his head pressed down on his knees, his tears dropping in the dust.

"I got to get back, Mr. Crowe," I said, and I started pulling him to his feet. He was limp, like Zock after the crash, but I pulled him up, holding him as steady as I could.

"Come on, Mr. Crowe," I said again. "I got to get back."

We started along the road, walking slow, my arm around his shoulder now.

"Zock loved you, Mr. Crowe. I swear to Jesus he did. He loved you. It wasn't your fault."

"He knew you best," Mr. Crowe answered. "I thought you might know why. He knew you better than me. Best of all."

"You don't believe that, Mr. Crowe. You know you don't believe that. He loved you. You were his father. He loved you best in all the world. Right before he died he told me. That he loved you. Me. I was just his friend. But you. You were his father. He loved you best in all the world," I said. "It wasn't your fault, Mr. Crowe. It wasn't your fault. He loved you best in all the world. He loved you best in all the world, in all the world," and I chanted it to him, saying it over and over and over as I carried him along, until he was able to walk by himself, until he'd stopped crying.

Finally, we got to his car. He looked worse than ever now, his face streaked with dust and tears. But at least he was smiling. Or trying to.

"So long, Mr. Crowe," I said. "Good luck in California."

We shook hands. "Good-by, Ray," he said. "Maybe I'll see you back in Athens."

"Swell," I said.

"What was it that Zachary called you?" he asked. "Euripides?"

"Right the first time," I said.

He got in the car. "I'm glad I came down to see you then, Euripides. And I'm sorry for what happened out there." He pointed toward the ranges.

"Forget it, Mr. Crowe. And I'm glad you came down too."

"Maybe I'll buy you a meal some other time." He turned on the ignition, started the motor.

"Like I said, Mr. Crowe, great seeing you."

Then, finally, he drove away.

I didn't sleep much that night, but just lay there, wishing to God he'd never come. I thought about him, broken; his wife, cracked up; Zock, dead.

All because of me.

I thought about it that night and the next morning and the next afternoon and I suppose it was around dusk when I first thought of committing suicide. Which always sounds heroic or stupid, never correct, never the right thing to do. But suicide's no different from murder, only more personal. And then a line in Shakespeare kept coming back to me, a good line, Zock liked it. Where Othello says he's going to knock off his wife before she destroys anyone else. Destroying is worse than killing. Mr. Crowe; he was destroyed.

The days went by and as they went I kept thinking about all the people I'd known in my life and where was the good I'd done any of them. The more I thought the more I kept ringing up a zero. So I was Desdemona now, and there wasn't any Othello around to do the job for me. And when you're a boy, and you get to thinking that you're Desdemona, you're in pretty bad shape.

Which I was, really bad, on the Sunday of our fourth week of basic. For the first time, the company was given passes and they all took off, most of them heading for Hastingsville, a typical Army town a couple miles from post, full of military stores, churches, and saloons.

I didn't go, but rather stayed by myself in the barracks, sweating from the heat, over 100°. I was all alone that afternoon, lying naked, my eyes closed. I kept staring up, seeing Zock's ugly face, hearing his voice, trying to figure out what he meant by the temple of gold.

Which is what he said to me just before he died, as we roared down the highway, out of control, Half Day Bridge looming just ahead, big as death, getting bigger all the time. And I know there's a lot of crap gets thrown around about what people say before they die. Such as: "I've got the answer, has anybody got the question?" Or stuffy Lord Chesterfield muttering: "Give the gentleman a seat." Because people don't like to admit they might die groaning, or just quiet, in their sleep. And you can't blame them for that; everyone would like to end his life with a punch line.

But what Zock said, he said. I was there. I heard him. Just before we smashed into Half Day Bridge; just before he died with his red bones jutting through his white shirt, he turned to me, frightened I suppose, and he whispered: "The temple of gold, Euripides. The temple of gold."

I heard someone on the stairs, but I don't think a ringside seat to the Second Coming could have roused me then, so I didn't move until the footsteps got closer and closer, stopping at the foot of my bed.

"Trevitt," somebody whispered.

I snuck one eye open and saw Kelly standing there in his underwear shorts, the flab of his belly hanging over. I closed my eye and tried a few snores, not very original, but it threw him for a while. Finally he said my name again, and then a third time, and then he shook me.

"Trevitt," he said. "Are you asleep?"

"Who wants to know?"

"Me. Kelly."

"Never heard of you," I said. "Anyway, Trevitt's gone AWOL. I'm only covering for him."

"C'mon," he said, excited. "Quit kidding around." He shook me again. Harder.

"You know, it's funny," I said, looking at him, "but I could have sworn I was trying to get some sleep." He didn't say anything. "I understand your old man won the Silver Star on D-Day," I went on. "Is that right? That's a story I'd really like to hear. You bet. A story like that is worth waking a man up for."

He was shaking, so I stopped, waiting for him to say something. He did.

"I'm going to kill myself," he whispered.

"You go do that, Kelly," I told him. "You couldn't have picked a nicer day." I shut my eyes again.

"I'm not kidding, Trevitt. I'm going to kill myself."

I sat up. "Well, what are you telling me for? I'm sure not going to stop you."

He swallowed hard. "I wanted company."

"Sunday is God's day," I said. "Leave me alone."

"I want somebody to talk to while I do it," he went on. "I don't want to die by myself."

I stared at him awhile. "O.K., Ulysses," I said finally. "I'm your boy. Go kill yourself. But do it here," and I pointed to the next bed. "Because I'm not moving."

"Then it's settled," he muttered. "I'll get my stuff."

"How you going to do it?" I yelled after him.

"I'm going to cut my wrists with my bayonet," he answered.

"Attago, Ulysses," I said. "That's a swell way." I lay down again, waiting. Not long after he clomped up the stairs and came over, sitting on the next bed. He held out his bayonet.

"Like a razor," he said. "I spent all morning sharpening it."

"Fine," I told him. "You do nice work."

"Here," he said. "Feel."

"I believe you," I said, but he kept holding it out so I did what he wanted. It was sharp.

"How about that, Trevitt? Isn't it like a razor?"

"Kelly," I said, closing my eyes, "I just paid for the main event. Wake me when the preliminaries are over."

"You better watch," he said. " 'Cause here I go."

He took the bayonet and very slowly, very carefully, he brought it down until the tip rested on the blue veins in his wrist. I waited. He began to exert a little pressure and the flesh of his wrist dimpled.

Then he looked at me. "I bet you wonder why I'm doing this, don't you?"

"No, Kelly," I said. "Can't say as I do."

"It's on account of my father," he began. "On account of all my life I've been filled full up to here with crap about the Army. I'm going to have to be an officer. Because he's going to make me. I got to be a career man. A career man in the Army like my father. And as far as I'm concerned, you can take the Army, fold it three ways, and . . ."

"Shove it," I finished. "O.K. You told me. Now do it."

"He even named me after a soldier, for chrisakes. Ulysses S. Grant."

"Be happy," I said. "He could have picked Pilsudski."

"What does your father do, Trevitt?"

"He's a Greek teacher."

"There," Kelly said, pointing the bayonet at me. "See?" I didn't, but I nodded anyway. "So I got a no-good bastard for a father. What can I do about it? I'd rather be dead than spend my life in the Army, so what's there to do? But this?" He gestured with the bayonet. "You tell me, Trevitt. What's the point of going on?"

I thought for a long time. "I don't know," I said, finally.

"Well then," he said. "This is it." He began pushing the bayonet down again. I watched his face. He closed his eyes. I waited.

Then he opened his eyes. "I mean, what's the point of living? You tell me, Trevitt. You're a smart guy. Go on. Tell me."

"Jesus Christ, Kelly!" I exploded. "Are you going to kill yourself or aren't you?"

"O.K.," he muttered. "This is really it. So long, Trevitt."

He took a deep breath, closed his eyes tight. It was stifling hot in the barracks right then. My bed was soaked with perspiration and as Kelly grabbed hard onto his bayonet, sweat ran across his knuckles. He pushed down on his wrist, farther and farther down.

Then he screamed "OWWW!!!," dropped the bayonet, and began to swear. "Goddammit! Goddammit! It hurts!"

I started laughing, kicking my feet in the air. "What did you expect, Ulysses?"

He stood up, bleeding a little at the wrist. "I'll bleed to death," he said. "Trevitt. What'll I do?"

"See the Chaplain," I told him. "Last rites only cost a quarter." He was licking at the cut with his tongue, making faces.

"Son of a bitch," he said, kicking the bayonet across the floor. And with that he took off down the stairs, and I heard water running in the sink. I stretched out, trying to think of Zock again, but the sight of Kelly yelling, "OWWW!!!" kept getting in the way and I couldn't help laughing.

Then he was back, walking stiff, looking determined as hell.

"Hi, Kelly," I said. "What's new?" He didn't answer. "You got any more games we can play?" I asked.

"Same one," he answered, more serious than ever. "I'm going to swallow a bedspring."

"I don't know," I said, scratching my head. "But I swear it sounded like you said you were going to swallow a bedspring."

He brought one out from behind his back. "I said it and I meant it."

"God damn, Ulysses," I said. "You pick the nicest ways. Did you ever think of roasting yourself over a spit?"

He looked at me. Then he started whispering. "I'm going to tell you something, Trevitt. Something I never told anyone else." He paused, looking around. Finally, he said it. "I'm going to die a virgin."

I shook my head. "Well, you can't blame the old man for that, Ulysses. It's nobody's fault but your own. Because there's a billion women in this world, Ulysses." I started drawing numbers in the air. "One-nine-zeros-billion. And out of all of them the law of averages says there's got to be one would do the trick for you."

"Well," he said, staring at the bedspring, "I never found her."

"First you got to look, Ulysses."

"It's too late now," he said, and with that, he stuck the bed spring in his mouth.

I won't describe what happened next in too much detail, seeing as it gets a little messy, even though it was pretty funny at the time. Kelly's face turned different colors, most of them green, and his eyes started watering, and then the bedspring hit the floor, quickly followed by his breakfast and lunch.

After it was over, we stared at each other. Then he broke out crying, turned, and tore away. I could hear him blubbering in the latrine, all the faucets going full, trying to blot out the sound.

I went to the head of the stairs. "Hey, Kelly," I yelled down. "Best you come back here and clean this. Because I'm sure not going to."

Then I sacked out again, waiting. Awhile later he appeared, carrying a mop and a bucket of water.

"Clean it up good," I told him. "All of it." He didn't answer so I just stared at the ceiling and listened to the mop make swishing sounds along the floor. "You know," I said, after a couple of minutes, "if you want a woman, I'll do what I can for you." He still didn't answer. "Goddammit, Ulysses. If you want to get laid, I'll see you get laid. Now don't say you were never asked." I could hear his brain working.

"How you going to do it, Trevitt?"

"I'm magic," was all I said.

"How you going to do it, Trevitt? How? You really going to do it? Naw. You're just kidding. You're not really going to do it. I know you're not."

"O.K.," I said. "I guess I'm not."

He grabbed me by the arm. "How? Go on. Tell me. How?"

"Get your clothes on and we'll go into Hastingsville and find somebody."

"Who?"

"How do I know who? Somebody. Just get your clothes on."

"O.K., Trevitt," he said, patting me. "O.K. Great." He was jumping around like a Mexican bean. "Terrific." He headed for the stairs. Then he stopped. "You mean with a whore?"

"I sort of had that in mind," I said.

"I don't know," he began. "What if I catch something?"

"Look, Kelly," I said. "Please. Make up your mind. You're not going to hurt my feelings, so don't worry about that. But please. One way or the other. Make up your mind."

"But what if I catch something?" he said again.

"If you do," I whispered, "we won't tell a soul. And we won't go to the doctors. And you'll get so sick you'll die. Then all your troubles will be over. See?"

"Sure, Trevitt," he nodded. "I get you."

So off we went.

The bus ride to Hastingsville took fifteen minutes and Kelly didn't say one word all the way. He just shook. Which is catching, because by the time we got there, I was a little tense myself. As soon as we left the bus his questions started again, faster than ever.

"Where is she, Trevitt? Where is she?"

"I don't know, Ulysses. We got to look."

"Maybe she's not here, Trevitt. What about that?"

"Kelly," I said. "If there's a God in Heaven, there's a whore in Hastingsville."

And with that, I started looking, moving from one bar to the next, Kelly always waiting for me on the sidewalk. Each time I came out, he bombarded me with questions, more and more of them as the afternoon went by.

Then, finally, in about the tenth bar I tried, I found her. She was sitting alone, sipping a beer, so I sat down beside. Her name, unfortunately, was Irma, and she was no beauty, being big and fat. But she laughed a lot as we chatted, haggling over this and that, mainly money. When she was done with her beer, we went outside.

Which was when Kelly started walking away.

"Hey!" I shouted. He stopped, his back to us. We walked around him. "Ulysses," I said. "Meet Irma. Irma, this here is Ulysses and he's virgin, so go easy."

Irma laughed.

Ulysses pulled me over. "She's not very pretty," he whispered.

"You're right," I said.

"Tell him he's no Adonis," Irma said.

"She says you're no Adonis," I told him.

"I heard," Ulysses muttered. "I heard."

"Let's get going," Irma said.

"What if I catch something?" he whispered to me.

"I'm clean," Irma said. "Tell him I'm clean."

"Ulysses," I said, "if you want to whisper, whisper."

"I can't," Ulysses said.

"Let's get going," Irma said again.

We started to walk.

Irma put her arm around Ulysses. "Quit shaking," she said.

"I'm not shaking," Ulysses said, sneaking away, putting me in the middle as we moved along. We got to Irma's apartment.

Irma stopped.

"This is it," she said, walking inside.

"I'll wait on the sidewalk, Ulysses," I told him.

"No," he said.

"Yes," I said, starting to push him.

Irma stuck her head out the door. "Come on," she said. "I ain't got all day."

"What'll I do, Trevitt?" Ulysses whispered. "What do I do?"

"Figure it out," I said, shoving harder.

"I can't do it, Trevitt," he pleaded. "Let's go back."

"Grab him, Irma," I said. "He's all yours."

She grabbed him.

I waited on the sidewalk. About ten minutes later, Kelly came out.

"Hi, Ulysses," I said. "What's new?"

"Not much," he answered, trying to be casual. He made it for about ten seconds, after which he began jumping around, whooping it up, throwing his arms around me, laughing like crazy. "Trevitt," he yelled. "Trevitt, hey Trevitt. I feel great!"

I pushed him away and started laughing too. "I feel pretty good myself," I said.

From then on, we were buddies.

Now, I'm not trying to say that sex is the elixir of life or anything like that. I'm not knocking it either, but it isn't the handle, not even close, because if it was, people like Irma would be running this country, and then where would we be?

In Kelly's case though, it worked miracles.

Mainly, I think, because it was the first time anyone had done anything nice for him. He didn't have many friends, either in the Army or out. But I had done the favor and afterward, I couldn't get rid of him. At breakfast, he ate next to me. The same at lunch. And supper. When he had any free time, he spent it with me. Wherever I went, there he'd come, a pace or so behind. None of which I minded, for he really wasn't so bad; just an overgrown lapdog, and there's a place for them in this world too, like everything else.

He told me all about himself, about his whole life until his father had made him enlist. About how he wanted to be a farmer, how he had a green thumb and dreamed only of living his life out on his own farm some place, growing crops and doing whatever else you do when you live on one. About how his mother had died and his father had brought him up, shipping him from one military school to the next, seeing as he never did well at any of them. About the time when he'd been turned down from West Point and how his father didn't speak to him for weeks after, even though they were living together at the time, alone under the same roof. I could have written Kelly's autobiography inside of a week, I knew that much about him.

In training too, he was different. He still made the same mistakes, still screwed up the platoon as much as before. But now he didn't care, didn't yell and holler; now he only laughed, blushing, looking over at me. He was in a good mood from Irma on, Kelly was; just another happy slob fumbling his way through the Army.

Then one night, more than a week later, I was lying in my sack, half asleep, when all of a sudden there he was, standing over me.

"Trevitt," he whispered. "I got to talk to you."

"You are talking to me, Ulysses," I whispered back.

"I got to talk to you," he said again. "In private. Alone."

Which is a hard thing to do around an Army barracks, so we left it and walked outside. It was a hot night, full of stars, cloudless, and we moved through it awhile, circling the company area. He was scared again, like he'd been that day on KP when the eggs went slopping. Still, I didn't say anything but just walked quietly beside him, waiting for him to come out with it. Finally he started talking.

"Tomorrow," he said. "After lunch. Major Sheffield's coming down here. He's a friend of my father, Major Sheffield. To talk about Officer's School."

"So what?" I said.

"We have to sign papers," Kelly went on, whispering even though we were alone. "Applications. For OCS. I heard about it just now. In the orderly room." He reached down and picked up a handful of dust, rubbing it in his hands. "What'll I do, Trevitt?" he said after a little. "What am I gonna do?"

"Well, Ulysses," I said, slapping him on the back, "I'll tell you. Tomorrow we'll go in there and we'll listen to the Major. And then when he's done, we'll leave. We won't sign a thing. Not you. Not me. But that's tomorrow. Right now, we're going to get some sleep." And I started toward the barracks.

He didn't budge. He just stood right where he was, rubbing that dust in his hands. I came back to him. "Come on, Ulysses," I said. "Let's stand tall. You got nothing to worry about. Not a thing. You want to be a farmer. Be a farmer. That's all there is to it."

He shook his head. "I'll never have a farm," he whispered. "I'll never get to have one."

"I don't know why not," I said, slapping him again. "Hell, Ulysses. I can see that farm right from here. I can see it plain as day, Ulysses, so I don't know why you can't." I picked up a stick, sauntered over to the supply-room steps, and sat down. Then I started drawing in the dust.

"The farmhouse," I began. "That goes here." I drew a big square. "And then I suppose you'll want a tractor. You want one, don't you?" He didn't answer. "Well, I'll give you one," I said, and I drew a smaller square next to the farmhouse. "And then you'll have to have a car, Ulysses, because you're such a slob you'd never walk into town." I put the car next to the tractor.

"And then, out behind the house, is the cornfield." I started drawing a bunch of wavy lines and while I was doing that, he came over and sat down beside me, his chin cupped in his hands, watching. "And over here, to the right of the house, you've got some barley going." I drew lines for the barley. "And here on the left, is wheat." I sat back and looked at it. "That sure is some farm you got there, Ulysses," I said. "I got to give you credit."

He didn't say anything, but bent over instead, looking at it carefully.

"Jesus, Ulysses," I said then. "I forgot the goddam silo."

"Silo goes here," he said, taking the stick, drawing a circle.

"You put it right on top of the house, for chrisakes." And I grabbed the stick, erased the circle.

"Then here," he said, making another circle with his finger.

"Not in the cornfield," I told him, erasing it. He bent down again, ready to put it some place else, but I grabbed his hand. "Ulysses," I said. "I'm sorry. You can't have a silo."

"I got to have a silo," he said.

"For what?"

"For fodder."

"Don't joke, Ulysses," I said, starting to laugh.

"Fodder," he said, louder this time. "To feed the animals."

I stared down at the farm. Then I shook my head. "There's no room for animals, Ulysses," I told him. "Sorry."

"I need animals," he said, louder still, grabbing the stick out of my hand, erasing what I'd drawn. "Anyway, you got the whole thing wrong. The farmhouse goes here and the silo goes here," and with that, he was off.

We stayed up all that night, talking about his farm, me asking questions, leading ones, to keep him going. He talked and he talked and every so often he'd reach down and pick up another handful of dust, kneading it in his hands as if it wasn't dust at all, but rich black topsoil just aching to give birth.

Along about three in the morning he started pooping out, his eyes half closed. But I kept him going, nudging him every once in a while, joking around some, mostly just listening to him.

Then, when he was almost out on his feet, I started talking. About how that afternoon, when the time came, neither of us was going to sign any papers. And nothing his father or anyone else could do would make us do any different. He was so exhausted he began to believe me, sitting there on the steps, nodding his head, half in agreement, half because he was too tired to do anything else.

When reveille blew, I got him back to the barracks, splashed water in his face, herded him out for formation. He was really dragging all that morning, but around lunchtime he started snapping to. And when that happened, the fear came back. So there he was, just like he'd been the night before, except that now I didn't have the time to talk him out of it.

I sat beside him at lunch, horsing with him, pouring salt in his coffee, hitting him, but it didn't do any good. He just sat there, not touching his food, staring straight ahead. I stayed with him after lunch, doing what I could—not much, because now the minutes were ticking away and he was so scared I thought he might shatter apart, right in front of me. I knew I had to do something. But I didn't know what.

At the start of training in the afternoon, Sergeant Muldoon called some names, Kelly's and mine and a lot more, and we waited while the rest of the company marched away. Then he told Kelly to march us down to the auditorium at the end of the company street.

When we got there, the Major was waiting for us.

He was all smiles, the Major, grinning from ear to ear, nodding to each of us as we came in, calling Kelly by name. "Make yourselves comfortable, men, make yourselves comfortable," he said, over and over as he stood up on the platform, leaning on the lectern, that smile still plastered on his face. I sat down in the front row, Kelly beside me, and waited.

We all got quiet and the Major started to talk. "Men," he began, "I'm here to speak to you about something important, something that may make a world of difference in your lives."

"Our discharges, Major?" I said, out loud.

He stopped and looked at me for a second. After which he chuckled. Something I've always hated. I mean, if you can't go all the way and laugh, why bother?

"No, soldier," he said. "I'm not here to talk about your discharge. I'm here to talk about the life you can have if you choose the Army for your career."

I groaned.

This time he didn't chuckle, but only smiled, hurrying on, getting to the main part of his speech. Telling us all about the benefits, the honor, the responsibility, the satisfaction of serving your country, of a job well done. And while he talked, I began to yawn, stretching out, sprawled in my seat, drumming my fingers on the armrest, my eyes closed. It wasn't long before he noticed me.

"Am I boring you, soldier?" he snapped, not smiling any more.

"Not exactly, Major," I said, standing up. "And no disrespect meant on my part either, but I don't want to be an officer in the United States Army.

I figure it's a good life and all that, Major. Like you say, it's just crammed full of honor and responsibility and the satisfaction of a job well done. But me, I don't want all that responsibility. And all that honor would probably just go to my head. Because some people aren't cut out to be officers, Major, and I guess I'm one of them. So it's not so much that you're boring me as you're just wasting my time."

"Then you better leave, soldier," he said.

"Yessir." I nodded. "I guess I better. But I'd sure hate to leave alone." I looked down at Kelly. He looked away, then back, then at the Major.

Then he stood up.

We filed our way out of the auditorium, the silence thick enough to sit on. The minute we were outside, I turned and slugged Kelly on the arm.

"Hello, farmer," I said.

We went to the barracks, laughing and joking, horsing around, waiting for the others. The Major must have talked for close to an hour, but then, when he had finished, the bunch of us marched out and joined the rest of the company for training. It was almost six o'clock before we got back to the company area.

And when we did, he was there.

I saw him the minute we turned into the company street. He was standing by his jeep, his back straight, his arms folded, waiting there in the afternoon sun, looking like a god.

When we broke formation, Kelly didn't move. I waited alongside him while the others rushed by us, going this way and that, streaming past like ants from a burning hill.

He strode up to us, quickly, his swagger stick beating a tattoo against his trouser leg, those eagles glistening on his shoulders as they caught the sun. He strode up to us and when he got about two feet away, he stopped. He didn't say a word, not one word, but just stood there, starring at Kelly, slapping his swagger stick into his open palm. All of a sudden there wasn't a sound to be heard except the crack of his swagger stick against the hard flesh of his hand.

I started counting those cracks. *One. Two. Three. Four.* We stood there. *Five. Six.* Waiting. *Seven.* Still nobody talked. *Eight. Nine.* His eyes, almost a colorless blue, burned up into Kelly's face. *Ten. Eleven. Twelve.* Kelly stared back into those colorless blue eyes, held them with his own. *Thirteen. Fourteen.* They were coming faster now, sharper, snapping off his hand into the afternoon heat. And still neither of them said a word.

Then Kelly broke.

"O.K.," he whispered, so soft I could hardly hear him. "O.K. O.K."

With that, the Colonel wheeled, hurrying away, his shoulders set. And I think if I'd had a gun in my hands then, I would have shot him. I hated him that much. You work and you work to get something done, you try as hard as you can, and suddenly somebody comes along, snaps his fingers, and everything crumbles like a house of cards.

But I didn't have a gun, so all I could do was watch as he vaulted into his jeep and sat back, straight, his arms folded in front of him. The jeep's motor roared and it jumped forward, gathering speed. He didn't so much as give us a glance as he whipped on by.

Kelly watched until the jeep was out of sight. Then he turned to me, a smile on his face. "What the hell," he muttered. "What the hell. It's not going to be so bad."

And it wasn't.

Not for a week or so anyway. Because during that week, Kelly talked to me all the time about going to Officer's School, and how he was going to knock them dead. None of which I believed, naturally, seeing as Kelly wasn't the kind of guy that knocks anybody dead at anything, most of all Officer's School. But I let him talk, agreeing with him, making him feel as good about it as I could. We joked a lot together and when the weekend came, we went back in to see old Irma, me serving again as chaperon. He was a lot less nervous about it and walked into her room by himself, unaided. When he came out, he wasn't excited or anything like he'd been before. This time he was calm, as if it was something he'd been doing for years, daily. And after a minute or two of horsing, we didn't talk about it any more. So everything went along fine, without a hitch.

Until that afternoon on the grenade range.

It was a scorcher, 100° or more. During the morning, the whole company grumbled and moaned, sweating as we went through our paces, practicing with dud grenades, getting ready to throw the real thing in the afternoon.

At lunchtime, I turned to Kelly. "Let's get in the chow line," I said. "Come on."

He shook his head. "I got to go to the latrine," he told me. "You get in line, Trevitt. I'll be with you in a while." He started walking away.

"Sure, Ulysses," I said. "I'll do that."

But I didn't. I stayed right where I was, watching him as he walked over and talked to the Lieutenant in charge of the range. I saw what he did and when he left the Lieutenant, I followed him.

He walked as fast as he could, never looking back, me trailing some distance behind. He walked across the range and then onto the road in back of it and then past that, heading for the big field of weeds beyond.

Once he got there, I yelled to him. He didn't stop. I broke into a run, tearing through those weeds full tilt, closing the gap.

"Hi, Kelly," I said, coming up behind him. He didn't answer. "You got some sense of direction, Ulysses. The latrine is back there. On the range."

"You better get away," he said.

I laughed. "Why? Just because you hocked a live grenade?" He turned and faced me then. I laughed louder. "I saw you, Ulysses. You'd make a hell of a thief, you would. Now, let's go." He fumbled around with his hands for a second.

Then he pulled the pin, his thumb pressing down on the release lever.

"Now will you go, Trevitt?"

I shook my head. "Not without you."

We stood there, facing each other, standing waist high in the weeds, him with his thumb on that lever, pressing it down, his thumb white, his hands squeezed against his stomach.

"Get out of here!" he yelled. I didn't move. "Get the hell out of here, Trevitt! Get the hell away!"

We were both drenched with sweat, standing there in the hot sun, five feet apart. I stared at that grenade awhile, and his thumb, looking like a ladyfinger against the rest of his red hand. Then I started talking to him.

"You got this wrong, Ulysses. You got it all wrong. This isn't the way. You're not going to find anything this way. Honest to God, Ulysses. Don't you see. You got it all wrong. I know. I know, Ulysses. Because you're not the only one ever thought about it. I did. Me. Honest to God, Ulysses. I was going to do it. But it's not the way. And you know why? I'll tell you. On account of you, Ulysses. On account of you. Don't you see? Back there in town. That's the way out. Not like this. Back there. That's the way. I found you and you'll find somebody and then everything's O.K. It all makes sense then. So don't do this, Ulysses. Not to me. Because that's who you're doing it to. Please, Ulysses. Don't do this to me."

He blinked some sweat away from his eyes, staring down at the grenade. Then he looked at me. "This'll fix the sonofabitch," he muttered.

Then he let go of the lever and the bomb was alive.

I dove at him, trying to get my hands on it, but he turned, shoved it harder against his stomach while I clawed at him.

The blast came a second later and I blacked out, deaf from the sound. I was flying backward, spinning in the air, and then I hit, tumbling down, my arms and legs tangled, lying there in a heap. When I came to, I could hear a lot of screaming, people running up, some crying, some vomiting as they stood around us.

But I couldn't open my eyes. All I could do was lie there, helpless, my leg throbbing. All I could do was lie there, thinking, saying it in my mind: "They're dying on me, everybody's dying on me, everybody's dying on me." Over and over and over.

Then I screamed once with the pain and blacked out for good.

VI . . . . The Town

I don't remember much about my first few days in the hospital.

I just lay there in bed, half asleep, half not, my knee stitched, my leg bandaged. Time slipped by on me as I lay there, listening to the orderlies walk along the halls, sometimes staring out the window at the sky. Then, the third day, I started snapping out of it, my head clearing. By evening, I was feeling pretty good again. Except for my leg.

He came to see me on the fourth day, a Captain from main post. He took off his hat and smiled at me as I sat up in bed. "You're Private Trevitt," he said.

I nodded.

"I'm from the Provost Marshal's office, Trevitt. I'd like to ask you a few questions."

I didn't say anything.

He smiled again, going on. "I'd like to know what happened, Trevitt. Out there in the weed field. I'm in charge of the investigation and there are a number of things that need clearing up. So why don't you tell me what happened. In your own words."

"Maybe some other time," I said.

"Now's as good a time as any," he said, pressing it. "So why don't you tell me what happened."

"Kelly got blown apart by a hand-grenade," I said.

"We know that."

"I thought you wanted to know what happened, Captain. That's what happened."

"I'd like a few more details, Trevitt. Now. What went on in that weed field?"

"Just what I told you," I said. "Kelly got blown apart by a hand-grenade."

"How?"

"He pulled the pin and held it against his stomach. The rest was easy."

113

"How did he get the grenade?"

"I suppose he stole it. I don't know. Maybe he made it in his spare time."

"Look, Trevitt," he said. "I just want to ask you some questions. That's all."

"Well, you're asking the wrong guy, Captain. It's not me you ought to talk to."

"No?" he said. "Who then?"

"Go see the Chief of Staff," I answered. Then I lay back down and closed my eyes. He left me.

It was about an hour later that I first heard the news.

Major Downes, my doctor, told me. He came in humming, snipping away in the air with a scissors he always carried.

"Afternoon, Trevitt," he said, faking a few snips at my head.

"Afternoon, Major Downes."

He didn't say anything for a while, but just smiled at me, almost laughing, grinning from ear to ear. I waited. "Trevitt," he said, finally. "I envy you. Always envy lucky people. And Trevitt, you're lucky. Me, I'm not. There I was, the most successful gynecologist in Dayton, Ohio, and what happened? I got drafted again. How's the leg feel?"

"Fine, Major. Why am I lucky?"

He slapped me on the back. "Because you've got the million-dollar wound, Trevitt. You're getting a medical discharge."

"Why?"

"Your knee, Trevitt. That's why."

"What's the matter with my knee?"

"Nothing fatal. But some of that shrapnel cut it. You'll be walking with a limp, so just as soon as you're able, out you go."

I nodded, staring up at him while he fiddled with his scissors. Then I asked him. "For how long, Major? How long will I limp?"

"Permanently," was his answer. After which he left me alone to think about it.

Nineteen days later, I was discharged.

They went fast, those nineteen days. There was so much to be done. First my bandage came off. Then the stitches. I was getting stronger again, but still at night I had no trouble sleeping. Because it was hard work, learning to walk. In the beginning I used crutches, until I could put weight on my left leg. After that I hobbled a day or two with a cane. Finally I was on my own, without help, limping around the room, falling back on my bed, cursing, trying it again, getting better at it all the time.

Processing didn't take long. I went to see the Provost Marshal, told them what happened. I had a physical, turned in my clothes, filled out a million forms—limping slowly around the post, from one office to another, getting set to go.

Once I saw Colonel Kelly. From a distance. He was riding in his jeep, sitting just like he always did, straight up, his arms folded on his chest. He whizzed out of sight and that was the last of him. He never came to see me; not one time those nineteen days.

Then, on a Tuesday afternoon, I was out.

Major Downes saw me to the main door of the hospital. We shook hands, said good-by, and that was it. I was a civilian again.

So I picked up my bag and headed for the main entrance to Camp Scott. It took me about fifteen minutes to get there, walking slow, sweating in the sunshine. But finally I made it, stopping a second by the MP stand to catch my breath. I nodded to the MP on duty and, in a little, I picked up my bag again and walked those last steps to the road outside. When I got to that road I looked first one way, then the other. There wasn't a car in sight, nobody, nothing, just me standing there alone. It was right then that it hit me.

I didn't know where I was going.

I looked up and down that road again, shaking my head. Because I just wasn't sure. I'd thought about it some, back in the hospital, figuring this answer and that, never coming to any conclusion. But now the chips were down and I hadn't picked a winner. I stood there a long time, looking first to my right, then to my left, then to my right, then to my left. Cars passed me. I didn't hail any of them.

Finally, my leg began aching, so I went back to the post entrance. I found a little grass to sit on and flopped down, facing the sun. I stayed there awhile, eyes closed, basking, not a thought in my head. Then the MP came up. A private, maybe eighteen years old; he looked me over, trying to make up his mind.

"What's the story?" he said, finally.

"No story," I answered. "I just thought I'd like to sit here awhile."

"Nobody's allowed to sit here," he told me.

"Come on," I said. "Please."

"You're on Government property."

"I know."

"You're on Government property," he came again, reaching down this time, grabbing my arm.

I jerked free. "Get your hands off me," I said. "You're touching a civilian."

"What are you doing here then?"

I held up my bag. "I'm going to blow up Camp Scott," I whispered. "I got the biggest bomb in here you ever saw. It weighs 500 pounds and the minute you turn your back, BOOM!"

He hurried back to his stand and when he picked up the telephone I saw I'd better get, so I headed for the road. In a minute, the bus for Hastingsville came by. I flagged it and got on.

I took a room in Hastingsville, a room with one big window right across from an Army-Navy store. That store had a huge neon sign in front and it flashed all night long. ARMY. NAVY. ARMY. NAVY. ARMY was red. NAVY was blue. All night long as I lay there in bed, the room kept changing color before my eyes. First red, ARMY. Then blue, NAVY. I stayed in that room for one day and two nights, not sleeping, not eating, but just lying flat, my hands behind my head, watching the colors change. ARMY. Where do I go, Zock? NAVY. Which way do I go? ARMY. And the temple of gold, Zock. NAVY. What about that? ARMY. Tell me, Zock. NAVY. Tell me. ARMY. Where do I go from here, Zock? NAVY. Which way?

Then finally, the second night, I knew. It came to me gradually, because I suppose I'd known all along, from the minute Major Downes had told me I was getting out. Just as simple as A.B.C.

Where do you go when there's no place to go?

You go home.

So I started off, thumbing my way North. It was still dark when I began, but I got a ride without any trouble, and by daylight I was speeding through the Indiana farmland. I had a lot of rides, and all in all, I made good time.

Because it was dusk when I got off at the main highway from Chicago and started the walk in, to Athens. It was a beautiful night, cool and clear. As I walked along I heard the birds still singing in the trees, the insects buzzing around in the bushes. I continued on, setting a slow, steady pace. Then the road opened and Athens College was right in front of me.

There's nothing like a college town when the college is closed. Quiet, deserted, it looks almost dead, as if it had never seen students riding around on bicycles, or teachers hurrying along, carrying briefcases. Only the buildings themselves remain, dark and squat against the setting sun.

Off in the distance I saw some kids playing ball, running and screaming, but I didn't stop to watch. I just went on, past the college, into Patriot's Square, also deserted, except for the yellow lamplights beaming on its corners. When I got to the center, I stopped and turned around, taking it all in: the college behind me, the town on my right, the Lake out in front, and on my left, home.

They were eating supper when I got there. I opened the front door as quiet as I could, listening.

"So I told her that if she didn't want to work at the Red Cross Wednesday afternoons, it was quite all right with me. Because there were plenty of others to do the job. And when I said that, she turned as meek as a lamb."

"Indeed."

Which was so funny I broke out laughing. For there wasn't any doubt about it. I was home. And nothing had changed.

"I'm sure glad things are going good at the Red Cross," I said, walking into the dining-room. She dropped her spoon and stared at me. I nodded to my father. We shook hands.

"Raymond," my mother said, smiling now. "We weren't expecting you. We had no idea. What are you doing here?"

"Mother," I said, "it's a long story. But if you'll get me some supper, I'll tell you."

And I did. After she'd come back from the kitchen with a plateful of food, I began. Skipping most of the details, concentrating more on the explosion and my knee and the medical discharge. She sat there, listening carefully, while my father leaned forward in his chair, muttering "Indeed" every once in a while, to show he was interested. When I'd finished, I excused myself, said I was tired, and went up to my room. I undressed, turned out the light, and lay down, staring at the ceiling. Then my mother came in.

"Raymond," she said. "Are you asleep?"

"No, Mother," I answered.

She stood in the doorway. "I didn't mean to bother you," she whispered. "But Raymond. I'm glad you're home."

"So am I, Mother," I said.

And corny as it was, it was true. So turning over once, I reached out, touched the wall, pressed against it, dropped my hand, and fell asleep. . . .

I didn't wake up until noon, and when I went down to the kitchen, my mother was there. The minute I walked in, she ran over and kissed me. "Good morning, Raymond," she said. "Did you sleep well?"

I nodded, pointing to the clock high on one wall.

She laughed. "Just sit down, then. I'll have your breakfast for you in a minute." I sat down. "It's so good having you here," she went on. "You'll never know just how wonderful it is. Your father thinks so too. He told me."

"Where is he?" I asked.

"In his study," she sang. "Trying to keep body and soul together." Then she started humming, smiling to herself, almost giggling every once in a while.

Pretty soon I knew something was up. "All right, Mother," I said. "Tell me. What is it?"

"Raymond," she answered, "I want to give you a party. I thought about it all night long and that's what I decided to do. Not a big one. Just for a few close friends."

"Such as?"

"You make out the list, and I'll tend to the arrangements. I think we ought to have it on the lawn. We'll set up tables and—"

"And serve ice cream and cake? On paper plates? Maybe play some games?"

"Yes," she said. "That kind of thing. Because it's so wonderful having you home. I want to announce it."

"Please, Mother," I said. "I don't want any party. I'm sorry. But please. Don't talk about it any more."

"Why, Raymond? Why not?"

"Because there's no one to ask," I told her. Then I started eating.

After breakfast I went upstairs to unpack. I wasn't there more than a minute when I heard her calling me, coming to my room.

"What is it, Mother?" I asked.

She walked in. "I have to go do the shopping, Raymond. How would you like to come along?"

"I'd rather not," I said.

"But you always go shopping with me."

"I never go shopping with you, Mother. I haven't been shopping with you since I was eight years old. And you know it."

"You could start now."

"I don't want to."

"That's no reason, Raymond. Come shopping with me. You can look around and see what's been going on. And get acquainted."

I waited a long time. Then I nodded. "I guess you're right, Mother," I said. "Now is as good a time as any."

She smiled. "Mr. Klein will be so glad to see you."

"Who's Mr. Klein?"

"The butcher, Raymond. You remember Mr. Klein."

"Can't say as I do," I answered, and with that we went downstairs.

Stopping for a minute in front of the door to my father's study. "Raymond and I are going to do the shopping, Henry," my mother said.

"Indeed," came the answer from inside.

"We're going shopping together, Henry. Isn't that wonderful? Isn't it wonderful having Raymond home?"

"Yes, my dear," he said. And that was all.

We parked in town a few minutes later. My mother took out her shopping list. "I thought we'd have roast beef for supper," she said. "How would you like that?"

"Fine," I said.

"Wonderful," my mother said and we started for the butcher's, her leading, me right behind. The second we were inside, she began talking. "Mr. Klein," she said. "Look who's here."

He was hacking up some chickens, his hands bloody, but he stopped to look at me. "Who?" he asked.

"Raymond, Mr. Klein. You remember my son Raymond. Raymond, say hello to Mr. Klein."

"Hello, Mr. Klein," I said. "How the hell are you?"

He nodded, still looking at me. "Glad to meet you."

"Raymond just got out of the Army, Mr. Klein. He's come home."

"Do tell, Mrs. Trevitt." He turned to me. "How long were you in for, son?"

"Eight weeks," I said. I saw it come into his face then, so I answered it for him. "I caught a piece of shrapnel." Which is a great thing to say—"I caught a piece of shrapnel." But you have to do it casually, as if it happened to you all the time.

"Really," Mr. Klein said. "How'd you do that?"

"We had a shrapnel-catching contest on the base. The guy who caught the most shrapnel got a discharge. I won."

"A shrapnel-catching contest," he said, scratching his head. "I never heard—"

"They have them mostly down South," I explained. "Like cockfights. Most every county down there has a shrapnel-catching champion."

"Raymond," my mother said.

"Do tell," Mr. Klein said.

"I'd like some roast beef, Mr. Klein. Enough for four. The very best you have."

"I'll cut you some, Mrs. Trevitt. Just take a minute."

My mother looked at her shopping list, then at me. "I'll have to hurry," she said. "I have a meeting at two. You wait here for the meat, Raymond. Then come to the A&P."

I nodded and she went out. There was a big fan blowing over in one corner. I walked up and stood in front of it while he got to work. Neither of us said a word. Then, when he was almost finished, he called to me over his shoulder.

"Your mother's a fine woman," he said.

"She sure is."

"A fine woman," he came again. I waited. "Meat's all done," he went on, holding it over the counter. I went up and put a hand on it but he held tight, didn't let go, and started whispering to me. "She's the best there is," he whispered. "And the whole town knows it. Ain't a person in this town wouldn't bend over backward for your mother."

"Swell," I said.

"So you just forget it, son," he whispered. "Forget the whole thing. Just drop it from your mind."

"Forget what, Mr. Klein?"

"What happened with the Crowe boy," he said, softer still.

"Oh, the Crowe boy. Hell. I forgot about that already." And I grabbed the package and took off for the A&P.

It was the same there. This time from the cashier. And in the shoe-repair shop. Every place we went, somebody said it to me. Or you could tell they were thinking it. From their faces.

That I was the boy who killed Zachary Crowe.

Finally we finished shopping and started home. "Wasn't that wonderful?" my mother said, once we were under way. "They were all so glad to see you. They told me."

I didn't answer.

But she rambled on just the same, jabbering about this and that, asking me questions, answering them herself. We were almost home before she put her hand on my arm.

"Is something wrong?" she said. "Why are you so quiet?"

"No reason."

"Then why are you so quiet?"

"I just made a mistake, Mother. That's all."

"Mistake?" she said. "Mistake?"

"Nothing, Mother," I answered, and then I swung the car into the driveway.

So I didn't go shopping any more. And I didn't have a party. My mother got the hint, left me to myself, and my father was forever working in his study or his office at school. Everything went along quietly for the next couple of days, nothing much happening, one way or the other.

And then, that afternoon, Sadie Griffin came back.

I was alone in the house, my father at school, my mother at a meeting, when I heard a car stop next door. I didn't get up to see, didn't move, but stayed where I was, lying on my bed, smoking, staring at the trees outside my window. A few minutes later, the doorbell rang. I answered. She was standing there.

"Hello, Euripides," she said. "Do you remember me?"

I nodded. "You're Sadie Griffin." We shook hands. "What are you doing here?"

"I'm going to be living next door for a while," she said. "Sort of keeping Uncle Willard company, while his wife"—and she paused—"while his wife is away. Didn't anyone tell you?"

"No. Nobody told me."

"He won't be home until tomorrow. So I thought I'd drop over and say hello. Besides, I've never much liked empty houses. Do you?"

I shrugged.

"It's wonderful seeing you again, Euripides."

"Nice seeing you," I said, edging away. "And I'd like to talk with you but I'm awful busy now, so you better excuse me."

"Let me come along," she said, following me inside. I just couldn't get rid of her. And then before I knew it she had me cornered in the living-room and was telling me the story of her life, of what had happened since I'd last seen her. About how her folks had died, her father first, her mother close after. And how she'd had a kid. And how her marriage had gone to pieces. And the divorce. She went on like that, talking quiet, staring down at her hands most of the time but occasionally up at my face, to see was I still listening. And if she'd been through hell in those years, it didn't show. For she looked the same as she had that day we first met, long before, when Zock and I were stranded in Chicago and she came roaring up from out of nowhere in that white convertible.

I never looked back at her, but instead out the window, hoping my mother could come home and break it up. She didn't. So I had to do the job myself.

"What the hell are you telling me for?" I said.

Which stopped her. "I thought you'd be interested," she told me first. Then she fiddled with her hands awhile, kneading them, watching them move. Finally, she looked square at me, gave me the answer. "Nobody around here," she whispered. "Nobody here . . . knows me. Not from before. You do. And I thought . . . I thought . . ."

"I can't bring back the old days, Sadie Griffin," I cut in. "You can't expect me to do that."

"I know," she said, still whispering. "But—"

"I'm sorry," I told her. "But I've got a lot of work to do, and I'm not getting much of it done here." I stood up and was almost out of the living-room when she called to me.

"I've some letters from Zachary," she said. "If you'd care to see them."

I went to my room and lay down. A little later the front door opened and closed and I was alone again.

My mother came home about an hour later, yoohooing, calling my name. I heard her tramping up the stairs and when she got to my room, she was beaming.

"Sadie Griffin's back," she said to me.

"Is that right?" I said.

"Yes. She's here this very minute. Next door. She's going to be living there. I've known about it for a week. I was saving it as a surprise."

"Swell," I said. "Now we have someone to invite to my party."

My mother shook her head. "You had your chance, Raymond. There's no point to giving you a party now. But I am going to have Sadie Griffin for dinner." I started to interrupt but she went right on. "I'm having Sadie Griffin for dinner tonight and you are going to invite her."

"Mother—" I began.

"No ifs, ands, or buts, Raymond. You are going to invite her and that's all there is to it." She left me.

I stayed in bed awhile longer, until it started getting dark. Then I left the house and went next door. Sadie Griffin was sitting alone in the living-room, a drink in her hand.

"O.K.," I said. "Show me those letters."

Nodding, she stood. "I'm staying in Zachary's room."

"I know the way," I answered and I led her up.

It was all changed, made over. The bed was different; the pictures on the walls were different; there were frilly drapes around the windows. If someone had shown me a picture and asked: "Guess what?" I never could have come through with the answer.

"Here we are," Sadie Griffin said.

"That's right," I said. "Now show me those letters."

"Let me see," she mumbled, going to the bureau, putting her drink down, talking to herself. "Where did I put them?"

I stood in the middle of the room, watching her, listening to her talk. First she searched the bureau, muttering away, and when she was through she went to the desk and started on it. And right then I began to realize she was lying, that there weren't any letters, that there never had been.

"Where's your kid?" I asked, stopping the monologue.

"With him," she answered after a while, opening one desk drawer, then another.

"Why is that?" I went on.

"I don't know."

"Why don't you have the kid?" I said again.

She slammed the desk drawer all she had, the sound exploding in the room. Then she stood up, staring straight at me. "You want to know why?" she said, almost yelling. "I'll tell you. Because I didn't divorce him. He divorced me! Because it got into all the papers. Didn't you read about it? I thought everybody read about it. I'm famous."

"You didn't have to come here," I said. "There are other places."

"I've never been much good at taking care of myself," Sadie Griffin said, her voice softer now. "I've always needed someone else to take care of me."

I didn't answer.

"Anything more you want to know?"

"You don't have any letters, do you? You lied about that."

"There were some. A few. But I threw them out. I threw out a lot of things before I came back here."

"You never had any letters."

"I told you. I did. I threw them out."

"You couldn't do that," I said. "I don't believe you."

She started laughing.

"I'm sorry," I told her. "Good-by."

"Wait!" She shot the word at me. I stopped. "Stay with me for a second. I want to change clothes. I chose the wrong dress to wear. Here it is summertime, and I still think it's spring."

"You're a big girl now," I said.

"Isn't it funny," Sadie Griffin whispered. "I've done it all wrong. I've done everything wrong." She shook her head, trying to clear it. Then she smiled. One last time. "Start over," she said. "That's what we'll do. We'll start over. Now. Please. I've just rung your doorbell. Please. 'Hello, Euripides. You remember me?' "

I didn't say anything.

"You've got to answer," she said. "You've got to help me." And all of a sudden she was crying, hysterical, her face red, contorted, tears streaming down her face. "Help me. Please."

Then she started coming toward me.

"Please. Please. You've got to help me. Help me. Help me! Please God, help me!" She reached out, tried to take my hand, but she was crying too hard. She couldn't see.

I made it to the door before I stopped. "My mother wants you for supper," I said, not turning. Then I went on down the stairs, holding tight to the banister all the way, listening to her as she wept, standing there alone in what once had been Zock's room.

When I got home, my mother and father were waiting. "What did she say?" my mother asked. "Is she coming?"

"I don't think she'll be here," I answered. "Not tonight. I don't think she's very hungry."

"Raymond," my mother asked, "are you all right?"

"Me?" and I laughed. "I'm fine."

But I wasn't and I knew it and inside of five minutes I knew I couldn't stand it, being with them a second more. Because my mother chattered away, mostly about the Red Cross, and my father just poked at his food, muttering answers when he had to.

"Eat, Raymond," my mother said then, pointing to my plate. "Before it gets cold."

"I guess I'm not so hungry either," I told her, and with that I got up from the table and left them. I headed for the car, jammed it into reverse, swerved onto the street and took off.

Inside of ten minutes, I was at the Crib.

It was like Old Home Week. All the lushes at the bar mumbled hello to me, asked me where I'd been, and the bartender gave me a couple of quick ones, on the house. Nothing had changed there either; it was still as dark and dirty as before. I started drinking, gulping them down one after the other, as fast as I could. They hit me right away and pretty soon everything began getting blurry. Within an hour I was as drunk as I've ever been. But I have no memory of it.

I woke up in bed the next morning, feeling terrible, my head throbbing and my knee, where I guess I must have smacked it on something. I went to the bathroom, drank some water and showered, which didn't help much. Then I got dressed and went downstairs.

He was waiting for me.

Standing at the foot of the stairs, his hands clasped behind his back, looking up. I stopped. We nodded to each other. Then he spoke.

"Perhaps I might have a few moments of your time," my father said.

"Later," I answered.

"I think now," he told me and with that he turned and walked into his study. After I'd sat down he went over, shut the door, returned to his desk, staring across at me.

I waited.

Still watching me, he reached for his pipe, put it in his mouth, drew on it a couple of times. Then he took it out of his mouth, rolling it between his dry hands.

"Where to begin?" he muttered. "Where to begin?"

He toyed with the pipe awhile longer, looking at it now, not me. Finally, he pursed his lips, wrinkled up his forehead, and started talking.

In Greek. He said a few lines, not bothering to translate, and when he did that, I glanced around the room, sweating, because it was so stuffy inside, with the door and the window closed, the smell of leather and tobacco hanging in the air. He was going on about how I got home, about how the bartender at the Crib had called him, told him I wasn't in shape to drive, how he'd taken a taxi out there, loaded me in the car, driven me home. I didn't listen close, but instead stared at that spot by the door where the guppies used to be. How many years ago? Twelve? Or was it thirteen? I couldn't remember. But whichever it was, it was the only thing different. There were still books piled up all over the room, on the floor, on tables, overflowing, jammed sideways into the bookcases all around me. Hundreds of books, thousands, some new, some dog-eared, some . . .

"What happened last night between you and the Griffin girl?"

"What?" I said.

"I asked you what happened with the Griffin girl."

"Nothing."

"Please," he said. "I know that isn't true. I'm not such a fool, my boy. You may think so, but I'm not."

"Nothing happened."

My father shook his head. "I gather she turned out to be—" And he stopped, looking for the word. "I gather she turned out to be a courtesan."

At which I started laughing. "Courtesan. Courtesan for Christ sake. Sadie Griffin is a whore! Why don't you say it?"

"Indeed," my father muttered, his pipe back in his mouth. "Terminology is, at best, of but peripheral significance."

"What does that mean?"

"I'm sorry," he said, very low. "I—I lack adroitness. Where to begin? Where to begin?"

Felix Brown. That was the last time I'd been in his study. Five years. No. Four. You live in a house all your life and it's been four years since you've been in one of the rooms. Four years. One thousand days.

"The Garden of Gethsemane," my father said. "Yes. The Garden of Gethsemane." He looked across at me. "Please. Listen. My boy. Please."

"I'm listening," I said.

"The Garden of Gethsemane," he repeated. "The Agony of the Garden."

I waited, staring back at him.

" 'My God. My God. Why hast thou forsaken me?' Christ said that. To his Father. Don't you understand?"

"No," I said.

"God failed. God failed His own son. God failed His own son in the Garden of Gethsemane."

"So what?"

"Please, my boy. I am trying. I lack adroitness. But I am trying. Please." He closed his eyes for a second. Then he reached out his hands, reached out across the desk, toward me. "My boy," he said finally. "Ray. Answer me. Do you think I've failed you?"

"No," I said.

"You are mistaken." He leaned forward, his hands still held out, closer. "Don't you see? You are wrong. I have failed you. I have failed you constantly, continually. And I will go on failing you. Don't you see?"

"See what?" I said, sweating now, pulling at my T shirt, for it stuck to me like skin.

"Everyone fails," my father said. "Everyone fails everyone. It must be. Failure is a fundamental law of living. We all have our own lives to lead, separately, so when you cry out for help, I can't give it. No one can. We are all human, Ray. All with our own lives, duties, complexities, problems, torments. Now do you understand?

" 'My God. My God. Why hast thou forsaken me?' Don't you see? You will, someday. I pray you see it now. And understand it. And accept it. For once you do, then you may forget about it and concentrate on what you can control, on what is within your power."

"Such as, Father?"

"Here are my books," he said. "Look at them. Think. Think of the wisdom contained therein. The understanding. Think how far we have come. Think how much farther we can go."

"You've got all the answers, haven't you, Father?"

"No," he said. "No one has all the answers. No one can. I don't. I don't pretend—"

"So everybody fails you. Is that right?"

"Yes, my boy. That is right."

"Well, Zock never failed me. Not once. Never."

"Only because you killed him," my father said. "Before he had the chance."

I sat there a second, staring.

"Facts must be faced," he went on. "I'm sorry, but facts—"

And then all of a sudden I was standing up, yelling, for the first time in my life yelling at my father. "I hate guys like you! I honest to God really hate guys like you. I've met you before. In the Army there was a Colonel and the worst son of a bitch in the world, but he had all the answers too. Well, you can keep your answers! Tell them to your students when they come sucking around. But don't tell me. Don't try helping me. Because back there in the Army I tried helping somebody. I wet-nursed him for weeks—and you know what happened? He blew himself up. So keep your advice and everything will be fine. And save your understanding for your wife, because she sure as hell can use it. But don't ever tell me anything! Don't ever try!"

I ran for the door, him calling to me: "My boy, my boy, my boy—" Over and over, calling for me to come back, his voice ringing in my ears. I opened the door, then turned on him.

"Shove it, old man!" I said, and I left him there.

My mother was waiting in the hall. I tried brushing by, but she caught me and held on. "What's the matter?" she said. "What is it?"

"I'm going away for a while," I said, pulling loose.

"Where?" she asked, following me. "Where?"

"Away."

"When? For how long?"

"Now."

"You'll come back soon," she said. "You'll come back soon."

"I don't know, Mother," I told her.

Five minutes later I was packing.

Ten minutes later I was gone.

But this time, I knew where I was going. Just the same, though, I didn't hurry getting there. Because it's beautiful in late September, and there were afternoons, as I hitchhiked my way East, when I just had to get out of whatever car I was in and walk for a while, limping along, the sun at my back, the smell of burning leaves always coming from somewhere off in the distance.

Then, early one evening, I got to Harvard.

Which isn't nearly as nice-looking a place as I thought, being crammed full of old buildings, one flush against the next. As a matter of fact, Harvard is ugly, comparing favorably to Athens in that respect, only bigger. I wandered around for a while, getting my bearings. Then I took out Zock's letter, checked the address, and found my way to his dorm. I went in, located the proctor's room, knocked on the door. He said to come in, so I did, holding the letter in my hands.

"I'm looking for a guy named Zachary Crowe," I said. "I think he lives here."

The proctor thought some, then shook his head. "Not any more," he answered. "This is a freshman dorm."

"I got a letter from him," I said, waving it. "It gives this for an address. So I thought he'd be here."

"He was here," the proctor told me. "Last year. But this is a freshman dorm. Zock's a sophomore now. I don't know where he's living. Maybe at Lowell. Try there."

"Zock?" I said.

The proctor laughed. "It was his nickname."

"Oh," I said.

"What did you want to see him about?"

I shrugged. "Nothing much. I was just passing through and my mother told me if I did I ought to stop in and see him. My mother's a friend of his family."

"Give Lowell a try," the proctor said, and he turned back to his desk. "It's as good a bet as any. Sorry." He started reading. I watched him.

"Do you know Zock?" I asked.

"What?" he said, looking up.

"I asked did you know him."

"I was proctor here last year. Sure I knew him."

"What kind of a guy was he?"

"Never gave me any trouble," he answered, starting to read again.

"But what kind of a guy was he?" I said, walking up, standing over him. "My mother told me to be sure and find him. She told me he was a great guy and to be sure and find him."

"Well," the proctor said, getting fidgety. "Everyone liked him, if that's what you mean."

"Why did everyone like him?" I asked.

"How do I know why?" he said, closing his book, trying to get up. I put my hand on his shoulder, pressing down.

"Maybe because he was such a great guy," I said. "Maybe that was it."

"Sure," the proctor said. "That was the reason. He was such a great guy everyone liked him."

"That's what I figured," I said, and I took my hand away. He watched me as I left, his eyes still on me as I nodded good-by and closed the door.

I didn't go to Lowell House. Because Zock wouldn't have been there; never in a million years. Instead, I just stood on the sidewalk, reading his letter over and over. Then I put it away.

"Hey," I said to the first kid who walked by. "I'm looking for somebody named Clarence that writes epic poetry."

He wasn't hard to find. Since no matter where you are, you're not going to meet too many people named Clarence. And when you tag the epic poetry on, it gets easier still. So, hardly a half-hour later, I was knocking on his door.

"Hello," I said.

"Come in, come in, come in," someone bellowed. I opened the door and there he was, huge, with bright-red hair, pacing the room in his underwear shorts, a pad of yellow paper in his hands.

"Congratulate me," he said. "I've just rhymed hideous with gaseous."

"How?" I asked.

"It's all in the pronunciation," was his answer, and with that, he began to read to me. He was trying to make an epic poem out of *War and Peace*, and I got there just in time for the battle of Borodino, which, judging from what I heard, must have been a long one. After a little, I sat in a chair, watching him as he walked around the room, reading away at the top of his lungs, playing all the parts, waving his free arm in the air, firing shots, drawing his saber, riding his horse, dying.

When the battle was over, he put the pad down. "What do you think?" he asked.

"It's something, all right," I said.

"Inarticulately put," he answered. "But it has the ring of sincerity." He went to the bureau, grabbed a picture, shoved it at me. "And what do you think of her?"

I looked. "She's something, all right," I said.

"Something!" he roared. "Something!" He cradled the picture in his arms. "She is my muse."

Which was the truth, but she looked more like his mother. Still, he showed me her picture again and again, just as though she was the goddess Aphrodite in the flesh.

"Unfortunately," he muttered. "She goes to Radcliffe."

"I'm sorry," I said.

He looked at me then. "Who the hell are you?" he asked. "There's nothing about you remotely familiar."

"My name is Ray Trevitt," I told him. "And I'm looking for a guy named Zachary Crowe."

For once, he quieted down. "Didn't you know?" he said. "Zock's dead. He was killed in a car crash last summer. I'm going to write a commemorative poem in his honor, just as soon as I finish this goddam thing," and he kicked the battle of Borodino across the room.

"Was he a friend of yours?" I asked.

"Friend?" Clarence laughed, pointing to the next room, which was empty. "He was going to live right there."

"I didn't know him very well," I said. "He—"

"I'll tell you all," Clarence interrupted, putting on his pants. "But now we must away."

"Where?"

"To meet my muse," he answered, and he took off out the door.

Her name was Martha and that photographer should have been paid double for the job he did on her. She had long dirty hair stringing down her back and an enormous nose and she was wearing a gray T shirt when I met her, in a crowded college bar a little way from Clarence's room.

"Muse, muse, muse," Clarence said, coming up behind her. "I just finished the battle of Borodino."

"He rhymed hideous with gaseous," I said, sitting down.

"How?" Martha asked.

"It's all in the pronunciation," I told her.

She looked at me. "Who are you?"

"Tell her," Clarence cut in. "I'm off for some beer."

"Who are you?" Martha asked again.

I told her my name.

"Where you from?"

I told her that, too.

"Illinois," she answered, and that was all we said until Clarence came back.

"You're looking particularly beautiful tonight," he whispered, slopping some beer on the table. "You've a wild, raving beauty tonight, my sweet. I love you madly." He kissed her hand. "Have you got the history notes?"

Martha sighed and handed him some papers.

"Without you I would die," Clarence said, stuffing them into his pocket.

"Tell me about Zachary Crowe," I said.

"Who's that?" Martha asked.

"A prince," Clarence answered, raising his glass. He'd gotten about two sentences out when Martha stopped him.

"You're ignoring me," she said.

Clarence patted her arm. "Muse," he said. "I have my reasons."

And then he began.

Martha left awhile later, but we didn't. We stayed right where we were, drinking beer, me listening to Clarence as he went on and on. He told me how he and Zock met, their first day at Harvard. And Bunny, and how the three of them had gone out a lot together as the year wore on. And pretty soon, he was talking about me, Euripides. How Zock and I had gotten drunk that night in high school. And my first date with Sally Farmer and the phone call that went before. And Felix Brown. I never stopped him, never said a word, only listened while he told about the two of us, Zock and me, growing up together. And as I listened I felt pretty great, almost as though I wasn't there at all but way off some place, high in the distance, looking down like God.

They threw us out when the bar closed, except by that time it didn't matter, seeing as we were both drunk. We left the bar and walked until Clarence sagged against a lamppost.

"I may be ill," he said.

"Don't you worry, Clarence," I said, coming up to help. "You're among friends."

"Am I, Euripides?" he said.

I nodded, waiting.

"You were driving the car, weren't you?"

I nodded again, watching him, both of us covered with yellow light. Then he smiled.

"Don't you worry, Euripides," he muttered, starting to fold. "You're among friends." With that he crumbled.

I got him back to his dorm, half carried him up the stairs, led him to bed. Then I stood by the window awhile, looking out at the quiet street beyond. Finally I lay down, eyes open, fighting sleep, cozy, drunk, and warm, lying there, in what would have been Zock's room.

I spent the next three days at Harvard, talking with Clarence during the afternoons, listening to his poetry, drinking with him at night. Martha hopped over all the time, bringing him notes and outlines and whatever else was needed to keep him in school. For he never took it seriously, only his poems, bad as they were, and I had to respect him for that.

Then, the fourth morning, we went out for breakfast, mainly coffee. Clarence bought a copy of *The New York Times* and we split it, sipping away, not talking. It was the early edition and I thumbed through, noting mostly the sports results, which were pretty incomplete. So I went on, glancing here and there, and suddenly I saw my father's picture staring out at me.

HENRY BAXTER TREVITT. AUTHOR AND EDUCATOR. That was the headline. I read every word, very slow, pausing after each sentence. Graduate of Harvard, it said. And it told about his Ph.D from that unpronounceable school somewhere in Italy. And how he was the head of the Classics department at Athens College, Athens, Illinois. And how he had lectured all around the country. And his books: *Euripides and Modern Man, The Euripidean Hero, The Medea Myth*, plus a couple of others I didn't even know about. And his translations of all the Greek plays. And the honors and prizes he had won. They listed everything there was to list, including my mother and me. I read it through twice and my only thought was: "Everything's here. They got it all right."

Then I quit the crapping around and realized it was my own father who was dead. And I knew, just as sure as God made green apples, that I was going to be there when they put him in the ground.

The next hour or two are pretty jumbled in my mind. I showed the clipping to Clarence, ran to his room, got my bag, said good-by to him, and headed for the airport. Once I got there I had more trouble, what with only five dollars in my pocket—not enough. But I talked and waved the paper and somebody must have taken pity on me because somehow I got a ticket.

I waited around the airport awhile before I could board the plane, getting more and more nervous. Finally we took off and I tried to sleep but never made it. Instead I just thought about my father and how mad he must have been when he knew he was going to die, with all those books left unwritten, all that work left undone, piled up there, on his desk. And what was the funeral going to be like. And facing my mother.

And would Mrs. Crowe be there. And what would I say to her if she was. And on I went, trying to sleep, not being able to.

We were about an hour away from Chicago when the announcement came. Because of fog, we were not going to land in Chicago at all, but instead were going north to Milwaukee. And be calm because the bad weather is moving south across Lake Michigan and won't bother us.

I started up to the pilot's room but a stewardess stopped me from going in. "You'll have to sit down," she said. "And don't worry about the weather."

"It's not the weather," I said, waving the clipping in her face. "But my father's being buried this afternoon and I've got to be there."

"I'm sorry," she answered. "You'll just have to sit down."

I went back to my seat, tensing up inside. My stomach started aching so I hit it, swearing quietly, trying to concentrate on something, anything at all. I knew that Milwaukee wasn't any farther from Athens than Chicago, but that didn't matter. Nothing did. I called to the stewardess and asked how long it would be before we landed. She said probably less than an hour. "Tell the pilot to hurry," I said. "Tell him I haven't got much time. Tell him my father's being buried this afternoon."

She didn't, naturally, but I kept after her, asking her every two minutes how long until we landed, and when we finally did get there, I know she wasn't unhappy being rid of me.

As soon as we were on the ground, I grabbed my bag and ran. I tore through the airport out to where the cabs were. "Athens, Illinois," I said, hopping in.

The driver looked at me awhile. "Forty bucks," he said. "In advance."

I checked my wallet, pulled out the five. "Here," I said. "Give you the rest when we get there."

"In advance," he repeated.

"Please."

"Look, buddy," he said, staring at me in the mirror.

"You son of a bitch!" I yelled, getting out. "My father's being buried this afternoon." I slammed the door all I had, hoping it would snap off at the hinges. Then I tried another cab, but it was the same thing. So I stood there, not knowing what to do, thinking: "If only I could find Mr. Hardecker. He'd drive me home all right. Mr. Hardecker would never let me down."

Then somebody honked at me and I jumped out of the road. Scared, alone, with only five dollars in my pocket and no train that made any time at all, I just wanted to sit down there by the cab stand and die.

Because my father was being buried that afternoon, and it began to look as if I wasn't going to make it.

Finally I got the idea of hitchhiking, so I ran to the main parking lot and stood at the exit, yelling, "Athens, Illinois" to all the cars going by. But nobody answered and nobody stopped, not for a long time. Then, maybe half an hour later, the law of averages came through. A car pulled up. "You want to go to Athens?" the driver asked.

"I sure do," I answered. "Yes, sir. Please."

"Well, get in," he said. "I'm going by there. And I'm in a hurry."

"So am I," I told him, opening the front door. "You can't get there fast enough for me. Because my father's being buried there this afternoon."

We took off.

I never found out his name, but whoever he was, he could drive. We tore down the highway hitting eighty miles an hour, never talking but staring instead at the road as it stretched on ahead or the telephone poles that blurred by on either side. "I got a chance," I told myself over and over. "If only we don't get a flat, I got a chance."

When we reached the Athens turn-off, I spoke to him. "Let me out here," I said.

"I'm not in that much of a hurry," he answered, and he made the turn toward town. I directed him on how to get to my house and in a few minutes we were there. "Thanks," I said, jumping out. He nodded and drove away. I ran inside.

They were all there in the dark living-room; my mother, Mrs. Janes, Mrs. Atkins, the wife of the college president, plus half a dozen more, sitting in a semicircle with my mother in the middle, talking softly, hushed. When I came in, they stopped.

I went up to her, staring because she looked so awful. Pale and tired and almost dead; not crying any more but puffy still around the eyes. My mother looked to be about one hundred years old that afternoon and I couldn't watch her, so I glanced out the window, over toward Zock's house.

"I came as fast as I could," I said.

"You're too late," she told me. "We buried him this morning."

"Oh," I said. That was all. Then I turned and went up to my room.

I lay on my bed, staring at the cracks in the ceiling, not able to feel a thing, but thinking: "I didn't have to hurry at all. I could have walked. I could have walked all the way from Boston, Massachusetts, because they buried him this morning." I had been there about an hour when my mother knocked on the door. "Come in," I said, not getting up but just lying flat, my hands behind my head, staring at those cracks in the ceiling.

It wasn't my mother who came in, though. It was Mrs. Janes, with the cloudy smell of alcohol trailing behind her. I didn't say a word.

"Your mother isn't herself," Mrs. Janes said. "She's very upset. It was a terrible thing."

"He was sixty years old, Mrs. Janes. You can't ask for more than that."

"A terrible thing," she repeated.

"*Hubris*," I said, for no good reason. But it stopped the conversation for a while, so we were quiet and just looked at each other. I began getting edgy, what with her standing over me. I turned away, but she didn't move.

"What is it, Mrs. Janes?" I said finally.

She fidgeted awhile. "That girl's back," she told me.

I looked at her. "What girl?"

"You know."

"What girl?" I said again, knowing who she meant but just wanting to hear her say it.

"Annabelle," Mrs. Janes whispered.

I nodded, waiting. I knew she had a whole spiel worked up, but the way I was acting upset her. She got that way easily, from her drinking and all.

"I thought you'd like to know," she said, heading for the door.

"Good-by," I called. "Thanks." But I really didn't care.

I stayed in my room until seven that night, lying on my bed, thinking about how it would have been to walk all the way from Boston, and what might have happened to me on the way. Which was silly, I suppose, but I couldn't help it. Then, at seven, I went downstairs. They were still there, a bunch of them, sitting around, talking quietly. Actually, they were different people than before. But they might as well have been the same, for they sat in the same chairs and said the same things in the same hushed voices.

"I'm taking the car," I told my mother. "I'm going out awhile."

"Where are you going?"

"Just for a drive," was all I told her.

I headed straight for the cemetery, speeding past the campus and beyond, to the edge of town. Athens Cemetery is very small. Quiet and beautiful, it is set on a hill overlooking a stretch of woods owned by the college. I parked the car and began searching for my father's grave.

It wasn't hard to find, what with all the flowers banked around it. I stepped over the flowers and stood on the grave, staring down.

Like Mrs. Janes, I had a whole spiel in mind, made up on the drive out. But I'd forgotten most of it. I didn't know what to say. It had turned into a beautiful night, Indian summer, with just that hint of autumn in the air, sneaking up on you whenever a gust of wind blew by. It was the same kind of night as when Zock died and I couldn't believe he was less than six months gone. I glanced around, trying to locate his grave. I couldn't right off, so I dropped my head again and looked at my father.

"Old man," I said. "I'm sorry." But that wasn't what I meant; not at all. "I guess you knew a lot about Euripides." And then I muttered: "Indeed," by way of finishing it off.

That was it. I took my time walking back to the car, looking around every few feet at my father's grave, covered with all those flowers. How he would have hated them, the smell and all. A pot of tea would have been better. With a pipe set alongside. But of course, when you got right down to it, it didn't really matter what they put there. Because he was dead. That was the hard thing to realize. I wasn't shaken and I never once came close to crying. It was just the realization that was hard. I suppose I had him figured as being too smart ever to die. But there he was, dead, lying under all those smelly flowers.

By that time I was at the car. And she was there, standing, waiting beside it, waiting for me.

"Hello, Annabelle," I said.

"I'm sorry about your father," she said. I nodded, not saying a word. She began to fidget. "I called your house. They said you'd gone for a drive. I thought you might come here." She stopped then, waiting for me to say something, anything at all, I suppose, so she could lead into whatever it was she had come to tell me. But I wasn't talking. She got worse and worse as the quiet stretched on, fidgeting more, staring out past me to the woods beyond, where her third man was, biting her lips, hands clenched, pale. I waited.

Finally, she cracked, everything pouring out at once. "I'm in trouble. Ray, I'm in trouble. I'm going to have a baby. His baby. I need help. Money. Three hundred dollars. I've got to have it. You've got to give it to me. You've got to give me three hundred dollars." I let her go on until she'd been all through it a couple of times. Then I stopped her.

"Your folks have money. Get it from them."

"I can't," she said, as if it was an explanation.

"Get it from Janes."

She shook her head. "His wife would find out."

I had to laugh. "His wife knows. She knows all about it."

"She'd divorce him."

Which was funnier still. "Not a chance," I said. "Not if he'd knocked up half a dozen girls."

"I love him," she whispered, shivering. "If that makes any difference."

"Well now," I said. "Why didn't you say so? Sure. That makes all the difference. Love does. I mean, I loved you once. Of course, being as I'm shy, I never told you. But now I can. I loved you, Annabelle. What do you think of that?"

"I'm sorry," she said. "About what happened."

"No need, Annabelle. It probably did me a lot of good."

She believed me. "I'm glad. That you feel that way."

"So you need money. Well, it's sure in a worthy cause. You might even start a fund. "Abortions for Annabelle.' " I think she was about to scream when I put my arm around her. "Hey now," I said. "Hey now, Annabelle. Take it easy." But feeling her body warm against me threw me for a little, and I didn't know if I could go through with it. Finally, I started to move.

"Where are we going?" she asked.

"For a walk," I told her. "Just for a stroll."

We began moving silently among the graves, going up one row and down the next. We did that about ten minutes with never a word spoken. Then I found it.

"Zachary Crowe," it said. "1934–1954. R.I.P."

"Here's a nice place," I said, pushing her down on the grass. "Here's a swell place. It's beautiful here." I knelt beside her and my hands shook as I started to undo the buttons of her blouse.

At first she didn't stop me. Then she tried pushing my hands away. But I went right on, finally pulling her blouse off, slipping it over her tanned arms, throwing it aside. "Relax," I whispered, blowing softly on her neck. "Relax, Annabelle."

"Don't," she said. "Don't do this to me."

I went right on. "An exchange," I whispered. "For services rendered. Now that makes sense, doesn't it, Annabelle? You want three hundred dollars. Isn't that right? Well, guess what I want."

But I didn't want it. Because all the time I kept thinking to myself: "This is for you, Zock."

Even as I listened to her groaning underneath me, I kept on thinking it. "This is for you, Zock. This is for you." Over and over and over.

And then it was done.

I looked down at her. She was almost smiling. But when I jumped up, she stopped. And when I started walking away, she got afraid, kneeling there naked in the cemetery, on Zock's grave, trying as best she could to cover herself with her long black hair.

About twenty feet away, I turned and called to her.

"If it's a boy, name it after me." Then I ran.

When I got back to the house, everyone had gone except Mrs. Atkins, who was to spend the night. I paid my respects, excused myself, headed for my room. Even though I wasn't tired, I went to bed. I was still wide awake when my mother came in, sitting down close beside me, staring.

"That Mrs. Atkins is very nice," I began. My mother nodded. "How long is she going to stay?"

"How long are you going to stay?" my mother whispered then. I didn't answer. "When you left," she went on. "When you left, you weren't coming back. Isn't that right?"

"Yes, Mother," I said. "That's right."

She started to cry softly. "Please," she whispered. "Don't leave me again. Raymond, don't leave me now."

I looked at her for a second, then away, out the window at the night. I thought for a long time, finally turning, holding out my hands to her. "All right, Mother," I said. "I'll stay home."

And I did.

I stayed home, inside the house, mostly in my own room, for the next ten months. Sometimes, at night, I'd slip out and drive to Crystal City for a visit with Terry Clark, but that never took long, seeing as Terry was a pretty busy girl. Otherwise, I never left the house.

My mother resumed her club work, worse than ever. She'd get up at the crack of dawn, zip through breakfast, and then off she'd go to the Red Cross, or some place else, crammed full of energy. But that energy drained as the day went on, so that when she'd come home, there wasn't much left. We'd have dinner together, the two of us, and then talk or watch television until it was time for her to go to bed. She was looking better, but it was a long process, a slow one, getting back to normal. And nothing either of us could do could hurry it along.

Still, things happened in those ten months.

Sadie Griffin left town in November, heading for New York. Two weeks later Mr. Crowe sold his house and everything in it. He came over to say good-by and we chatted some, mumbling about this and that, both of us smiling. Then he drove away, picked up his wife, and went to live in California. I got a postcard from him later, from Los Angeles, in which he said that he was fine and his wife was fine and they had a fine apartment and he was working in a clothing store in the downtown area, and good luck, Euripides. Mrs. Janes was sent away for the cure. My mother told me that, and also how proud she was of me for having a friend who was also a friend of hers. Because I was the last person Mrs. Janes asked about before she went.

So life went on. People kept busy. And I kept busy too.

By reading.

Just as soon as I was awake in the morning I started, and I read all day long. I began with the Greeks, working forward, from Homer and Sophocles to that bloody Roman, Seneca. After him a jump to Shakespeare. All his plays, even *Hamlet* again, which improves, I guess, as you get older.

Then I took up poetry. First Shakespeare and his sonnets, then Milton, who is worse than the Chinese Water Torture, no matter what anyone says, and Tennyson, and Browning, together with his phony wife. Then Chaucer, who is worse than Milton, and Spenser, who is worst of all. And the Romantics—Wordsworth, Coleridge, Shelley, and Keats. Then Donne with his ladies and Herrick with his broads. Then Eliot and Housman and Yeats and, naturally, Kipling.

I read everything, anything I could get my hands on, understanding some, but not all, which is par. I read most of the books in my father's study, the English ones anyway, and when I began running low, my mother got more out of the library for me. I read for ten months solid, one day slipping easily into the next without a hitch of any kind.

Then one night, late in April, my mother came into my room, smiling but nervous, standing over me.

"Raymond," she said. I looked up. "Raymond." And she paused, walking around to the other side of my desk. "Raymond."

"What is it?" I asked.

"There's someone downstairs I'd like you to meet," she answered, blurting it out. I nodded. "Be polite," she whispered as we headed for the door. "Please, Raymond. Please. Remember your manners."

"I shall endeavor to try," I said, following her down.

"Adrian," my mother said, when we got there. "This is my son, Raymond. Raymond. This is Adrian Baugh."

"Jolly glad to meet you," he said.

"Jolly glad myself," I answered.

"Adrian's from England," my mother said.

We shook hands.

Adrian Baugh stood nine feet tall. Actually, that's not true. Actually, he only stood six foot six, but he looked nine feet tall, he was that skinny.

And English. He said "chaps" all the time. I was a good chap; the students were good chaps; even my mother was a good chap. And I'm sure that no one has really used that word, except in movies, since the dear, days of old Victoria. But Adrian Baugh did. He was so English you almost couldn't stand it, never wearing anything but tweeds and never smoking anything, naturally, but a pipe. Aside from that, though, he wasn't a bad guy at all.

"Adrian has taken over your father's position at the college," my mother said. "As head of the department." We walked into the living-room and sat down. My mother smiled at Adrian; he smiled at her; they both smiled at me. But nobody said anything.

Finally, my mother broke the ice. "Would either of you care for anything?" she asked.

"Tea," Adrian replied. "If you have it."

"I'll make some," she said, standing up. "You two stay here and get acquainted. I want you to get to be pals." She left us.

"So you're from England," I said, after a minute or two more of silence.

"Righto," Adrian said.

"Well," I asked. "How are things over there?"

And believe it or not, he told me. Starting with Churchill and working down. I sat there, nodding every so often while he chattered nervously on, lighting his pipe, letting it sit, then knocking the ashes into the fireplace.

We were in the middle of the House of Commons when my mother came back. "How are we getting on?" she asked.

"Fine," Adrian answered. "He has a genuine interest in England."

They sat across from each other, balancing teacups on their knees, smiling. I watched them. The silence dragged on and on, with nothing to break it up but the sound of their sipping.

"Adrian loves sports," my mother said then. "He played cricket in college."

He nodded. "I don't believe you play it much over here."

I pulled away at my lip awhile. "No," I said.

"It's a delightful game," he began. "You see, in cricket, the pitcher bowls the ball, attempting to knock over the wicket. Meanwhile, the batsman—"

"Wait a minute," I interrupted. "You got a wicket in cricket?"

"Raymond," my mother said.

So I sat back and listened while he told me about cricket, which is a game I think I could really learn to hate if given half a chance. Adrian talked on and on, gesturing to me, explaining, smiling at my mother. Finally, gym class let out and he had to go home. My mother walked him to the door. "Delightful chap," I heard him say just before he left. The door closed and my mother came back humming.

"Mother," I said, beating her to it. "We're great pals already. But what difference does it make?"

"No difference, Raymond," she answered. "No difference at all." Then she started to hum again.

From that day on she pestered me.

"Raymond, you're staying home too much," "Raymond, you ought to go out more." "Raymond, why don't you bring someone home to dinner?" "Raymond, Adrian and I are going to the concert. Come along." "Raymond, Adrian and I are going out to dinner. Come along." "Raymond, Adrian and I are going for a walk. Come along."

All of which was easy enough to ignore, at least in the beginning. But then one night they both cornered me in the living-room.

"Raymond," my mother said, "I'm worried about you."

"Yes," Adrian said. "Katherine"—and he smiled at her—"Your mother feels that perhaps you might use your time to some better advantage."

"So we thought"—she went on, taking over—"Adrian and I thought that it might be easier for you if we all went out together."

"You mean the three of us, Mother?"

"No, Raymond. I mean four. You know. A double-date." She giggled.

"Mother," I said, "you're kidding."

"Raymond," she answered, "I've never been more serious."

"Who would you like me to bring?"

She smiled across at Adrian. "Surprise us," she said.

At which I started laughing. "Mother," I told her. "I will."

And so, three nights later, we were driving out to Crystal City, me behind the wheel, my mother and Adrian in the back seat. When we got to Terry's place, I parked, honking the horn. We waited awhile. Then Terry appeared, walking toward us.

"Why, Raymond," my mother said, "she's adorable."

Which was the truth. Terry Clark's face was her fortune. She had a wonderful smile, dimples, a perfect, straight nose. And the greatest eyes I've ever seen. Round, innocent, pure; they were doll's eyes.

She got in the car. "Terry," I said, "my mother and Adrian Baugh. Meet Terry Clark."

"Pleased," Terry said, and we drove off.

"I thought we'd go to the drive-in," I told Terry.

"Good deal," she nodded. Then she turned around and faced the back seat. "Apologies for keeping you waiting," she said. "But I was reading the *Digest*."

"*Digest?*" Adrian asked.

"*Bedside*," Terry explained. "Honest to God, I get so wrapped up in that sheet I don't know what's going on. Just now I read about this dope peddler who found God. How about that? There he was, pushing 'H' in the back of this church, when whammo! it hits him. So he—" She stopped, staring at Adrian. "What're you sittin' on?" she asked.

"Nothing," he answered.

"Adrian's very tall," I put in.

"You're not whistlin' Dixie," Terry said. She turned back to him, smiling. "It's good, y'know. Being tall. Females prefer it. Tall men. The *Digest* took a poll. The tall men came out best." She patted his knee. "I like tall men myself."

"How nice for you," my mother said, ice cold. Which killed the conversation for a while.

When we got to the drive-in, I heard Adrian fumbling around in the back seat, but I raised my hand. "This is on me," I said, and I paid for all of us. We parked, adjusted the mike, and relaxed. A Western was playing and we got there just in time for the barroom brawl.

"Brain him," Terry muttered. "Kick his teeth out."

"What's going on?" Adrian asked. The car was full of punches, broken bottles, grunts, groans.

"Shhh," I said. "You're spoiling the love scene."

"I can't see," Adrian said. I turned around. He couldn't. He was too tall.

"I'll give you a play by play," I said. There was a terrible splat as the hero unloaded on somebody. "He just told her he loved her," I said. Somebody else broke a chair on the hero's head. "She says she loves him too." The hero knocked a third guy over a table. The table collapsed. "Now they're kissing," I said. The sheriff appeared in the doorway and fired a shot at the ceiling. "Wow," I said. "Some kiss."

"Kiss," Adrian said.

"Raymond," my mother said.

Adrian bent down. Or tried to. All he really managed was to graze my mother on the temple with his elbow. He sat up again. "Dreadfully sorry, Katherine," he said. "But I can't see."

"Quiet," Terry put in. "You're spoiling the mood."

"Raymond," my mother said, "Adrian can't see."

"Did we come to look or did we come to talk?" Terry asked.

"Raymond," my mother whispered, "Adrian can't see."

"He wouldn't like this picture anyway," I whispered back.

"I might," Adrian said. "I might."

"Chatter, chatter, chatter," Terry said, very loud. "I'm going to get me some popcorn." She got out and slammed the door.

"Raymond," my mother said, "where did you find that girl?"

"She's a friend of mine," I answered.

"Really, Raymond," my mother said.

"I hate to be a stick," Adrian sighed. "But I do wish I could—"

"All right," I said. "All right." I opened the door and changed seats with him. "Now I can't see," I said. "Adrian. Will you bend down?"

Adrian bent down. Terry came back. "Whatsamatter?" she said. "Don't you feel good?"

"Raymond can't see," Adrian said.

"Why don't you bend down?" Terry asked.

"I am bending down," Adrian told her.

At which she giggled. Then she moved up, sitting right next to him, her head resting on his shoulder. "You don't mind?" she said.

"No, no," Adrian coughed. "Perfectly all right."

"Come on, Mother," I said, putting my arm around her. "Let's us get cozy."

She pushed me away, glaring. "Raymond," she said.

So we sat there for an hour or more, during which time the Western ended and the other picture began, a spy movie taking place in Europe. From the first, Adrian liked it. "That's the Louvre," he said, turning, smiling at my mother. "The Arc de Triomphe, of course. On the left there, is . . ." And he was off. Throughout most of the movie he talked away, explaining where we were, the museums nearby, on and on, talking a mile a minute.

Then Terry interrupted. "Time?" she asked.

"Nine forty-five," I told her.

"I gotta go," she said, all excited. "I'm entertaining at ten."

"Couldn't you possibly wait until the conclusion?" Adrian said.

"I'm sorry," Terry told him, shaking her head. "I can't."

So Adrian got out and I got back in the driver's seat and we left. Nobody said a word until we got to Terry's place.

" 'Night," she said, smiling at them. "Awfully pleased." She turned to me. "See you next Tuesday."

I nodded. We left her.

And after that my mother didn't pester me any more.

I kept to my usual routine, sticking to myself, staying in the house, reading. Nothing happened, one way or the other, until the afternoon of the 12th of September.

When Harriet called me.

I was up in my room, alone, my mother being off at a meeting. The telephone rang. I answered.

"Let's go swimming," Harriet said right off, as if we'd talked about it all day yesterday, when actually I hadn't seen her for more than a year.

"No," I said.

"Fine," she answered, hanging up. "I'll be right over."

And she was. In about fifteen minutes she was pushing away at the doorbell, rat-a-tat-tat, until I had to go down and talk to her.

"Hi, Euripides," she said. "What's new?" She looked the same as ever, standing there in a bathing suit, a towel curled around her shoulders.

"Nothing," I said.

"Get your suit on," she told me. "I'll wait."

"Harriet," I said. "I'm not going swimming."

She laughed. "You just think you're not going swimming." I turned and went upstairs. She followed me. I sat down at my desk. She looked around at all the books. "Pressing butterflies?" she asked.

"Goddammit," I began.

"Oh, you have changed," she said. "It's positively startling." Then she came over and started pulling off my shirt.

"Harriet," I said. "Please."

But she kept pulling away at my shirt, finally getting it caught around my neck.

"You're strangling me, for chrisakes," I said.

"I've only just begun," she answered, not stopping. She got it off. "You do the rest," she told me. "I have some pride."

I looked at her as she stood over me, smiling down. "All right, Harriet," I said after a while. "You win."

"I knew you wanted to all the time," she answered, applauding. And when I was getting ready, she told me about herself. About the boys she'd gone out with, the girls she knew; about how she'd been appointed editor of *The Athenian*, which was why she'd come to Athens a week early, to start getting things organized.

We left the house together, walking slow. It was a beautiful day, warm, almost hot, and in a few minutes we were at the road that led down to the Lake. The minute we turned onto that road, I started tensing.

Because I could see the beach below me, and it was jammed; hundreds of people from the town, mothers with their babies, old women, high-school kids. My stomach knotted more and more with each step. Then the noises met us, beach sounds, laughter and splashing, the roll of waves. I jabbed at my stomach, jabbed at it hard, trying to make it relax, not being able to.

Then we were there.

Harriet took my hand, led me along a few steps. I stopped. She tugged at me. I didn't move, but just stood there, sweating and cold, taking it all in. The people, running or laughing or lying around; the yellow sand, the water beyond. And above, framing it, that cloudless blue sky.

"Come on, sissy," Harriet said then. "What have you got to be afraid of?"

I didn't answer. Instead, I took her by the hand and together we walked toward the water.

It was a great afternoon. We swam and horsed around some, having a gay old time. Then we flopped on the sand and I listened while she told me more of what she'd done the past year. When she was through, I started. Harriet lay alongside me, nodding, smiling, interrupting every so often, asking me questions. I don't know how long I talked, but when I had finished, the sun was going down, the beach almost empty. Still we stayed on, both of us talking now, until finally it got a little chilly.

I took her to her dorm. On the steps, she held out her hand to me. "Thanks," she said.

I pushed her hand away, holding her in my arms, hugging her tight. "Don't mention it," I answered. Then she went inside.

I walked home slowly, taking my time, singing out loud. It was after eight when I got there. I heard voices from in back so I started around.

But I stopped.

Because there, standing by the ravine, half in shadow, were my mother and Adrian Baugh. And as I watched, he reached down, pulled her close. Then he kissed her. She leaned against him, smiling.

I snuck up to my bed as quietly as I could, so as not to disturb them. I lay there awhile, thinking. Then I got up and walked into my mother's room and looked out at them. They were still standing there by the ravine, holding each other just as tight as they could.

And as I looked out the window, it hit me. I didn't mind; I wasn't upset. But all of a sudden I realized that there was my mother, in love again. And where was I? I stared across at Zock's house, empty, deserted. And where was I? The same as before. No different. Standing still while everything else was moving, leaving me, passing me by.

I thought about it all night long, tossing and turning, the books on my desk silhouetted in the moonlight. It was almost dawn when I figured out what to do. So I made a phone call right then, at five o'clock in the morning.

And when my mother came down for breakfast, I was dressed and packed, ready.

"Mother," I said. "I'm going away for a while. But not long," With that, I left her, standing puzzled in the kitchen.

It was three days before I came back. Not alone. "Mother," I yelled, opening the front door.

She was in the living-room. "What is it, Raymond?" she called.

We walked in.

"Mother," I said. "Meet the wife."

VII . . . . The Wife

Terry Clark moved into my house with all her wordly possessions. Namely, a closetful of clothes, eleven pairs of lounging slippers, and sixty-six copies of the *Bedside Digest*.

I watched her unpack. We were up in my room, me sitting on the bed, her wandering around, putting things away, neither of us saying much of anything. She took her dresses and suits and shoved them into my closet. She took her lounging slippers and dumped them on the floor, beneath the clothes. She took her stockings, slips, etc., and stuffed them in the dresser.

Then she went to my bookcase and began pulling out books, stacking them on my desk.

"What are you doing?" I asked her.

She didn't answer but just kept on pulling away at the books. When she'd gotten about two shelves cleared, she went to the hall and brought in a beautiful red leather suitcase with a dial combination, humming as she fiddled with the dial, opening it.

She took out a copy of the *Bedside Digest*, dog-eared and torn, blew away some make-believe dust, and stuck it on one of the empty shelves. Then she backed away, staring at it, her head tilted to one side.

"They're gonna look fine," she told me.

She took another copy from that red leather suitcase, blew again, and set it on the shelf. I was about to say something but she beat me to it. "These books," she said, waving at the desk. "We got to find some place else to put them."

I got off the bed and tried to hug her. She pushed me away. "Please," she said. "I'm busy."

"Terry," I said. "Which is more important? Me or the *Bedside Digest*?"

"Trevitt," she answered. "Don't ever ask. Now, do something about those books. 'A tidy home is a happy home.' Abe Lincoln's wife said that." She gnawed on her finger awhile. "I think it was her. Maybe it was Martha

Washington. It's in last February's issue. I'll check it." She snapped her fingers. "Bess Truman."

"Swell," I said, and I gathered up a big armful of books.

"Don't hurry," she told me as I headed for the door. "This is gonna take a while."

I shook my head and went downstairs, turning down the hall toward my father's study.

It wasn't empty. My mother was sitting there, at his desk, in his chair, alone, sitting in the dark.

I switched on the light. She blinked a few times, then forced a smile. "Hi," I said, putting the books down.

"What are you doing, Raymond?" she asked.

"Terry needs space for the *Bedside Digest*," I explained.

My mother didn't answer. Instead, she kept on staring straight ahead to the spot behind the door where the guppies had been. I set to work, sliding the books back on the shelves. It took me a long time. Still, my mother didn't say a word. Finally, when I was done, I went over and sat on top of the desk close by her.

"You want to talk?" I asked.

"Talk?" she answered. "Talk about what?"

Then it was my turn not to say anything. I waited, sitting there on top of my father's desk. Pretty soon, she started.

"It must be my fault," my mother said, whispering.

"What is, Mother?"

"I don't know." She pushed her hair away from her face. "I've been sitting here, trying to reason it out. Your father always did that. Whenever something went wrong, it was right here that he'd come, sitting and thinking, reasoning it out."

I nodded.

"I don't know," she said again, staring up at me. "I suppose it's just that I always planned . . . I always wanted . . . I wanted my son to have a church wedding. With the organ playing, people crying. And you in a tuxedo, your bride in white. And then you elope. With that girl. I don't know, Raymond. I'm disappointed, that's all."

"I'm sorry you feel that way," I told her. "Really. I am."

"With that girl," she said again.

"Terry's all right," I said. "You'll see. Once you get to know her."

"All right?" my mother whispered. "Is that what you wanted in a wife? Someone all right? What would your father have said?"

" 'Indeed,' " I answered, at which she smiled. So I left her like that.

Back in my room, I stopped in the doorway. Terry was standing quietly, staring out the window, her arms crossed in front of her.

"Bedtime," I said, walking in.

She spun around, her great blue eyes wide open.

"Relax," I said. "It's just your loving husband."

"You should knock anyway," she told me. "Else you'll scare a person half to death."

"I'm sorry. But like I said, it's bedtime."

"You look smelly," she answered. "Why don't you go take a bath. Take a shower. Take both."

I laughed, lifting her high in the air, squeezing her just as tight as I could. "T. T.," I said. "You know what that stands for? It stands for—"

"Tough Titty," Terry said.

"Terry Trevitt," I finished. Then I put her down, taking a step away, still holding tight to her hands. "Listen to me a second," I said. "Listen to me, Terry. I mean this. I don't want you talking like that. Not any more. Please."

"Why?"

"Well," I told her. "Well. Because it's not ladylike."

She laughed. "So who's a lady?"

"You are," I said.

"Sure, Trevitt."

I picked her up again, cradling her in my arms, whispering. "Oh, maybe not now," I whispered. "Maybe it'll take a lot of doing. But someday, Terry."

"Yeah," she said. "Sure. I'll be Queen of the May."

"That too."

"You're strangling me," she said. "Lemme go." I let go. "And take a shower," she went on, sitting at my desk. "Don't rush."

I bowed low and headed for the bathroom.

I suppose I hadn't spent so long getting cleaned up since my first date with Sally Farmer years before. I showered and scrubbed myself, shaving, showering again, drying off, combing my hair, even throwing on some talcum. All the time I was in there I sang away at the top of my lungs, sang all the words to all the songs I knew, as loud as I could. When I was finally finished, I tucked a towel around me, opened the door and went back to my room. Terry was still sitting at the desk.

"All clean," I said.

"You're practically naked," she answered, very loud. "Go put some clothes on. Get dressed."

"I was sort of thinking of going in the other direction," I said.

"Men," she muttered. "All the same. All you ever think about is sex, sex, sex. The *Digest* says—"

"Terry," I interrupted, "you're talking to your husband."

"Please," she said, holding up one of her hands. "Don't remind me."

"Well, Jesus," I said. "Then what did you marry me for?"

"I been thinking about that," she answered, very soft, staring out the window. "I been thinking about that a good deal. While you were yapping in the shower."

"And?"

"I don't know," she told me. "I had lotsa proposals. Seventeen, total. Starting from when I was nine years old. One guy I turned down owns his own gas station. Right now he owns it. Outright. And another guy—"

"You're a liar," I said.

She waited awhile, then nodded. "O.K.," she said. "But when I was nine the kid next door, he wanted to marry me. He did. His name was Wilford something or other. Nine years old and he had pimples. At that age. I never had pimples. I got a beautiful skin. My beautician told me that. 'Terry,' he said. 'You got a beautiful—' "

"Tell me about it there," I interrupted, pointing to the bed.

"You don't own me, y'know," she said. "I'm still a human being. Free as the birds."

"Terry," I said. "Don't you even like me?"

She thought some. "Sure," was her answer.

"Thanks."

"You're a nice enough guy. And nice-lookin'. And you come from a nice family. With a nice house. And you got standing in the community." Then she was quiet for a long time. I waited, watching her as she sat there, huddled in my desk chair. "Trevitt," she said finally.

"What?"

"Tell me you love me."

I was about to answer but I didn't. Because my mother was standing in the doorway, looking at us. "I just stopped by to say good night," my mother said.

"Come in," Terry told her. "Please do." She stood and my mother walked in, taking her by the hands. None of us said a word until Terry spoke up, very soft. "Remember, Mrs. Trevitt. Remember it this way. You're not losing a daughter, you're gaining a son."

"That's backward," I said.

At which my mother started to cry. She turned from Terry, flinging her arms around me, her tears dropping onto my shoulders. "Raymond," she said. "I want you to know that I love you." Then she hugged Terry. "I love you both," my mother said. "And more than anything else, I want you to be happy."

"We'll try, Mother," I told her. "We'll try just as hard as we know how. We can't promise more."

"That's right," Terry echoed.

My mother looked straight at Terry. "I'm proud to have you with us," she said, and you could tell from the way she talked that she meant it, every word. So, muttering good night, she left us alone.

I waited a second, then started taking off the towel.

Terry panicked. "Hold the phone," she said, and she tore around the room, turning off lights, until we stood in darkness. "Strip away," she told me then.

I got into bed, leaning up on one elbow, staring across the dark room to where Terry was.

"Now," she whispered. "Tell me you love me."

"O.K.," I said. "I love you."

"Say it like you mean it."

"I love you," I said again.

"No good. Say it like this: 'Terry, my rose, my flower, my sweet. I love you.'"

"Like hell," I said.

"Listen," she told me. "That was how Mr. Tarkington proposed. And if it's good enough for Mr. Tarkington, it's good enough for you."

"Terry," I asked, "who's Mr. Tarkington?"

"He was the most unforgettable character I've met last August," she answered.

"Please," I said. "Please. Will you come here?"

"This is my wedding night," she said, talking very fast. "A girl's got a right to sweet talk on her wedding night. That's the night she's most in love with her husband. Don't you understand about love, Trevitt? It's the most important thing in the world. I was in love once, and it was the greatest thing ever happened to me. With a steelworker from Gary, Indiana, when I was sixteen years old." She stopped.

"What happened?" I asked.

"He got me impregnated."

"He got you pregnant."

"That's what I said."

"No, Terry. You said he got you impregnated. It doesn't make sense."

"It made plenty of sense to me at the time."

"I meant grammatically."

"Grammatically, crap," Terry said.

"Please. I asked you once already not to talk that way."

"Listen here," she cut in. "If this is how you're gonna act, we can call the whole thing off right now."

"Terry," I said. "Are you scared?"

"Fat chance," she answered.

"You are, aren't you?"

She waited a long time, and when she finally did talk, I could hardly hear her. "So what if I am," she whispered. "A bride's got a right to be scared on her wedding night. Mrs. Tarkington was so—"

"Only one way to get over that," I said, standing.

"Stay away from me, Trevitt."

"Naturally," I said and with that I picked her up and carried her to the bed, setting her down gently, starting to undress her.

"Please," she whispered. "Please, Trevitt."

"Please what, baby?"

"Go easy."

"I'm not going any place at all," I answered, putting my arms around her, pulling her close. With that she kissed me, one time, high on the cheek. We lay there next to each other, holding hands under the blankets, her head resting on my shoulder.

We were still like that when we dropped off to sleep . . .

All of which took place on a Saturday night, making the next morning Sunday. I woke pretty early, but not as early as I'd planned. I shook Terry. She didn't budge. "Terry," I said, shaking her again. "Rise and shine."

"Mumble," she said.

"Time to get up," I said, pulling the blankets off her.

Again she came with the "mumble, mumble, mumble." I shook her harder, talking all the time. After a while, she opened her eyes. "Hi, Trevitt," she said, still half asleep.

"Hi, baby," I answered. "Come on. Snap to."

"What time is it?" she whispered, stretching.

"Almost eleven," I told her. "And we're late."

"Late for what?"

"Church."

She smiled at me, stretching lazily, nodding her head. Then she sat straight up. "Church!" she bellowed. "Church! Are you crazy?"

"No," I said. "It's Sunday and we're late."

"Nobody goes to church," she said. "Me either." And she pulled the sheet over her head.

I ripped it away. "You've got to," I said. "You're my wife and if I go, you go."

"You're kidding."

"No sir," I said. "I'm very devout. I haven't missed church in years. Fifty-two Sundays a year. Rain or shine. It's an important thing in my life. God is love, you know. So come on."

"O.K.," she said, getting up. "I'm sorry. I didn't mean to make fun, Trevitt. I didn't know."

"I forgive you," I said. "Now let's get dressed."

Ten minutes later, we took off down the stairs.

"Where's your mother?" she asked me, half out of breath.

"She went early."

"What religion are you anyway?"

I thought awhile. "Presbyterian," I answered.

"I didn't know you come from a religious family, Trevitt."

"Oh yes," I said. "My mother and father were pillars of the church and I'm carrying on the tradition."

Terry stopped. "Y'know," she said. "I admire you for that."

"Thanks," I answered and I pulled her along. We got to Patriot's Square and shagged a left, heading for the big church in the middle of the block.

"Here we are," I said, going up the steps.

Terry didn't follow. Instead, she just pointed to the big sign out in front. "I thought you was Presbyterian?"

"Correct," I said.

"Well, this here is the Methodist church."

I read the sign. She was right. "Damn," I said. "I'm not awake yet. The Presbyterian's a little farther down."

We walked a few hundred yards. Terry stopped again, pointing. "That it?" she asked.

"It sure is," I answered. "That's the good old Athens Presbyterian Church."

"In your hat," Terry said. "It's a synagogue."

"Synagogue," I said, forcing a laugh. "Synagogue. I don't get it. Here you go to a church all your life and then one day it disappears on you."

Terry stuffed her hands in her pockets and walked on ahead. "It's goddam amazing, that's what it is," she mumbled.

We finally got to the Presbyterian church. It took a lot of walking, but we finally got there. Arriving just as the service was breaking up and all the people were streaming out. I stood on the sidewalk, shaking my head.

"I guess you sort of ruined your attendance record," Terry began.

"It's O.K.," I told her.

"No, it's not. It's a shame. A devout Presbyterian like you."

I shrugged, took her by the hand, and made the turn toward home. Getting only about two steps before somebody called my name.

"That's a church, Euripides," Harriet said, running up, giggling.

"Very funny," I told her.

"Don't you feel well? It's not even noon and you're up. You must be sick. Here," and she put her hand on my forehead, still giggling away.

"Terry," I said. "This here is Harriet. Harriet. Meet my wife."

Harriet stopped giggling. She looked at my face a long time, studying it. Then she turned to Terry, gave a quick smile, and walked off.

"Hey," I called, starting after her, but she didn't stop. I went back to Terry.

"Who's that?" Terry asked.

"A friend of mine," I answered.

"I'd hate to meet your enemies," she said.

My mother was waiting for us when we got there, along with Adrian, sitting in the living-room, chatting, both in their Sunday best.

"Raymond," Adrian said, standing, "your mother informs me that you're married."

"Hi," Terry said, going over and sitting next to him. "You want to kiss the bride?"

Adrian coughed, looked at my mother, then touched his lips to Terry's forehead.

"Y'know," she told him, "you're really cute."

"Thank you," Adrian said.

"I mean it," Terry went on. "No kidding. Maybe a little tall, but you know about women and tall men. Mr. Tarkington was—"

"I hate to interrupt," my mother interrupted, "but where in the world have you been?"

"Church," Terry answered.

"Church!" my mother exclaimed, smiling. "How wonderful. But I didn't see you there."

"Oh, we hit 'em all this morning," Terry went on.

"How wonderful," my mother said again. "Terry, I just know you're going to be a wonderful influence on Raymond."

"She sure is," I said. "But maybe you didn't know she was interested in social work."

My mother beamed.

Terry didn't.

"Yes," I finished. "And she wanted me to ask you if there wasn't something she could do. Can you find anything for her?"

"Of course I can," my mother said. "We need you at the Red Cross right away. Tomorrow afternoon. Answering the phone. Helping the girls here and there. Is that the sort of thing you wanted?"

"It's perfect," I said.

"Yeah," Terry echoed. "Perfect."

My mother clasped her hands in front of her. "I had no idea you liked social work. I find it fulfilling, of course, but so many don't." And with that she was off, talking about the Red Cross, the work they did, how Terry could help, the people she'd meet, the committees she could join. She talked on and on, smiling, gesturing, happy as a mother hen. "You'll never know how pleased this makes me," she said. "It's so wonderful having you here, Terry. Won't you stay for dinner? There's plenty."

"Mother," I broke in, "Terry lives here."

At which my mother blushed. "Of course," she said. "I keep forgetting." She stood. "I'm sorry. You'll have to excuse me. I have a few things to do in the kitchen. Raymond. Set the table."

I nodded. We went out and as I put the plates down I could hear my mother puttering around on one side of me, Terry and Adrian laughing on the other. My mother came into the dining-room.

"Terry is all right," she said. "All it takes is getting to know her."

I yelled that dinner was ready. They walked in a minute later, both of them laughing. "I just heard the most delightful joke," Adrian began. "It seems that there was this rabbit farmer—"

"Perhaps we ought to start," my mother said.

"Certainly," Adrian answered, pulling out the chair for Terry. Then he did the same for my mother. "You know, Katherine," he said, bending over her, "you should be a very happy woman. Twice blessed. Because you haven't lost a daughter, you've gained a son."

"That's backward," Terry said.

We sat down to eat . . .

The next morning I let Terry sleep, getting dressed as quietly as I could. My mother was in the kitchen when I got there. "How do I look?" I asked her.

She turned, facing me. "Where are you going, Raymond?"

"Out," I answered. "How do I look?"

"I can hardly believe it," my mother said, smiling. "Terry working at the Red Cross this afternoon. You up early. Wearing a necktie."

"I'm a new man," I told her, gulping down some orange juice, starting for the door. "In a while, you probably won't even know me."

"Where are you going?" she asked again.

"Big surprise," I said, and I left her there.

It was a beautiful day, just like the one before, and the minute I hit the street I just knew sure as God made green apples that it was going to work, that everything was going to turn out the way I wanted. So, singing out loud, I headed for Patriot's Square.

Returning home a little after twelve. Letting the front door bang shut, I stood in the foyer, shouting for Terry.

"In here," she answered from the dining-room. She was finishing her lunch, munching away on some toast. I came up behind her, kissed her on the neck.

"Get away," she muttered. "It's bad to interrupt the digestive processes while eating. Dr. Spock said so last April."

"Terry," I said, kneeling down by her chair. "I've got some news."

"Tell me," she said.

I told her.

"A schoolboy!" she bellowed, after I'd said two sentences. "My husband's gonna be a schoolboy?"

"That's right," I went on, laughing. "I just snowed President Atkins. I told him how I'd changed, how much more mature I am and all. He's letting me back into school. Probably as a sophomore. And he said—"

"Did he say how you're gonna support me? I'm your wife, y'know. A wife needs support."

"Don't worry," I told her. "The Government's taking good care of me. I got the G.I. Bill. I got Disability. I got—"

"A hole in the head's what you got," Terry interrupted. "A common, everyday schoolboy. How'm I gonna hold my head up?"

"With your neck," I answered, putting my arms around her, holding her tight. "Now say you're glad."

"I dunno," Terry sighed. "I got no one to blame but myself. That's an awful position to be in."

I looked at my watch. "Come on," I told her. "The Red Cross is calling."

"I ain't going," Terry said.

"You just think you're not going," I answered, picking her up from the chair, carrying her into the foyer. She kicked and hollered but I didn't stop until we were outside.

"Trevitt," she whispered then. "Please. Lemme alone. I don't wanna work for the Red Cross and the Red Cross don't want me working for it. Why not let things be?"

"You'll knock 'em dead," I told her and I took her by the hand and led her downtown. She grumbled all the way, but when we were almost to the office, she quieted.

"Please," she said. "I promise to be good but don't make me go in there. They'll make fun of me and I don't wanna do it. Please. I'll talk nice and I won't swear any more but please don't make me go in there."

"I'm doing you a favor," I answered, pulling at her. "You'll see."

We got to the office. My mother was sitting at a big desk, talking on the phone. She waved. "Take good care of her, Mother," I said, and I kissed her good-by.

When I hit the street I turned toward the college, going as fast as I could, heading for the dorms.

Arriving at Harriet's a few minutes later. I had somebody buzz her room and she buzzed back and I waited at the bottom of the stairs. She appeared. I nodded.

"What is it?" she snapped.

"Let's have a talk."

"Busy," she said, and disappeared.

I had the bell girl buzz again but this time there wasn't any answer. So I put my thumb against the buzzer and pushed, holding it there, whistling away. A couple minutes later she came skipping down the stairs. I smiled at her. She zipped right past me, out the door, without so much as a look.

I banged through the door after her. She was already on the sidewalk heading toward Patriot's Square. I almost caught up to her but then stopped, walking about two paces behind as she hurried along.

"Don't look now," I said, when we were inside the Square. "But I think you're being followed."

She whirled around. "Will you stop it?" she said. "Will you please stop it and leave me alone?"

"Sure thing," I answered, but as soon as she started walking, I did too. "I'm sorry," I said. "I want to stop. My brain says yes, but my feet have a mind of their own."

She whirled again, tears in her eyes, almost yelling at me. "Dammit, Euripides. There's nothing to say. And I'm busy. Now will you please stop it?"

"I've got to talk to you, Harriet," I said.

"You've got a wife now," she answered. "Go talk to her."

At which point I lunged up and grabbed her, lifting her, walking over to a tree, setting her down. "This is my afternoon for picking up girls," I said. She didn't answer. "That's a pun, Harriet. I thought you liked them." I sat down beside her.

She still didn't say anything.

"What's the matter with you, Harriet?"

"What's the matter with you?" she said.

"Me!" And I laughed. "Nothing's the matter with me. I've never been better. You've got to believe that. I'm a new man, Harriet. I'm even going back to school. Only this time, I'm going to knock them dead. You'll see. And right this second, Terry's down working at the Red Cross."

"By her own request, I'm sure."

"No," I said. "As a matter of fact I made her. But it's the best thing for her. And she'll like it, once she gets to know her way around."

Harriet quieted then, relaxing some, taking a twig, holding it gently in her hands, as if it was alive. She stared at it a long time, then finally she put it down and looked at me. "Euripides," she said. "Euripides. Why did you do it?"

"I had to get married, Harriet. I just had to."

"But why to her? Why in the world to her?"

"Terry's a good girl," I said. "You'll like her. She's really a nice girl. Everyone likes Terry when they get to know her."

"Why to her?" Harriet said again. "Why not me? Or somebody else? Anybody else?"

"Don't you understand, Harriet? Don't you? I thought sure you'd be the one to understand. Hell, there's no point in marrying you. You're there, Harriet. There'd be no point. But somebody like Terry. That makes sense. To make it with someone like her. That's something." I took her hands, held them, waiting for her to look at me. "It's going to be something, Harriet," I said then. "Don't you see?"

She broke loose, threw her arms around me, holding me just as tight as she could. "I see, Euripides," she whispered. "I think I do. I think I do." We stayed that way awhile.

Finally, I stood up. "Do me a favor, Harriet," I said then. "Will you give me a tour of the lit magazine?"

"The Athenian?" she asked. "What for?"

I laughed. "Because I'm going to be editor next year. That's what for."

She smiled at me, quickly. "I'm on my way there now," she said. "To see the advisor."

"What's he?" I said, as we started walking.

"He's in charge," Harriet said. "He has the final say-so on everything."

"I guess I better get to know him then."

Harriet stopped, pointing to a little barnlike building, wooden and rotting, across the street. "That's the office," she told me. "And if you think it looks bad from here, wait until you see the inside." We left the Square and approached the building. "Gets worse as you get closer, doesn't it, Euripides?"

I ignored her. "Let me get this straight," I said. "Is the advisor the guy who made you editor this year?"

"Yup."

"Who is it?" I asked, opening the door to the building for her.

"Professor Janes," she told me, stepping inside.

He was there, sitting down, waiting for us.

"Hi," Harriet said, going over to him. I stood in the doorway. She was about to say something more but she stopped and stared at the two of us as we stared at each other. I suppose she guessed it right then. "Why don't you wait outside," she said to me. "Private conference and all that. It won't take long."

"I'll be in the Square," I said, and I left them, closing the door. I walked back across the street and lay down on the grass, my hands behind my head, looking up at that blue sky. I wasn't thinking, not at all, but just lying there, muttering to myself "boy oh boy oh boy oh boy oh boy," with that sky, blue as blue, covering me.

I don't know how long I stayed like that, but some time after, I heard footsteps and then Harriet was prodding me in the ribs.

"Hey, wake up," she said. "No loitering."

I sat up, rubbing my eyes. "Give me a tour now?"

She shook her head. "He wants to see you."

"Why?"

"I don't know," Harriet said. "But inside there, he asked me who you were and I told him, and what you'd told me, about wanting to work on the magazine, and he said he'd like to have a talk with you."

I nodded.

"Shall I wait?"

"This may take a while, Harriet. You better not."

"Euripides," she said, "he knows who you are. Doesn't he?"

"We have mutual friends," I said, and then I waved good-by, crossing the street to *The Athenian*, stopping in the doorway.

He was still sitting in the same chair, his chin balanced on the tips of his long, thin fingers. "Come in," he said, not looking at me.

I closed the door and sat down on the other side of the desk, watching him. He was a handsome guy, Janes. Trim, dark-haired even though he must have been pushing fifty. With a soft, slow way of talking and an easy smile.

I sat there, nervous, my stomach beginning to tense, waiting for him to say something. He didn't, so after a minute or two, I started. "Harriet told me you wanted to see me," I said.

"Yes," he answered quickly, smiling that way too. There were no windows open and the room was full of warm, dead air. I began to perspire.

"My name is Ray Trevitt," I said.

"I knew your father," he told me.

I nodded, waiting for him to continue, staring at him. I suppose it was then I first realized he was nervous too. I went on. "I met Harriet on the way down here and—"

"Charming girl," he interrupted. "Do you know her well?"

"Pretty well," I said. "I went out with her awhile before I—"

"Before you what?" he said, interrupting again.

"Flunked out," I finished. He nodded.

"But I'm back in school now," I told him. "I had a talk today with President Atkins. He okayed it. And—"

"What do you plan to major in, Mr. Trevitt?"

"English," I told him, and he nodded again and asked me why and I told him that too. We went on for a couple of minutes, making chit-chat, hedging around as if we'd never met before, never known anything about each other; as if we were complete strangers. My stomach got worse as we talked, knotting so tight that finally I couldn't stand it any longer.

"Look," I said. "I don't know what you want from me, but I'll tell you what I want from you. I want to be made editor next year."

"Well, Mr. Trevitt," he said. "Perhaps—"

"I want to be editor and I'll work for it," I said. "I just want you to know my hat's in the ring. That's all."

"I was going to say that perhaps you're making a mistake, Mr. Trevitt. A look at your previous record might indicate that what we do here is a bit, shall we say, out of your line. Perhaps some other extracurricular—"

"Please," I said.

"Perhaps some other extracurricular activity would be better suited to your talents, Mr. Trevitt." He was talking louder now, glaring across at me.

"Professor Janes," I said. "I'm going to be editor next year. You might as well know that now." He was about to talk, but I went on. "I'll make it on my own, Professor Janes. So you don't have to worry. Just a fair shake is—"

"Mr. Trevitt," he said, leaning toward me, "there is no chance."

"What's over is over," I said. "The slate's clean as far as I'm concerned. You can relax. You've got nothing to be afraid of. Just relax and give me what I deserve. That's all I want."

"Mr. Trevitt," he said, and both of us were close to yelling, our words shoving their way across through that dead air, "I don't want you working around here. This is my magazine and I don't want you near it. I know what happened in the cemetery, Mr. Trevitt. Does that make it all clear?"

"Sure," I said, standing up. "That makes it all clear! But you listen to me anyway. Because I know what you did to Annabelle and I know why your wife's a dipso, so you don't rank too high on my list either. But just the same, when the time comes, I'm going to deserve to be made editor. You're going to go right in to President Atkins and give him my name. Because I'm going to work my ass off down here. I'm going to work harder than anybody else and when spring comes, you're going to have to make me editor. So you better get used to seeing my face, because I'm going to live here. I'm your boy, Professor Janes, and you better know it now."

"Whatever you wish, Mr. Trevitt," he said, smiling at me. "Whatever you wish."

I ripped the door open and ran.

I tore across Patriot's Square. Then all of a sudden I sagged, making it over to a tree, falling against it, my eyes closed. "Why does it have to be so hard?" I said, right out loud. "Why does everything have to be so hard?"

Finally, I snapped out of it and headed for home, my leg aching and my head, my stomach worse than ever. I walked inside and went to the kitchen, holding my head under the faucet, letting the cold water spray over me. It didn't help much so I climbed up the stairs to lie down and wait for Terry.

But she was there already.

Sprawled on the bed, sniffling, a wet handkerchief in her hands. "Hi, baby," I said. "What are you doing here?" At which she really started to cry. "I guess it didn't go so well for you either, huh, baby?" She managed a nod. I took her in my arms, cradling her, kissing her swollen eyes as soft as I could. "Don't you worry, baby," I told her, lying back, pulling her down against me. "You can cry, but don't you worry."

"Why?" she asked.

"Because, baby," I whispered, squeezing her, holding her tight. "Because we got no place to go but up. . . ."

Which was the way we went—up. From that day on, at least for a while, things got better. But we worked for it.

I was carrying a full load at the college and then some, seeing as I'd talked them into letting me have an extra course to speed things along. So in the morning, I'd get dressed, grab a cup of coffee and then off to the library, my arms practically breaking with books. I took English and history and a lot more, including a goddam geology course that I really hated. I studied at the library, went to classes, then came home and studied some more, reading and remembering, reading and remembering, day after day, week after week. With only *The Athenian* serving to break up the routine.

We had our first meeting at the start of October. Harriet put a notice in the college newspaper that anyone interested in working for the literary magazine should report to the old barn at four the next afternoon. Naturally, I was there.

Arriving early, pulling up short by the door. Because Janes was inside, talking with Harriet. I watched them until Harriet waved to come on in. Janes smiled at her, turned to me.

"Nice seeing you, Mr. Trevitt," he said. Then he left us. I went over and sat down by Harriet's desk, waiting for the others to show.

They came, one by one, straggling in. Maybe twenty-five in all. And an uglier bunch of people I never saw. Mostly girls. Sporting ponytails. And blue jeans and dirty sweaters. All of them smoking away a mile a minute, jabbering on about Proust, who I'll never forget; and what did Yeats mean there; and how about roses in Eliot? There were some boys, too, mostly with horn-rimmed glsses, standing around smirking, as if they'd found the handle but left it outside so as not to get it dirty. Tall, short, thin, fat, they all had one thing in common: pimples. Millions of them. And why some skin doctor didn't set up shop next door, I'll never know.

Anyway, Harriet fiddled at her desk until it got quiet, after which she stood up and gave a little talk. About how this was the office of *The Athenian* and *The Athenian* was the literary magazine of Athens College. And how there were four issues per year, in November, January, April, and June. And how glad she was to see everyone because she could use all the help she could get, and if you've written anything, submit it, please, stories, poems, essays, anything, because we need it. Then she stopped, took our names, and asked if there were any questions. There were a few, scattered here and there, and then this girl raised her hand, a freshman if ever there was one, straight from some progressive school, without a doubt.

"What sort of thing do you publish?" she asked.

Harriet laughed. "It depends on what's submitted."

"Well," the girl went on, "I think we should publish good stuff."

"I agree," Harriet said.

"Well, I've written a story and I think you ought to print it."

"Fine," Harriet said. "If you'll just submit it, we'll be—"

"I spent last summer in Greenwich Village," Good Stuff cut in. "And I wrote a story about two college girls who go to Greenwich Village. They meet there. They come from good families but they find themselves irresistibly attracted to each other. Irresistibly. Lesbians, you might say, except really, they're not. Really, they're both nice girls who are attracted to one another."

"Irresistibly," Harriet said.

"Yes." The girl nodded.

"Do they get married?" I asked.

"They do not," she answered, glaring at me. "They make a suicide pact and—"

"We try to skirt the controversial," Harriet said.

"And what?" I asked.

"I'm not sure," Good Stuff said. "I haven't finished it yet."

"Why not give it a happy ending?" I said. "How about if one of the girls is really a boy, disguised? Then they could live happily ever after."

"Euripides!" Harriet said. She smiled at the others. "Submit whatever you want," she continued. "Anything at all. And have your friends do the same. Are there other questions?"

"Yes," Good Stuff said. "Who's he?" She pointed in my direction.

"He's sort of my court jester," Harriet answered, giggling. "You can ignore most of what he says. He's harmless and if you bring him a lump of sugar, he'll be your friend for life."

"Thanks," I said.

"Well," Good Stuff muttered. "He talks as if he owns the place."

"Not yet," I said.

"You think you're pretty smart, don't you?"

"Sure," I answered. "I'm a regular wizard."

"O.K.," she said. "All right. If you're so smart, who wrote *Biographia Literaria*?"

"You really want to know?" She nodded. I closed my eyes. "Samuel Taylor Coleridge," I began. "1772 to 1834. In 1798 he wrote *Lyrical Ballads* with Wordsworth. But he wasn't much of a poet and don't let anyone tell you he was. He never finished anything, Coleridge, except maybe the 'Ancient Mariner.' He threw in the sponge on poetry and since he loved gassing on, he became a critic. *Biographia Literaria* came out in 1817 and it's a book of criticism. Wordsworth gets the short end of the stick, except not really. Because Coleridge was a good critic and Wordsworth was a good poet and—"

"My God!" Harriet yelled. "Meeting's over. Class dismissed."

They all filed out, mumbling. I sat there, looking across at Harriet. "You feeling all right?" she asked. I nodded. "How did you know all that?"

"How do you think? I read that goddam book. I read most of Coleridge. I can't stand him but—"

"Euripides"—Harriet laughed, coming over and sitting in my lap— "you may be a genius after all."

"Naturally," I said. Then we both started laughing.

I walked home singing, letting the front door bang shut behind me, calling for Terry. She didn't answer, so I went to our room, dropped my books on the desk, and began cleaning up for supper. I was getting undressed when she came in.

"Where were you?" I asked. "I yelled."

"Thinkin'," she answered. "I been thinkin' a lot lately." Which was the truth. Ever since that afternoon at the Red Cross, about ten days before, she'd been spending all her time in the house, moping around, thumbing through old copies of the *Bedside Digest*. "Trevitt," she said then.

"What?"

"Educate me."

"How?"

"Well," she said, "I been thinkin'. And I decided to go back to the Red Cross. You want that?" I nodded. "So, I figured—I figured if maybe you'd help me along a little, I'd do better."

"You do fine now," I said.

She shook her head. "That's a lie and you know it. When those biddies down there get to blabbing, I don't understand what the hell's going on. So I want you to educate me. Maybe give me something to read. A classic. Something I can talk about with the biddies. Make conversation. A real classic's what I want."

Right then my mother called out that dinner was ready, so we went down. We sat around, eating, discussing the problem, Terry listening very close to what we said.

After supper we went back to my room and I gave her a copy of *Hamlet*, then started on my homework. I didn't get very far.

Because Terry began laughing. "Is he kiddin'?" she said.

I turned. "Who?"

"This Shakespeare. Ophelia. Who ever called anybody Ophelia? He must be kiddin'."

"Go on reading," I told her. "It takes a while to get into it."

About two minutes later she called me again. "How come nobody's got a last name in here?"

"What?"

"Nobody's got a last name," Terry said again. "Hamlet who? Didn't people have last names then?"

"Of course they had last names. It was just a convention not to use them."

"Some convention," Terry said.

"Please," I said. "Just read the play."

"I am reading. And I don't understand one word. And why does this Hamlet always talk to himself? Is he nuts?"

"Those are soliloquies," I told her. "It's another convention."

"Somebody ought to write a book on conventions then. So a person could know what's going on."

"Just read the play," I said. "Remember. It's a classic."

Which shut her up. She lay in bed a long time, flipping the pages, giggling a lot, while I sweated away on my Geology. Adrian and my mother were downstairs. Pretty soon I heard him leave, the front door close.

It was right then that Terry slammed the book on the floor.

I turned. "Finish it?"

"I should say not," she answered. "That's trash. I been brought up better than to read trash."

"Terry," I said, "what's the matter?"

She picked up the book, thumbed through it. "What's the matter?" she bellowed. "Listen. Right here. Hamlet's talkin' to Ophelia. And she says: 'I-think-nothin'-my-lord.' And he says—catch this—he says: 'That's-a-fair-thought-to-lie-between-maid's-legs.'"

"So what?"

"It's dirty, that's so what! Dirty talk is all it is. And I asked you for a classic. Smut! Smut! Smut!"

"Terry," I said.

"What is it, children?" my mother asked, standing in the doorway.

"Your son got a dirty mind, Mrs. Trevitt. Listen to what he gave me to read. Right here, Hamlet says: 'That's-a-fair-thought-to-lie-between-maid's-legs.'"

"We mustn't take things too personally, dear," my mother said.

"I ask you," Terry went on, "is that dirty or is that dirty?"

"So what if it is?" I said.

"You hear that, Mrs. Trevitt? He admits it."

"Good night, children," my mother said, and she was gone. Terry banged *Hamlet* down on my desk and walked to the bookcase. I went on with my work.

"Purity of Soul *Is* Attainable," Terry said, suddenly.

I jerked up. "Huh?"

"Purity of Soul *Is* Attainable," she repeated. "By Maxwell P. Carter. August. Last year." And with that she began to read to me. Fortunately, it was a short article, in which Mr. Carter told how he got his soul purified. When she was through reading it, Terry undressed and went to bed. I studied awhile longer, then did the same thing, going right out.

It must have been three in the morning when I felt her shaking me. "Trevitt," she whispered. "You asleep?"

"What is it, baby? Don't you feel well?"

"Trevitt," she went on. "I been thinkin'. About that play. How does it come out?"

"What play?"

"*Hamlet,* for chrisakes. How does it come out? What happens to Ophelia?"

"She dies."

Terry was quiet for a while. "I'm sorry," she said finally.

"We'll send a card in the morning," I said, rolling over.

She shoved me. "How about her old man? Polonius. Does he get all shook up when she dies?"

"Nope," I said. "He dies first."

"How about her brother?"

"Him too. Now, will you let me go to sleep?"

"How does her brother die?"

"Hamlet kills him."

"Is he brought to trial by the king?"

"Hamlet kills the king too."

"You're makin' this up, Trevitt."

"It's the truth," I told her. "So help me."

"I hope that Hamlet got his," Terry said.

"He does. Laertes kills him."

"I thought you said he killed Laertes. Now I know you're lying."

"Terry," I said. "Jesus. They all die. The queen dies too. She poisons herself. Hamlet's buddy is the only one left."

"And I thought you said it was a classic."

"It is a classic. It's the most famous play ever written."

"Then read it to me, Trevitt," Terry said. "Read it to me so I'll understand."

"Maybe some other time."

"Now, Trevitt."

"You're crazy."

She started pushing me out of bed. "Please, Trevitt. Read it to me. Please." She kept on pushing until finally I stood up.

"All right," I said. "O.K. It's my fault anyway. I should have let you stick to the *Digest*."

"Nobody dies in the *Digest*," Terry said.

"Well, they sure do here," I told her, and with that, I began to read. I read her the last three acts of *Hamlet*, playing all the parts as well as I knew how, me sitting at my desk, her in bed, covered up, biting away at her fingernails. At the end, she started to cry.

"It's beautiful," she said. "It's so goddam beautiful I can't stand it." I went over to her. She pulled me close. "Just wait," she whispered. "Wait 'til those biddies start talking today. I'll knock 'em dead. I will, Trevitt. So help me God."

"You're going to be a lady," I said.

"I'll work on it," she promised.

"So will I," I told her.

And we did.

We set ourselves a routine and stuck to it. I studied hard at school and helped out at the magazine, getting the feel. Terry went to the Red Cross every afternoon, and she must have done well, because she got put on a couple committees and even was invited to teas every once in a while.

And at nights we spent most of the time up in my room, both of us reading or horsing around. I put her on a steady diet of the classics and she came through fine. She read Dickens and Thackeray and Jane Austen who she really ate up. She tried some poets too, Dowson and Kipling and Housman, and she didn't mind that either, once she got used to it.

All in all, those months were pretty happy, quiet months without much happening. Except for two things.

Both of which took place in December.

The first was when the Peabodys moved into Zock's old house. They came on a Saturday and my mother went over to pay respects, welcoming them to the neighborhood. Mr. Peabody was a real-estate man, a nice enough guy, from Chicago. His wife was nothing special. They had one kid, a boy sixteen years old, named Andy.

My mother told us all about them after her visit and suggested that it might be nice for us to meet them. So the next morning, while my mother was at church, we walked over. I rang the bell. After a minute, the front door opened. Just a crack.

"Who's out there?" somebody asked.

"I'm Ray Trevitt," I answered. "And this here's my wife, Terry. We're your neighbors, come to pay respects."

"My folks aren't home," the voice behind the door said.

"You're good enough," I said. "Open up."

He did, standing there in the foyer, watching us as we walked in. He was a short kid, Andy, blond and ugly and shy. When we took our coats off, he didn't bother looking at me any more, but only at Terry. He gaped at her, mouth half open. She smiled at him.

"You're Andy," I said. He nodded. "How are things going?" He shrugged, still staring at Terry.

"Whatsamatter?" she asked. "Somethin' on my face?" He blushed, turning away.

"Nice house you got here," I said.

He shrugged again and the three of us stood around, trying to make conversation. He asked us would we like some coffee and when we said yes, it turned out he didn't know how to make it. Terry grabbed the chance and volunteered, dashing to the kitchen, me telling her the way. When she was gone, Andy stuttered a little, before he asked me.

"How did you know where the kitchen was?"

"I spent some time in this house once," I answered. And then: "Would you let me see your room?" He nodded, and I followed him up.

It was Zock's old room he led me to, like I'd figured. I stood in the center of it awhile, thinking about all the hours I'd spent there, all the things that had happened there, both good and bad. I don't know how long I thought, but pretty soon he was tugging at my shirtsleeve.

"Mr. Trevitt," he said. "Are you O.K.?"

I nodded. "This is some room you got here, Andy."

"It's all right," he said. And, very fast, before he'd had time to stop himself: "That really your wife?"

"She sure is," I told him. "Why?"

"No reason," he muttered.

I sat down on the bed, looking at him, feeling paternal as hell. "You go out with girls, Andy?"

"I don't like girls," he said. "They make me sick."

Terry yelled up that coffee was ready.

"Well," I said, "when you change your mind, I've got a few tricks I'll be glad to show you," and, taking one last look at Zock's room, I went downstairs. We chatted some, until Mr. and Mrs. Peabody came home, after which we chatted some more, about nothing in particular. Finally I stood up to go. Andy walked us to the door.

"So long," I said. "See you around."

" 'By, Andy," Terry said.

He nodded and mumbled something.

"Andy thinks you're cute," I said, as we ambled home.

"I am cute," she answered. "He's got good taste."

I turned for another look and he was still there, standing by the front door, staring at us, every step of the way. . . .

The second thing that happened took place on the 25th, which is Christmas, and a big deal under any circumstances. But this one was even more special.

We were down by the tree, sitting in the living-room—my mother, Terry, and I—when the doorbell rang. I answered. It was Andy.

"Merry Christmas," I said. "Come in. Say hello."

"Here," he answered, shoving a package into my hands. Then he turned and ran. I watched him go, tearing across our lawn to his house. I closed the door and went back to the living-room.

"Who was it, Raymond?" my mother asked.

"Andy Peabody," I said, fiddling with the package, tossing it to Terry. She started unwrapping it, muttering to herself.

"How sweet," my mother said. "Terry. I think he has a crush on you."

Terry nodded and opened the package. It was a bracelet he'd given her, silver, with her name engraved on it. She stared at it awhile.

Then she began bawling.

"I'm sorry," she whispered, trying to stop. "But all of a sudden it's like I'm nine years old and the kid next door's proposing."

"How sweet," my mother said again, and there were tears in her eyes too.

"Aw, come on," I said. "It's Christmas. You know. Christmas. Merry. Please, will you both cut it out."

"Raymond." My mother sniffed. "You wouldn't understand. You're a man." She got up and went over to Terry, sitting down beside her.

"It's beautiful," Terry said. "Honest to God, it's so beautiful I could cry."

"You are crying," I told her.

"Hush, Raymond," my mother said. After which they both went to it harder than ever.

It was at that second that Adrian made his entrance, his arms full of packages. "Merry—" he began, then stopped.

"Adrian," I said. "Meet the happiness girls."

"What happened?"

"You wouldn't understand," I told him. "You're a man."

"Leave us alone," my mother managed to say. "Both of you."

Adrian nodded, and we left. The minute we were out of the room, he grabbed me by the arm. "Raymond," he whispered, "it is imperative that I speak to you. Privately." With that he walked up the stairs to my room, me a step behind. I closed the door and turned.

"What's the matter, Adrian?" I asked. "You look green."

"Raymond," he whispered, "I want to propose to your mother."

"Propose what, Adrian?"

"Please," he said. "No jokes."

"I'm sorry," I said. "But don't talk to me. I'm not going to marry you. Go ask her."

"Raymond," he said. "I haven't eaten for two days. Help me."

"You want me to make you a sandwich?"

"I'm forty-seven years of age," Adrian went on. "I've been a bachelor all my life. A man acquires habits in forty-seven years. I feel that to be understandable. After all, if a man did not acquire habits in forty-seven years, it would be most unusual. Consider. I—I—" He stopped.

"Should I ask her for you, Adrian? Would you like that?"

"Marriage," he mused.

"Face it," I said. "You're scared."

He nodded.

"I got just the thing for you, Adrian. Don't move." And I dashed out of the room.

Returning with a bottle of Scotch and a water glass. "Courage," I said, pouring him a stiff one. "Coming right up."

He held the glass of whisky a minute, peered at it, then drank it down. "How do you feel?" I asked, after he'd stopped coughing.

"Horrible," he answered. "Positively horrible."

"It takes time," I said, pouring him another.

He drank the second glass. "You know," he told me, "it's really not so bad, if you don't mind the taste."

"Here," I said. "You'll be a tiger in no time."

"More?"

"More."

Inside of fifteen minutes he was drunk.

Which is also understandable, seeing as he hadn't eaten in so long. He stood there, a silly smile plastered on his face, as if he'd just cornered the market on composure.

"Raymond," he said to me, talking very slow, pausing between each word, "I . . . shall . . . do . . . it."

"Attago, Adrian," I said.

"Yes," he continued. "I shall propose to your mother this very day. I may even get down on my knees. I believe your mother would appreciate such a gesture."

"She'd love it. Why not give it a try?"

"There is plenty of time," he said, pouring himself another drink. "When a man has waited forty-seven years, he—"

"You may not have as much time as you think," I said, and I took the glass from his hand. But when I reached for the bottle, he backed away, holding it about nine feet in the air. Terry came in then, looked at us awhile.

"What's up?" she said.

"The bottle," Adrian answered, after which he began to laugh. "I . . . think . . . that . . . rather . . . funny," he said.

"It's a riot," I told him. "But now's your chance, Adrian."

"By George," he said, "you are absolutely correct." He gave me the bottle, shook my hand. "Raymond. I shall never forget this. I thank you."

"Where you going?" Terry asked.

"To claim your mother-in-law for my wife," he answered, heading toward the door.

"Good luck," Terry said.

"Confidence is all one needs," he told her. "And now good-by." He left the room.

We waited about five minutes before starting down. The first thing we heard was my mother's voice. Loud. And every once in a while, Adrian, going, "But . . . but . . . but . . ."

"Drunk," my mother said as we walked in, pointing at Adrian, who was sitting slumped on the sofa. "And on Christmas Day. Raymond, was this your doing?"

"More or less," I admitted.

"More," Adrian said.

Terry went over and sat down beside him. "Didja proposition her yet?" she whispered.

"She allowed me no opportunity," he whispered back.

"Drunk," my mother said.

"Kate," Terry said. "Adrian here wants to marry you."

"My own son playing jokes on Christmas," my mother went on. "My own son . . ." She stopped, looking at me. Then she looked at Adrian.

He nodded.

Naturally, my mother started to cry.

"I'm going back to bed," I said.

"You got no heart," Terry told me, also crying.

Adrian got down on his knees, which took a while, and my mother walked over to him. Even on his knees, he was about as tall as she was.

"Katherine," he began, "it has come to my attention of late that—" He stopped, sweating. Then he started again. "Katherine. Perhaps it may come as something of a surprise to you to learn that my—" He stopped again. "I am a man of habit, Katherine. But I feel that to be understandable. After all, if a man did not acquire habits in forty-seven years, it would be most unusual. Consider. After all . . ."

"Adrian," my mother whispered. "I will."

"Hallelujah," I shouted and I dashed upstairs for the bottle, grabbing glasses on the return trip. I filled them, handed them out. We raised them high.

"God bless us every one," Terry said.

We drank to it. . . .

Which, in a couple of ways at least, was the high point—that moment when the four of us stood in the living-room, Adrian tight, Terry and my mother sniffling away, me watching them all, happy as hell.

The next day, when Adrian was in better shape, he and my mother made plans. To get married just before spring vacation so they could have a ten-day honeymoon and then spend the time between April and June packing and saying good-by. Because he was returning to England, Adrian was, and my mother with him. Terry went back to the Red Cross, sitting in the office during the day, answering phones, going to meetings, working up. And me.

I hit the books. For final exams were coming lickety-split and I had a lot to do. I spent hours reading away at geology, the worst subject in the world, bar none. I kept at it, though, learning how to spell "Pleistocene," remembering that the Mesozoic was the Age of Reptiles, plus other interesting facts no one should be without.

I studied and I studied and when exams came, I did well, getting a B in geology, better in the rest, making the honor roll, to the wonderment of all. Once exams were over, I really got to work.

At *The Athenian*.

I spent all my time there, morning until late at night, dashing out when I had class, then coming back, taking up where I'd left off the hour before. The first thing I did was to clean that barn of a building. I swept the floors, waxed them, washed windows, cleaned off desks, waxed them, too, filing, dusting, making everything ship-shape.

Once the office was a decent place to live in, I started learning about the magazine. Harriet was great about that, telling me everything she knew, making things as easy for me as she could, the two of us sitting there every night, going over and over details until I understood which end was up.

The April issue was staring us in the face and I don't think I'll ever forget it. Mainly because the two of us put it out alone, Harriet and me. There were some others helping at the start, but soon they dropped off, seeing as whenever there was anything to be done, I ran and did it.

I read stories, poems, essays. I helped Harriet with the layout, making suggestions here and there when something struck me. We planned the heads, read proof, set the type, hustled around getting the cover ready, the engraving done. I sold ads, going from place to place, making a nuisance of myself. Mr. Klein gave me an ad just to get rid of me, and so did the shoe-repair shop and the clothing store Zock's father used to own. I painted posters, held meetings, listened, talked, and listened some more.

I even wrote things for that issue, two of which were accepted. One was a story, about a kid at college who finds out his roommate is really a machine. Which may not sound like much but compared with most of what else was submitted, it was a masterpiece. The other thing accepted was a poem. This was the first line:

Love is the color of my love's eyes.

The rest of the poem I've forgotten, fortunately, seeing as it wasn't much good. But Harriet liked that first line a lot, so she printed it, mainly, I suppose, as a favor to me. We spent February and March together, the two of us, me learning, her teaching, with always the name of Professor Janes hanging in the air overhead, like the sword of Damocles. Sometimes, though, I even forgot about him, because things were going so well down there.

Which could not be said of things at home.

Terry was the first to give me trouble. By pestering, making fun of the magazine as best she could. Then she got sullen, not talking at all, but pouting, muttering to herself, acting like a baby. Finally, late in March, we had our first real squabble.

I got home about two in the morning, having spent the evening reading proof, managing to get a headache. I crept up the stairs, shoes off, so as not to wake anybody. But the light was on in our room and Terry was sitting in bed, reading the *Digest*, wearing a frilly white nightgown, her hair combed, her face scrubbed.

"Hi," I said, starting to undress. "You ought to be asleep." She didn't answer, but went right on reading, ignoring me. I finished undressing, headed for the bathroom, showered the dirt away, came back. She was still reading.

I sniffed. "Something smells awful."

Which got her. "Me," she said, glaring. "And it don't smell awful. It cost a small fortune per ounce."

"O.K.," I said. "Now that you're talking, let's have it."

"I got nothing to say to you," she answered, pushing the *Digest* in front of her face.

I nodded and crawled into bed, closing my eyes, breathing deep.

She smacked me with the *Digest*. "No, you don't," she said. "Wake up."

"Why? You've got nothing to say to me."

"Wake up," she said again. "Right now."

I opened my eyes. "I'm awake. Shoot."

She wrinkled her forehead, trying to think, not able to say anything. I waited. Then she started bawling, something she must have done five hundred times in the months we'd been married.

"Terry," I said, "you know I hate that. Will you please stop?"

"You don't care," she mumbled. "You don't care what happens to me."

"Sure I do," I told her. "Now please stop that crying."

"If you care," she went on, "why do you ignore me?"

"I don't ignore you. I think about you all the time."

"When you're down at that goddam magazine," Terry cried, "I hate that goddam magazine. I hope the goddam thing burns up."

"You're being irrational," I said.

"What does that mean?"

"Silly."

"Silly! Silly, for chrisakes. Here I put on my best nightie and my best perfume and I spend hours combing my hair and what do I get for it? 'Something smells awful.' "

"I'm sorry," I said. "I was just trying to make you talk."

"Sorry! You're sorry. You know what I am? I'm bored. B-o-r-d. Bored to beat hell."

"Go play with Andy Peabody," I said. "He's a nice boy. He gave you a bracelet for Christmas."

"I do," she said. "I see him all the time. He loves me. He writes me poems. He—"

"When do you see him?" I cut in. "When?"

She threw her arms around me then, pressing her body close, kissing me, holding me tight.

I pushed her away. "When do you see him?" I said again.

"Every afternoon," she whispered.

"What about the Red Cross? You work there afternoons."

She shook her head. "I quit. Three weeks ago."

"I don't believe it," I said. "Why didn't somebody tell me?"

"I was afraid you'd be mad, Trevitt. And Kate promised that she—"

"Maybe you'll go back tomorrow," I said.

She pressed close to me again, whispering so soft I could hardly hear. "I hated it, Trevitt. I only went because you wanted. That's the only reason. I always hated it. So I quit."

"You've just got to go back," I told her. "You've got to go back tomorrow."

"I won't."

"Then I don't give a damn what you do," I said and I lay down again, my eyes closed. Tight.

The next day, when I came home from school, my mother was waiting for me in the living-room, Adrian beside her. "Raymond," she called as I went by, "come in here." I did. "Raymond," she said, "we want to have a talk with you." She turned to Adrian.

"Yes," he began. "We feel, Raymond—Katherine and I both feel— and we reached this conclusion separately—we both feel that you are spending altogether too much time at the magazine and . . . neglecting other things. Such as your wife, Raymond, and your mother who, we must remember, is leaving you and going to England before too much longer. And you've been terribly nervous of late and . . ." He chattered away, with me listening politely, nodding when I was supposed to. As soon as he'd finished, I told them I'd think it over, thanked them for their kind attention, and took off.

For the magazine. Harriet was working. I threw my jacket at a chair, missed, swore, picked it up, crumpled it in my hands. Then I heaved it all I had against the wall, yelling, "Goddam it to hell," as loud as I could.

Harriet looked up. "A new poem you're working on?"

I grumbled something.

"You know, Euripides," she said, "come to think of it, I've never seen you looking better. All that weight you've lost and those wonderful shadows under your eyes. You're dreamy."

"Not from you," I said. "Please."

"I just thought you'd like one woman's opinion."

"Frankly, Harriet," I began, "you can take . . ."

"If you swear at me," she cut in, "I don't know what I'll do."

"O.K.," I said. "All right. I'm sorry. But Jesus, Harriet. Why can't they leave you alone?"

She got up then, came around the desk to me. " 'Cause hims is such a cutie pie," she answered. After which we both started laughing. . . .

The magazine was printed on the night of the 10th of April, and a pretty great night it was. At least I thought so at the time, standing there in the basement of the college newspaper, Harriet beside me, the two of us filthy dirty, black with ink. I stared straight ahead, listening to the presses, watching as those sheets of glossy paper came slapping out, clean, printed, done.

Finally, Harriet turned to me. "You did it," she said, laughing. "That's your baby." And she pointed at those presses, shouting over the noise. "All yours, Euripides, and you'd better take care. Because next year you're going to be editor, so you ought to practice feeling like a father."

"You really think so?"

"I know so," she went on, yelling louder, laughing more. "There's no one else Janes can put up. Just you, Euripides. You've made it! It's all over but the shouting! You've won!"

.   .   .

My mother was married on Friday the 14th of April in the college chapel at four o'clock in the afternoon.

By eleven that morning she was in a state of panic. Everything was going wrong. The reception was to be held at our house after the wedding and here it was eleven already and the food hadn't arrived. And what should she do about the way she looked? And she'd tried on her dress and it didn't fit and her girdle hurt and where oh where was that food?

I did what I could to calm her, but she just went on and on, nervous, scared, tears in her eyes, giggling every once in a while when she couldn't think of anything else to do. Terry wasn't much help either. There were tears in her eyes, too, as, muttering to herself, she followed my mother around.

So finally I gave up and went to the kitchen, made a bunch of sandwiches. I carried them out to my mother and Terry and they looked at me as if I'd committed a cardinal sin. I shook my head, returned to the kitchen, and ate alone.

When the caterers did come, my mother really took off, zipping around the house, from living-room to dining-room to kitchen and back again. The punch bowl goes here, the this goes there, the that goes over in the corner. Watching her, I couldn't help laughing.

"Raymond," she said, "there is nothing funny."

"I wouldn't say that, Mother."

"Raymond, please. If you can't help, don't hinder. Do you remember when to give Adrian the ring?"

"Ring?" I said. "Do I have to give Adrian a ring? Why didn't somebody tell me?"

"Trevitt!" Terry said.

"Why don't you two go off and play," my mother suggested. "Do something. Is your suit pressed, Raymond? Have you bathed? Are you clean?"

"Yes, Mother."

She turned to Terry. "Have you shown Raymond your new dress?"

Terry's face lit up like a Christmas tree. "I was saving it for a surprise," she said. "At the wedding."

"Surprise him now," my mother told her. "Please, Terry. Right this minute."

Terry nodded, grabbing me by the arm, leading me upstairs, talking a mile a minute. "Kate bought it for me last week. It's all pink. With lace. Pink and lace all over. With a great big skirt that swirls around. And I got new shoes to go along with it. They match. And a new hat. And—"

"Where is it?" I said, sitting on the bed.

"I can't just show it to you. It's gotta be modeled."

"O.K.," I said. "Model it."

"I gotta clean up first. You can't just model a dress like this. I gotta bathe and clean up." She pushed me flat on the bed. "You wait right here, Trevitt. I'll hurry."

I stretched out, listening to the water running in the bathtub. I closed my eyes and thought about a nap, but two minutes later my mother was calling my name.

"What is it, Mother?"

"Phone," she told me. "As if I didn't have enough to do. Be quick, Raymond. Don't block the line."

I hurried into her room and answered. It was Harriet. "What's new?" I asked.

"I have to see you," she said. "I'm at the office and I have to see you."

"Why? What's wrong?"

"I have to see you," she said again. "I can't tell you now. I have to see you."

"Be right down," I told her and I hung up.

Terry was still in the tub when I started getting dressed, putting on my suit, clean shirt, tying my tie. Finished, I knocked on the bathroom door. "I've got to go out," I said.

I heard her scrambling from the tub and then the door opened. She stood there, dripping, a towel draped around her. "I've got to go out," I said. "I'll meet you at the chapel."

She shook her head. "But I'm going to model my dress. You said that—"

"Harriet has to see me," I cut in. "I'm sorry. I don't know how long it'll take, so we better plan to meet—"

"You said you wanted to see my dress."

"I do," I told her. "But this is important. I'll see the dress at the wedding."

"You promised," Terry said, her voice rising.

"Don't make such a big deal out of it. Please. And don't start bawling."

"Which means more to you, for Christ's sake? Me or that goddam magazine?"

"Don't ever ask," I laughed, grabbing for her.

She stepped away. "Don't go."

I headed for the door.

"Don't go," she said again, following me. "Please. Don't."

"I don't know how you look in that dress," I said. "But you're pretty damn cute in that towel." And waving, I left her.

It was a beautiful day, almost too warm for April, as if summer was getting tired of waiting and had decided to give spring a run for its money. I began perspiring the second I got outside, so I slowed, picking up stones every once in a while, skipping them along the street. The afternoon sun slanted in at me as I walked along, from shadow to light, light to shadow. It must have been twenty minutes before I reached the office, and when I did, Harriet was waiting for me, sitting alone.

"Hi," I said, walking in. "Do I look like a best man?"

"Wonderful," she told me. "You look wonderful." After which she started to cry. I hurried around the desk, taking her gently by the shoulders.

"Hey, Harriet," I whispered. "Stop that. Please, Harriet, cut it out. Ever since Christmas people have been crying at me. The minute I come near them they cry. I'm getting a complex, Harriet, and you wouldn't want that to happen to me. So stop it now. Please. Stop."

And she did, gradually, with much blowing of nose and drying of eyes. I sat across from her, smiling, telling her everything was fine. But all that time I was tensing, knotting up, waiting for her to say it.

"Janes was here earlier," she whispered finally. "And he didn't do it, Euripides. He didn't make you editor."

I nodded.

"I argued with him, Euripides. I did. I tried, but he kept saying you weren't capable, you weren't capable."

"Who got it, Harriet?"

"I did," she answered, very softly. "He said I was the only one that could do the job. I told him I wouldn't. He said if I didn't, he'd only get someone else, because you weren't capable. And then I got to thinking that if I were editor, you could help me, like you've been doing. But I'd let you make the decisions. So it will be the same as if you were editor. There's no difference, Euripides. Just a title is all. Just a name."

"I deserved it," I said. "I worked for it. I deserved it."

"I know you did. God knows. And I'm sorry, but I couldn't tell you on the phone. I had to explain it to you. It's just a title, and it's a lousy magazine anyway, so it doesn't matter."

I didn't answer, but just sat there in that dark, musty office, staring out at all that sunshine, thinking over and over: "I deserved it. I deserved it. I deserved it." Harriet came close, put her arms around me, holding me, rocking.

Right then I stood up, heading for the door. "Where are you going?" Harriet called.

"Terry," I told her, not turning. "Terry. I'm going home."

It didn't take me long, half running, half limping, cursing my leg out loud. It began aching, but I kept on, and when I did get there, the place was a madhouse. I yelled, but nobody answered so I went into the dining-room. A fat Negro lady was spreading silverware on a tablecloth for the buffet.

"Where's Mrs. Trevitt?" I asked her.

She laughed. "Mrs. Trevitt ain't gonna be Mrs. Trevitt long. She's gettin' married."

"The other one," I said. "The young one."

"Who are you?"

"I live here," I said. "I'm looking for my wife."

"She went off with your brother."

"What the hell are you talking about?"

"Little blond boy," she said. "Smaller than you."

I spun around, heading outside, cutting across the lawn, over to Zock's house. I went in. No one was home. I went upstairs. It was then that I heard them.

Voices.

Coming from Zock's room. I threw the door open, felt it smack against the foot of the bed.

"Who's out there?" Terry said.

I didn't answer, but just stared, stared across the room to the desk chair and the pink, lacy dress spread carefully across it.

Then someone left the bed so I turned, tearing down the stairs, tripping, falling the last few feet. But I got right up, not stopping, never once stopping even though from above I could hear my wife calling my name, screaming it as loud as she could.

I hit the street, my leg killing me, still going on, trying to run. I ran until she'd stopped yelling, until I couldn't hear her any more. Then I started to wonder. I'll never know how I found my way to the college chapel. But somehow, I did.

By the time I got there, the wedding was about to begin. Adrian was already at the front, standing very straight. I turned up the aisle toward him. He smiled. I stopped. The music started. My mother appeared at the far end of the aisle. The music got louder, louder, louder still.

And before I knew it, my mother was a wife again. She kissed Adrian. They ran down the aisle together. I stood still. Everyone swooped down on me, told me how lucky I was, and I smiled, said: "Sure am, sure am, thank you." Finally, the crowd thinned, all of them heading back to our house for the reception.

I waited in the church awhile, then walked home. The place was jammed. With faculty and students and a million friends of my mother. I watched them a second through the window, saw them drinking away, heard the laughter and the screaming. I turned, continuing on to the back door, sneaking in as quiet as I could, hurrying up the back stairs to my room. I opened the door, walked inside.

Terry was there.

I closed the door, not saying a word, but instead going to the bathroom, splashing some water on my face.

"I been waitin' for you, Trevitt," Terry said when I came back.

I nodded, listening to the roar from below as it came through the walls, filling the room.

"I'm sorry," Terry said.

"Nothing to be sorry about," I told her.

"I'm sorry," she said again.

"That sure is a nice pink dress," I said. "I guess it looks even better on you than folded over a chair. You folded it nice and neat over that chair. There wasn't a wrinkle."

"Trevitt—" she began.

"Maybe we ought to go into business," I said. "I'll pimp for you. We'll split fifty-fifty. That's fair. And you'll need a pimp. Whores need pimps, don't they? Don't whores need pimps?"

"Sure," Terry whispered. "Please—"

"And we won't work out of any of those Crystal City whorehouses either. We'll do it right here. Mother won't mind. And when we've got enough money, we'll go to New York. And then maybe we'll try Europe. There's a big market in Europe. And we'll buy a house and settle down on the Riviera with servants and cars and all the rest."

"Please," Terry said, starting to cry. "I told you I was sorry. Please. Don't be mad, Trevitt. I'm sorry, honest to—"

"Mad?" I cut in. "I'm not mad. You marry a whore and she turns out to be a whore. What right have you got to be mad?"

"Please," she sobbed. "Please. You got to help me, Trevitt. I'm sorry and you got to help me."

I just shook my head. "Why do you always ask for help when it's too late? Everybody's always asking for help when it's too late." I opened the closet door, took out a bunch of dresses, carried them over, dumped them on the bed. My back was to her when she said it.

"I love you, Trevitt. No crap. I really do."

I got some more dresses, carried them over, stacked them on the first pile. "You know," I said. "You're the first person ever told me that. In all my life. I used to daydream about it, about how it was going to be. I never figured on this." She was crying harder now, gasping, getting close to hysteria. Then she was up, brushing by me, tearing at the clothes in the closet, ripping her dresses off the hangers, throwing them wildly around the room.

"I guess you can pack for yourself," I said. She stopped, trying to look at me. "Don't forget anything," I told her, pointing to the bookcase.

"To hell with the *Bedside Digest!*" she screamed.

I closed the door and went downstairs.

The noise was terrible. The house was crammed with noise, drunken laughing, loud talk, and I waited a minute before I could force my way through it. People came up to congratulate me. Old women kissed me. Men shook my hand. I tried losing myself in the living-room, but Mrs. Janes, who was "much better now," got roaring and started a Charleston demonstration. I couldn't watch, so I began edging out and as I did, I saw her husband. He saw me too. We both smiled, nodding to each other.

Then my mother cornered me, asking questions, where was Terry, where was Terry, what happened to Terry? I tore loose and headed for the bar.

Swallowing drink after drink, throat open, pouring them down as fast as I could. It all got hazy very quick and I needed a chair for support, but I kept drinking. Then my mother was on me again, Adrian beside her, asking me questions, again and again. The noise was worse than ever and I started shaking as if I had a fever, that noise pushing at me, knotting me so I couldn't breathe. I felt myself going and I knew if I stayed in that house one minute more I'd split wide open.

Getting to my feet I headed for the door, bumping into people, into chairs, into walls, but I kept on going until I was outside. The air was cooler and it hit me hard so that I fell once or twice before I got my bearings. Finally I began walking, walking just as fast as I could, walking out there, to the cemetery, to where Zock was.

I never made it. Not that night. Patriot's Square was too big and I fell on the grass in the middle, helpless.

The sun woke me. I don't think I ever felt worse, but I got up all the same and, stumbling, lunging forward as best I could, I started again.

"I'm coming," I said out loud, over and over. "I'm coming, Zock. I'm coming. Wait for me."

By that time I was pretty cut up from falling every few feet, and my clothes were in shreds. But it didn't matter. I just kept going, falling, getting up again, making my way.

And then I was there, lying on the ground, just a little bit away from "Zachary Crowe, 1934–1954. R.I.P." I crawled those few feet, clawed the ground with my fingers, stretching out on top of his grave and, for the first time, I think, since the death of Baxter, I cried.

"I made it, Zock," I said. "I told you I was coming, and here I am. Just like I said. Just like I told you." I pulled myself over to the tombstone and grabbed at it, holding it tight, crying, squeezing it against my own body.

"Zock, I'm cracking. Help me. Help me for Christ's sake. I can't find the handle, Zock. Tell me what to do. Tell me now because I'm cracking. I can't go on much longer so for God's sake, help me. Please. In the name of sweet Jesus, Zock, help me. Help me now because I'm cracking and I don't know what to do."

I clung to that stone for a long time, sobbing, trying to talk, hunched against his tombstone, holding it tight until finally I passed out again.

The sun was high when I woke. I don't remember getting home, but when I did, they were waiting for me, my mother and Adrian Baugh. I said I was sorry and went up to wash. When I came down, I felt better.

"What are you doing here?" I asked, starting it off. "Don't you know you're supposed to be on your honeymoon?"

"What happened?" my mother said.

I laughed. "I guess I got drunk. Too much champagne. I'm sorry."

"Raymond," Adrian asked, "where is Terry?"

"She had to go home," I answered. "In a hurry. Her father's sick. She didn't want to worry you so she just slipped out. She didn't want to spoil your honeymoon, and neither do I, and if you're going to have one, you'd better get moving."

"I don't know," my mother said.

I went up, threw my arms around her. "I do, Mother," I said. "So take it from me. Get going. I'll hold the fort." She and Adrian looked at each other. I laughed, grabbed their luggage, carried it out to the car. Finally, they followed.

"Raymond," my mother said, "are you sure you're all right?"

"Never better," I told her. Then I opened the car door. She waited. I bowed low, laughing, smiling away. That did it. She got in one side, Adrian the other.

"Happy honeymoon," I said, waving.

My mother waved back. Adrian tooted the horn twice. Then they were gone.

I went back inside the house and up to my room. I took off my clothes and showered, letting the water splash over me, scrubbing my body as hard as I could. My knee was swelling some and it hurt, but I scrubbed it too. I stayed in the shower a long time, the water stinging me, my leg aching. Then I dried off, left the bathroom, and flopped down in bed, closing my eyes.

But I couldn't sleep. I was so tired I ached all over, but I couldn't sleep. I just lay there in bed, listening to the house. There wasn't a sound. No noise. Nothing. I tossed and turned and swore and flicked the radio on and off, always listening for some sound.

I got up and walked to the kitchen, opening the icebox. I wasn't hungry. I went back upstairs and lay down again, closing my eyes as tight as I could, the pillow over my head, my hands grabbing at the mattress.

I don't know when I figured out what to do, but it was late afternoon before I got to Crystal City.

I rang the bell to her old apartment, waited a minute until I heard footsteps. The door opened.

"I'm looking for Terry Clark," I said to the woman in the doorway. "She used to live here."

"She got married," the woman said.

"I know that. But is she here now?"

"She got married last fall. She hasn't been back since."

"Is she here now?"

"I just told you she hasn't been here since last fall."

"She didn't come back last night? You sure she isn't here now?"

The door closed. I turned, hurrying toward the center of town, going into the dress shop on the corner. "I'm looking for Terry Clark," I said. "She used to live in Crystal City."

But she wasn't there. And they hadn't heard of her. So I went next door to the grocery. But she wasn't there. After the grocery was a shoe shop. She wasn't there. I kept on, walking down the street, going into every store. I crossed the street, worked my way up. She wasn't there. Then I started on the bars. I went to every bar in Crystal City. But she wasn't there. Nobody had heard of her. Nobody had seen her. I kept going, asking the same questions, getting the same answers.

By then it was dusk. Neon lights began flickering. Red and Green. Blue and Red. Red and Blue. I stood in the center of town, turning around and around, reading all the signs, shivering, turning around, pulling up my collar, cold and shivering from the wind, standing there, turning around. EAT. Bar. Dance. Drugs. EAT. Eat. Dance. Drugs. Eat. DANCE. Dance. Dance. BAR. BAR. BAR.

Finally, I started looking in the whorehouses.

The first was on the edge of town. Music was playing on a radio somewhere upstairs. I stood there, shivering still, listening to the music, sweet and soft, drifting down to me. I waited and waited and then a tall, thin woman came downstairs, a shawl across her shoulders.

I want to see Terry Clark.

She don't work here no more.

The stars were out. Billions of stars. I counted them as I walked along. Ninety-five. Shivering. Five hundred. The wind got stronger. A million. I leaned over the curb, tried to throw up. Two million. Ten.

I'm looking for Terry Clark.

Never heard of her.

Why was the wind so strong? I couldn't figure it out. Where did it all come from? Where does the wind come from? Why doesn't it blow the stars away? Twenty million. Twenty billion. How many stars could there be? A trillion. Two trillion. Ten.

Is Terry Clark here?

Nobody here by that name.

Why weren't the madams fat? Madams were supposed to be fat. Why were they thin? I went to the curb again, put my finger down my throat. I couldn't throw up. I hadn't eaten. That was why. You can't throw up when you haven't eaten. Anybody knows that. I waited downstairs for the madam to show. This one was quiet. No music. That was wrong. There ought to be music in a whorehouse. I kept listening for it, but it wasn't there. I waited for the madam, but she didn't show. Then I heard footsteps. I looked up.

Felix Brown was coming down the stairs.

His arm around a colored whore. I stared at him. He was wearing an Army uniform. Sergeant First Class. A bunch of combat ribbons on his chest. And he was bigger than before. Not taller, but bigger, heavier, thicker. I shouted to him. "Fee! Hey, Fee!"

He stopped, looking down. Then he said something to the whore and left her. I ran up to him.

"Fee!" I yelled again.

"Hello, Trevitt," he said.

"Fee. What are you doing around here?"

"I came home to see Pa," he answered.

"What are you doing in that uniform? Whose is it? And those ribbons?"

"Mine," he answered. That was all.

"How'd you get to be an SFC in two years? Tell me. How'd you do it?"

"I enlisted five years ago," he said. "I'm a career man."

"You're kidding," I said. "You can't be serious. You've got to be kidding. You're getting out soon. Sure you are. What are you going to be?"

"I think I'll be a nigger," he said, starting to move away.

"I like your answer," I said, grabbing him by the arm. "Now quit the kidding. This is me. Euripides."

"I know that."

"Well then, quit the kidding around."

"I'm late," he said. "I've got to go."

"Invite me. I'll come with you."

"No," he answered and he walked away. I followed him outside.

"Fee," I said, grabbing him again. "What's the matter with you? I tell you it's me you're talking to. Remember? 'Pale amber sunlight falls across the reddening October trees.' Remember?"

"I already forgot that," he said. "Why don't you try." He pulled free. "So long, Trevitt." He started off.

"So long," I said. And then I let go. "So long, nigger!"

He stopped, turning to face me.

"Well, isn't that right? Aren't you a nigger? A big, buck nigger. Isn't that what they call you? You don't meet a big buck nigger every night. It's something special when you meet a real live buck nigger."

"Shut up, Trevitt," he said.

"Sure, nigger. I'll shut up. I won't say one more word. But you might have had the nigger courtesy to ask about Zock. You might like to know he's dead. He's dead, nigger. Aren't you glad to know? He's as dead as you'll be someday, but you didn't even have the nigger courtesy to ask. Or don't niggers have any courtesy? Maybe they only have thick skulls. How thick is your skull, nigger? One inch? Two inches? How about that, nigger? How thick is your skull?"

He walked away from me but I stood right there, yelling: "Hey, nigger! Hey, nigger! Hey!" until he was gone.

Then I started to run. I ran by the whorehouses and I ran by the stores and the shops and the bars in Crystal City. I ran along the road that led to Athens. I ran past the bushes and the trees and the lanes and the big highway leading to Chicago. I ran past the college and Patriot's Square. I ran until I saw my bed in front of me and then I lay down, staring up at the cracks in the ceiling or out the window at the sunrise.

I tried not to think, but the house was too quiet. I wanted to talk to somebody. I wanted to talk to somebody but I didn't know who. That was a lie. I knew. It was only a matter of admitting it.

So, finally, Sunday afternoon, I went to church.

I'm not even sure which one it was, but that doesn't matter. I rang the front doorbell of the rectory until the minister came.

Whose name was Holloway. He was very young, no more than thirty, short, and red-faced. I barged in and told him I wanted to have a chat. He nodded and he took me into the church to his office, a small room in the back, lined with books. He sat at his desk while I pulled up a chair.

"I don't think we've met before," he said, smiling.

"No, sir," I told him. "I've never been here. But my name is Trevitt."

"Fine, Trevitt," he said. "Now. What can I do for you?"

"I don't know. I thought we might have a talk, is all."

"Fine," he said again. "About anything special? Or what?"

I was trying to get hold of myself. My stomach was knotted and I hit it some, hoping he wouldn't see.

"Just relax, Trevitt. We've got all day. So relax."

I kept on hitting my stomach, harder and harder, concentrating on the books, trying to read the titles, which was easy, for they stood out plain as day. He didn't say a word and neither did I, but we both sat there, him watching me, me staring at the titles of those books.

"They stand out plain as day," I said.

"What?"

"The books." I pointed. "I can read the titles clear over here. They stand out plain as day."

"Yes," he said, and we were quiet again. "Perhaps I ought to leave you for a while, Trevitt. Perhaps you might use the time to think."

"No," I told him. "I don't need any time to think."

"Yes," he said.

I looked at him. "I killed my best friend," I said.

"How did it happen?"

"On Half Day Bridge."

"Why don't you start from the beginning, Trevitt?"

"I killed Zock," I said, louder. "Can't you understand that?"

"Just relax," he said, leaning forward. "Take it easy."

"Preacher," I said, "I can't find the handle."

He tried smiling at me. "Yes, Trevitt."

"What do you think of the temple of gold?"

"I don't quite know," he said.

"I asked you a question. What do you think of the temple of gold? Explain that. You're the preacher. So explain it. Tell me!" He started to say something but I stood up, grabbing him by the shoulders, shaking him. "I came for some answers," I said. "I'm twenty-one years old and I can't find the handle." And by then I was shouting, standing over him, pulling at his shirt, staring at his eyes. "And don't try telling me about God. That's all you know about is God. You and your goddamned God! I came for some answers, so just tell me about the temple of gold. That's all I want! Just tell me about the temple of gold and I'll be happy!"

He jerked free. "Sit down, Trevitt."

I sat down.

"And stay there."

I did. I stayed there while he picked up the telephone. I stayed there while he called the hospital. I stayed there, waiting, not looking at anything but those gold books in those nice clean rows on the shelves with the titles shining out plain as day. I stayed there while they came in, two of them, and talked to him. I stayed there while he told them. I stayed there until one of them said for me to come along. I got up. I followed them out, obediently, like a dog, followed them out of the office, on through the church to the street, into the ambulance.

It was only then, on the way to the hospital, that I started to cry. . . .

VIII . . . . The End

The room was rectangular. It was on the first floor and everything in it was rectangular, clean, and neat. On my left was a gray rectangular wall, a rectangular bureau set exactly in the center. In front of me was another wall, with two rectangular doors, a closet, and a washstand. On my right was a big window, divided in eight.

The sun poured through that window, past me, striking the mirror, rebounding, brightening the room. In the mirror you could see trees spreading green shadow on the ground. You could see green hedges, paper smooth, and beyond them, the rising, rounded tops of the buildings of Athens College. You could even see the edge of the sky, sliding down, gently touching the edge of Lake Michigan, so close together in color you couldn't tell where one stopped and the other began; lake and sky were joined at the end of my mirror. . . .

There wasn't much to the first day. I slept. That was about all. I slept and I don't know if they gave me anything or not, it didn't matter. I slept twenty hours through with the only interruptions being the nurses, tiptoeing in, bringing food, and a doctor who examined me, talking to me in a soft voice, telling me not to worry, telling me to sleep. And I did. Except that even after twenty hours, I was still tired.

Reverend Holloway visited me the second morning. He knocked and came in, stopping at the foot of my bed.

"I'm sorry," I said to him.

He nodded, smiling. "We tried reaching your mother," he said. "We couldn't get in touch with her so—"

"They're just driving around," I told him. "They'll be back soon enough."

"So I thought perhaps you might like to talk to me."

I shook my head.

"How do you feel, Trevitt?"

"Fine," I said.

He nodded again, clearing his throat. Then he started talking about God, telling me that he was always at the church, whenever I wanted him. I shut my ears, smiled back, thanked him when he left. Which he did, finally, and I was alone again.

But not for long. Because Miss Dietrich came bustling in soon after. Miss Dietrich was the college psychiatrist and a harpie, if ever there was one. Short, gray-haired, and pudgy, she got to me right off, smirking at me as if she was God and asking: "How do you feel?" When most people ask that, they mean it: "How do you feel?" Not Miss Dietrich. What she meant was; "Are you nuts or not?"

"I feel fine," I told her.

"Now Mr. Trevitt," she began, "I don't imagine that to be quite accurate. After all, if you felt fine, we wouldn't be chatting, would we? So why don't we amend that to say 'I feel better'?"

"I feel better," I told her.

"Better than what, Mr. Trevitt? Better than when?"

"It was your idea," I said. "You tell me."

And that was the way it went, her asking questions, me answering, her correcting, me agreeing. She left after an hour or so, promising to come back tomorrow, and the minute she was gone I closed my eyes and slept. I woke up for supper, ate a little, then got ready to sleep again.

I was lying in bed, eyes closed, when suddenly there was a rapping at my window. I opened my eyes and there was Harriet, standing outside, gesturing to me. I nodded, so she opened the window, started climbing in, grumbling away all the time. After she'd made it, she took a deep breath, walked over and put her face down next to mine, our noses almost touching, both of us cross-eyed.

"I'm disappointed," Harriet muttered. "You don't look crazy at all."

I pointed to the window.

"Crazy people can't have visitors," she answered, shaking her head. "I consider the whole thing sheer fraud. Here I walk all the way from my dorm, risk life and limb, and you don't look any different."

"I'm sorry," I said.

"Do you feel funny when the moon is full, Euripides? You know, strange? Flesh creep or anything?" I tried smiling. She sat on the end of my bed, bouncing up and down. After a while she stopped and looked at me. "What happened, Euripides?" she said then. "Whatever happened?"

I told her. Starting from when I left the magazine, hurrying home. What I'd seen in Zock's room, the marriage, the reception, the blow-off, coming home the next morning, the trip out to Crystal City to find Terry, the . . .

"Why did you do that?" Harriet cut in.

"What?"

"Why did you go to Crystal City?" I shrugged. "Did you want her back?" I shook my head. "Then, why?"

"What do you care?"

"I'm a girl and you're a boy," Harriet said. "We have mutual interests. Why did you go there?"

I thought a long time. "I don't know," I said finally. "I don't know."

"O.K.," Harriet said. "Now that you've cleared that up, go on."

I did. And when I had finished she looked at me, smiling, shaking her head and smiling. "How do you feel now, Euripides?" she said.

"Tired," I answered. "Honest to God, Harriet. I've never felt so tired in my life . . ."

I stayed in the hospital a week, "under observation," and except for my daily visits with Miss Dietrich, I didn't mind. It was quiet. I slept a lot and the food was good so I have no complaint.

Then, the eighth day, my mother and Adrian were standing in the doorway, holding hands, staring at me across that rectangular room.

"The newlyweds," I said, laughing.

My mother ran to me, throwing herself on the bed, holding me. Adrian looked very serious. "Raymond, old chap," he said, "how do you feel?"

"Miss Dietrich says I got a fifty-fifty chance of making it, Adrian. But the odds will go against me if the fits come back," and I jerked my head, squinting. "I sure hope they don't. I haven't had one now since yesterday. Those fits are no fun, Adrian, let me tell you."

"Katherine," Adrian said, coming over, resting his hands on her shoulders, "you can stop worrying. He's all right."

And in his own way, he turned out to be a prophet, Adrian. Because two afternoons later, I went home.

A wet April afternoon, complete with thunder and pouring down rain. My mother drove slowly, peering ahead, turning here, there, here again. Then we were in the driveway. She led me up to my room. My bed was ready, clean sheets and all, a mountain of white pillows piled at the head. I lay down. My mother started talking, but pretty soon she realized I didn't much want to. She asked me if I minded her going downtown for a little. I said I didn't. She kissed me on the forehead and left the house.

I lay quiet in bed, propped up by all those pillows. It wasn't comfortable. I took some of them out. It didn't help. The rain was coming down worse than ever, that thunder tearing up the sky. The room was hot and stuffy. I tossed and turned awhile longer, watching the rain die against my window. Then I threw the covers off and went downstairs.

To my father's study. I closed the door and right away that leather smell hit me and I swear his tobacco was around too, some place. I walked to the bookcase, glancing at the titles; Sophocles and Homer, Catullus, Theocritus, Pliny the Elder. The air was so thick and heavy I started to sweat.

I sat down at his desk, in his chair, my head in my hands, my eyes closed, listening to the rain. I stayed like that a long time never looking up, not even when the thunder seemed right on top of me, not even when the study door opened and someone came in.

"I've been waiting for you to get home."

Then I looked up. Andy Peabody was standing in the doorway, staring at me.

I nodded to him.

"I've been waiting for you to get home," he said again, kicking the door shut, never once taking his eyes away.

"Some other time," I said.

"I got a letter from your wife," he said. "Don't you want to see it?" He tossed me an envelope. I opened it. There was nothing inside. Suddenly he was laughing, high-pitched, the sound filling the room. "I burned it," he said. "I burned it before you could see it. You'll never see it now."

"Come on," I said. "I'm tired, Andy. Go home."

"Don't you want to know what was in it?"

I didn't answer.

His body shook as he came closer to me, staring. "She said she was sorry. How do you like that? She said she was sorry and she's gonna divorce you and she's never coming back. She's sorry and she's never coming back here again."

I didn't say anything and neither did he. We waited there in that stuffy room, me sitting, him standing across, breathing deeper and deeper, his body shaking more, about to explode.

Then he was crying, the tears flooding down his face. He turned. "I hope you die," he said. "I hope you both die."

I stood up and he wheeled around, not able to see, but still staring, screaming at the top of his voice.

"I screwed your wife!"

I came closer to him, tensing, listening to him as he screamed, "Whore!" at me. I didn't say anything. "Whore!" I didn't answer. "Whore!" My stomach was aching and it was hard to breathe, but I kept on, coming closer to him. "Whore!"

Closer.

"Whore!"

Closer.

"WHORE!!!"

I hit him.

All I had, the back of my hand against his cheek, my knuckles against the bone. He coughed, gasped, his body stiff. I hit him again and he sagged, suddenly limp, falling against me, sobbing.

"I'm sorry," I said, and when I did he tried getting away. I held him with all the strength I had left, held him until he quit struggling and just lay there in my arms, pushing his head against my chest, burying it.

"I'm sorry about what happened, Andy! I honest to God am! I'm sorry about what happened and I'm sorry you had to be there, but that still doesn't give you the right to go around calling her names. Not today or ever. Just because she did something you don't like doesn't give you the right to go around calling her names. Because everybody's going to do something you don't like sooner or later. Do you hear me, Andy? Do you hear what I'm saying? Everybody's going to screw up on you sooner or later. Everybody screws up. Everybody fails. Everybody fails everybody. Just like God. God failed. God failed on His own son in the Garden of Gethsemane. God failed His own son in the Garden of . . ."

And I stopped.

I led him over to my father's chair. I walked to the door. He was still sobbing when I called to him. "Stay as long as you want, you poor bastard. You got a right to cry."

I closed the door and stood a second in the hallway, stretching. Then I went up to my room. I walked in. There was a face looking at me in the mirror. I stared back at it, watched it as it started to smile, said one word to me.

"Indeed."

That's about all.

My mother and Adrian left for England on the 14th of June, two months to the day after they were married. And how my mother lived through those months, I'll never know, she was that busy. She put the house up for sale, held an auction on the furniture she didn't want, shipped the rest off to England. She attended to all her club work, getting things in decent order for whatever poor soul was going to take over after she'd gone. She went to a million parties, was constantly in tears. With Adrian always one step behind her, running, trying to keep up.

I took it easy. There wasn't much for me to do. Except wait. I spent most of my time in the back yard, throwing stones at the trees in the ravine, or just lying flat, sopping up sunshine. Harriet came over a lot, and we said good-by on the 8th of June, when she went home.

I walked her to her dorm. Neither of us said anything, but stood around instead, scuffing our shoes. Which got so ridiculous that finally she gave a giggle, kissed me, and dashed inside. I turned, heading for the sidewalk. She called to me before I got there, from the parlor window.

"I live in Rhode Island," she called. "And my name is Harriet."

"Raymond Euripides Trevitt," I called back, bowing. "And the pleasure is mine."

On the morning of the 14th we got set to go. It was a beautiful day, warm and clear, with just a couple of clouds speckled here and there, to break up the monotony. By ten o'clock we were ready, luggage in the car. But we didn't leave.

Because Mrs. Atkins appeared at the end of the block, coming toward us, followed by about twenty-five other women, all of them calling, "Bon voyage, bon voyage, bon voyage," over and over. My mother took one look and started bawling. The closer they came, the worse she got. Then they had us surrounded and began kissing my mother, giving her presents, hugging Adrian, smiling at me.

I dashed back into the house, stopping a second in the foyer, still able to hear that "Bon voyage, bon voyage." I went up the stairs to my room, looked around, went into my mother's room, did the same. I looked at every room upstairs and when I was through I went down and began with the kitchen. Just a quick glance and then to the dining-room. Then the living-room.

Finally I got to my father's study. Like all the others, it was empty. The books were gone, the desk, everything. But you still could smell that leather in the air. I closed the door and headed outside.

I managed to get my mother into the car. Adrian followed. I sat behind the wheel, backed out of the driveway, those twenty-five women standing in front of us, waving.

The drive to the airport was horrible. My mother cried and cried, sniffling away in the back seat, Adrian doing what he could to comfort her—not much. I drove as fast as I could, and when we got there we waited, stuttering, trying hard to grab onto some conversation. Finally their plane was announced.

I shook hands with Adrian. "Good-by, old chap," I said, which stopped him, seeing as he was about to say the same thing.

"Raymond." My mother wept, throwing her arms around me. "I'm going away."

"Not unless you get a move on, Mother."

"Raymond," she said. "Are you sure you're all right?"

"It's a hell of a time to be asking." I laughed, leading them toward the plane. They handed in their tickets and I followed to the steps. We looked at each other.

"I just knew you two would be pals," I said. "I just—"

"Good-by, Raymond," my mother interrupted. "Be a good boy."

I nodded, watching as they got on the plane, sitting by a window, looking out. They waved and I waved and they waved and my mother cried and we kept at it until the plane motored down the runway. Then I got in the car, heading North.

It was mid-afternoon when I reached the cemetery.

When I had parked, I tucked in my shirt and looked around. There were a lot of other people wandering aimlessly, walking among the graves. Way off on the right a funeral was ending, twenty or thirty people dressed in black.

I stepped onto the grass over him, bending down, kneeling, my eyes closed. "Zock," I said. "I've come to say good-by. I'm leaving Athens, Zock, for good. I'm taking off and don't ask me where, because I don't know. But there's a lot of places I haven't been, and I've been here." The sun was beating down on me as I knelt there, sweating, my collar wet against my neck. I opened my eyes, looked around at the cemetery again, up at the sky, then back to him. "And if that sounds like I haven't found the handle, Zock, it ought to. Because I haven't. But I don't feel bad about it. Because you were wrong, Zock. There isn't any handle, any temple of gold. You were wrong and I'm sorry if I failed you, but maybe it's a good thing you're dead, Zock. I don't know. But you can't keep expecting me to go on looking for something that isn't there. I got my own life to lead and God knows where it's going, but I have to follow along to see. And I'm sorry to be crying, Zock, and I don't know why I am, because I really feel good and you got to believe that." I stood up. "So long, Zocker," I said. "Maybe I'll see you sometime."

I left him there.

Afterword

WARNING: READ AT YOUR OWN PERIL

When I sat down, June 24, 1956, to be totally precise about it, to write what turned out to be this book, I was as lost as any Cortés. But I knew I had to write something, so I did.

What follows is that something.

It is the original first chapter of my novel. When I submitted the book to Knopf, rewrote and doubled it in length (it originally ended a few pages after the chapter called The Army), and they accepted it, the first thing the editor did was cut the first chapter. Totally. The book you hold now starts with what was then chapter two.

One thing you must know about me: I don't read what I've written. A slight exaggeration but only that. I never read what I'm writing while I'm putting it down, and I only read it through one time afterward, just before I meet with the editor if it's a book, the director if a flick.

So I have never read the original opening since I wrote it. Never will. So if there are typos in what follows, blame my editor, Peter Gethers.

If you hate the chapter, blame me.

One

MYSELF

First a few facts:

Name	:	Raymond E. (for Euripides) Trevitt
Age	:	21 years of age
Height	:	Five feet, nine inches tall
Weight	:	165 pounds
Scars	:	One. Along my right cheek from an accident I had.
Occupation	:	I don't work.
Place of birth	:	Athens, Illinois
Education	:	Athens Grammar School (graduated)
		Athens High School (graduated)
		Athens College (didn't graduate)

No. That's enough. I have a whole list of things I could put down, but there's no point in it I can see. I think you could put down a bookful of facts about yourself, all neat and correct and in order, and the whole thing together with a dime might get you a cup of coffee.

Because a simple fact in black and white doesn't tell a thing. Like the scar on my face. It's there all right, but that doesn't tell you what you want it to. Such as what it means. That scar means something to me, and every time I look at myself in the mirror I see it. And I remember. To live with something every day like my scar and to remember how you got it— that's important. It tells something. About me. So it's not the scar alone that counts; not the fact that it's there. But why it's there.

Now we all know that Medea killed her kids, which doesn't deserve a gold star in anybody's book, but still, you can't go around saying, "Why, that no-good Medea, killing her kids like that. She ought to be put away." Extenuating circumstances. In every single thing that happens, there's extenuating circumstances. And you've got to understand what they are and why they are, along with all the rest. Then, after you understand, if you still want to go around saying, "Why, that no-good Medea, killing her kids like that. etc. etc. etc," then it's O.K. But the understanding has to come first.

And you have to start at the beginning. That's why it's there. To start from. For example, just from the facts I put down, you might say that I'm a bum. Look. "There he is, twenty-one years of age and not working. He's a bum." Well, such may be the case and such may not, but you must be sure you know whereof before you speak. I could tell right now how I got the scar, point-blank. But it wouldn't be right, because that scar didn't come until later, and a lot of things led up to it. And you've got to know those things, at least the important ones, before you can understand why I'm twenty-one years of age and have no occupation, and why I never graduated from college.

But even that is not as easy as it sounds. Because I'm not sure what's important and what isn't. Not really. For example, my killing the guppies. When I put that down I want to say—There! Remember that! It explains something—but I can't tell you what. I feel it. Or these words: "So seize the moment." They are the first words of the first poem ever written by my friend Zock, who is now dead. Because of me. I killed him. Or what Felix Brown said to me that hot day down south; or what happened in the bedroom with Helen Twilly. There are lots of things, many more, that I feel are important, but can't say why.

Which is the main trouble with writing in the first place. You can never say what you mean to say. Not really. Sometimes you come close. And I suppose that coming close is all anyone has ever any right to expect. To want more would be *hubris*. Which, by the way, is a Greek word that you can't translate into English except by saying that it sort of means pride. Wanting too much. It's the reason Oedipus got into all that trouble, and why Antigone got hers. They wanted too much. *Hubris*. That's why.

All of which is just my way of saying that in my opinion, you can't get much across to anybody at anytime. Communication is in the same class with the elixir of life and the philosopher's stone. It just isn't. You can't explain yourself to anybody. Never in this world. Or why you do something. Or what makes you tick. You can't ever point to something that happened to you and say—There! That's me. Right in there. See? Now do you understand?—Because nobody's going to.

But if there's one thing that nobody can accuse me of, it's consistency. Because just to round things off, I'm going to point to something that happened. And I'm putting it here because I think it's typical. Of me. I'm in it. Somewhere.

It took place on a Sunday afternoon in Kentucky when I was in the middle of my basic training. Kelly was the other kid involved. Actually, he was the only one really involved, as I was just a spectator. But on his invitation. I was there.

I was lying on my sack that afternoon, sweating like a pig because it was so hot, over 100. I was all alone there that afternoon, with my thoughts, mostly of Zock. I was lying naked with my eyes closed, staring up and seeing his ugly face, when I heard somebody coming up the stairs. I don't think a free ticket to the second coming could have roused me then, and I didn't move until the footsteps came close, stopping at the foot of my bed.

"Trevitt," somebody said. I snuck one eye open and saw Kelly standing there in his underwear shorts, the flab of his belly hanging over. Kelly was a big blonde kid, our platoon leader, only not because of anything he could do, but rather on account of his father, who was a colonel and a West Pointer and a hell of a great guy. I knew all that and so did everyone else, since Kelly told us about him every chance he had. His old man won the Silver Star on D day, and I think every man in the company with half a mind, about ten of us, could quote the citation by heart.

I closed my eye and tried a few snores, which wasn't too clever, but it threw him for a while. Finally, he said my name again, and then a third time, and then he shook me.

"Trevitt," he said. "Are you asleep?" Which should show how bright he was.

"Who wants to know?"

"Me. Kelly."

"Don't know you," I said. "Anyway, I'm not Trevitt. Trevitt's gone AWOL. I'm covering for him."

"C'mon," he said, all excited. "Quit kidding around." He shook me again. Harder.

I opened my eyes and looked at him. "I could have sworn I was trying to get some sleep," I said. "I guess I must have been mistaken." He didn't say anything. "I understand your old man won the Silver Star on D day," I went on. "Is that true? That's a story I'd really like to hear. You bet. A story like that is worth waking a man up for." He was shaking a little so I stopped, waiting for him to say something. He did.

"I'm going to kill myself," he said.

"You go do that," I told him. "You couldn't have picked a nicer day." With that I shut my eyes again.

"I'm not kidding, Trevitt. I'm going to kill myself."

I sat up. "What the hell are you telling me for? I'm sure not going to stop you."

He swallowed hard. "I wanted company."

"Sunday is God's day," I said. "Leave me alone."

"I want somebody to talk to while I do it," he explained. "I don't want to die by myself."

I stared at him. He wasn't kidding. At least he thought he wasn't kidding, which is what counts. "Kelly," I said. "I'm your boy. Go kill yourself. But do it here." I pointed to the next bed. "Because I'm not moving."

"O.K.," he muttered. "Then it's settled. I'll get my stuff."

"How you going to do it?" I yelled after him.

"I'm going to cut my wrists with my bayonet," he answered.

"Attago, Kelly," I said. "That's a swell way." I lay down again, waiting. Not so long after he clomped up the stairs and came over, sitting down on the next bed. He held out his bayonet.

"Like a razor," he said. "I spent all morning sharpening it."

"Fine," I told him. "You do nice work."

"Here. Feel."

"I believe you." But he kept holding it out so I did what he wanted. It was sharp.

"How about that, Trevitt? Isn't that like a razor?"

"Kelly," I said, closing my eyes. "I only paid for the main event. Wake me up when the preliminaries are over."

"You better watch," he said. " 'Cause here I go."

He took the bayonet and, very slowly, very carefully, brought it down until the tip rested on the blue veins in his wrist. I waited. He began to exert a little pressure and the flesh of his wrist dimpled.

Then he looked at me. "I bet you wonder why I'm doing this."

"No, Kelly," I said. "No, I don't."

"I'll tell you why."

"Kelly, believe me. I don't care."

"It's on account of my father," he began. "On account of all my life I've been filled full of crap about the Army, and I'm going to be an officer someday, because he's going to make me. And as far as I'm concerned, you can take the Army, fold it three ways, and . . ."

"Shove it," I finished. "O.K. You told me. Now do it."

"What does your father do, Trevitt?"

"He teaches Greek in a little college in Illinois," I answered.

"There," he said, pointing his bayonet at me. "See?" I didn't, but I nodded anyway. "So I got a no-good bastard for a father. What can I do about it? But this." He gestured with his bayonet. "You tell me, Trevitt. What's the point of living?"

I thought for a long time. "Beats the hell out of me," I said, finally.

"Well then," he said. "Here I go." He began pushing the bayonet down again. I watched his face. He closed his eyes. I waited.

Then he opened his eyes. "I mean, what's the point of living? Tell me. You're a smart guy, Trevitt. Tell me. I'm asking you."

"Jesus Christ, Kelly," I exploded. "Are you going to kill yourself or aren't you?"

"O.K.," he muttered. "This is it." He took a deep breath, flexed his muscles and closed his eyes. I remember how hot it was in the barracks right then. My bed was soaked with perspiration and as Kelly grabbed hard onto his bayonet, sweat ran down across his white knuckles. He pushed down on his rigid wrist, farther and farther down.

Then he screamed, "Ouch," dropped the bayonet, and began to swear. "Goddamit, goddamit. That hurts."

I started laughing, kicking my feet in the air. "What the hell did you expect? Of course it hurts." He was standing up now, bleeding a little at the wrist, the blood dripping down red in a pool on the barracks floor.

"I'll bleed to death," he said. "What'll I do, Trevitt?"

"Try the chaplain," I told him. He was licking at the cut with his tongue and making faces.

"Son of a bitch," he said, kicking his bayonet across the floor. Then he ran down the stairs and I heard the water running in the sink. I lay back and began thinking of Zock again, and the temple of gold. But the sight of Kelly standing up and yelling "ouch" kept getting in the way and I just couldn't help laughing.

Then he was back, walking stiff and looking determined as hell.

"Hi, Kelly," I said. "What's new?" He didn't answer. "You know any more games?" I asked him.

"Same one," he answered, looking more determined than ever. "I'm going to swallow a bedspring."

"I don't know," I said, scratching my head. "Maybe I'm losing my marbles but I swear it sounded like you said you were going to swallow a bedspring."

He brought one out from behind his back. "I said it and I meant it."

"Goddamn, Kelly," I told him. "You pick the nicest ways. Did you ever think of roasting yourself over a spit?"

He looked at me. "I'm going to tell you something," he said. "Something I never told anyone else." He paused. "I'm going to die a virgin."

"You can't blame the old man for that," I said. "It's nobody's fault but your own." I started drawing numbers in the air. "There's a billion women in the world, Kelly, one nine zeros billion. And out of all of them the law of averages says there must be one who would do the trick for you."

"Well, I never found her," he said, staring at the bedspring.

"First, you got to look," I told him.

"It's too late now," he whispered. Then he stuck the bedspring in his mouth.

I'm not going to describe what happened next in too much detail, for it gets a little messy, even though it was pretty funny at the time. Kelly's face turned different colors, most of them green, and his eyes started watering, and then the bedspring hit the floor, quickly followed by his breakfast and lunch.

After he was done we just stared at each other, me trying not to laugh. He broke out crying, turned, and tore downstairs. I heard him blubbering in the bathroom with all the faucets going full, trying to block out the sound.

I went to the top of the stairs. "Hey, Kelly," I yelled down. "Best you come back here and clean this up. 'Cause I'm sure as hell not going to."

I sacked out again, waiting. A while later Kelly appeared, carrying a mop and a bucket of water.

"Clean it up good," I told him. "Every bit." He didn't say much so I just stared at the ceiling and listened to the mop make swishing sounds along the floor. "You know," I said, after a couple of minutes. "If you want a woman, I'll do what I can for you." He didn't answer. "Goddamit, Kelly. If you want a piece of tail I'll get you a pice of tail. Now don't say you never were asked."

"How you going to do it?"

"I'm magic," I answered and that was all. I could hear his brain working.

"How you going to do it, Trevitt? How? You really going to do it? Naw. You're just kidding. You're not really going to do it. I know you're not."

"O.K.," I said. "I guess I'm not."

He grabbed me by the arm. "Tell me. Go on. Tell me."

"Just get your clothes on and we'll go into town and find somebody."

"Who?"

"How do I know who? Just put your clothes on."

"What if you don't?"

"I will. I already told you once about the law of averages."

"O.K., Trevitt," he said, patting me. "O.K. Great." He was jumping around like a Mexican bean. "Terrific." He headed for the stairs. Then he stopped. "It means we'd be AWOL."

I started groaning.

"I don't know," he said. "What if we get caught?"

"Look, Kelly. Just make up your mind. I'm not going to come apart if you don't want to. If we're caught they'll probably blast us with a firing squad and all your troubles will be over. So make up your mind."

He thought on that for a while. Then he went downstairs.

We didn't get caught. . . .

All of which is, as I said earlier, typical of me. Not the taking into town part. That's just incidental. Anyway, Kelly was killed two weeks later when he froze up holding a grenade after he'd pulled the pin. The fact that he didn't die a virgin doesn't really count for much in the long run.

But what is typical is the fact that I let him try suicide in the first place. Instead of plastering him one, or trying to talk him out of it, or running for the H.Q. For I have always tried to cram as much into each and every day of my life as I possibly could. Once, just as an example, I ate a pound of grass from my backyard because someone told me it was good. I got sick to my stomach and had a case of diarrhea that Doctor Gunn still talks about back in Athens whenever the subject comes up. Which I trust isn't often. I never ate grass again, but the point is that I had done it, at least the one time, and I knew what it was like. I had experienced it. And I try for that, experience, whether it's eating grass or watching poor Kelly make a fool of himself trying to commit suicide.

Because, as I have already put down, communication is for the birds, and we all have our own lives to lead in the same place, here, but like concentric circles, they don't touch. So your life is yours and mine is mine and never the twain, etc.

And what follows now is mine. Put down haphazardly, more or less as I went through it, starting at the start and going to the end, which is as things should be. It might be called "my life so far," but that wouldn't be true, because my life so far is about as interesting as a toilet bowl. What follows is really more the people I have known as I knew them; other lives, other concentric circles that have come near to my own and, once or twice, because maybe there is a God after all, have touched my own. And if there is anything that makes life worth a hill of beans, it is those few times, those occasional moments of joy when two lives touch for just a little while, before passing on again, into their own individual paths.

ABOUT THE AUTHOR

WILLIAM GOLDMAN has been writing books and movies for more than forty years. He has won two Academy Awards (for *Butch Cassidy and the Sundance Kid* and *All the President's Men*) and three Lifetime Achievement awards in screenwriting. His novels include *Marathon Man,* which has made him very famous in dentists' offices around the world, *The Temple of Gold,* and *The Princess Bride.*